ROGUE PLANET

Revised Edition

By Ty Jodouin

3 1969 02303 4589

This book is a work of fiction. Places, events, and situations in this story are purely fictional and any resemblance to actual persons, living or dead, is coincidental.

ISBN-13:978-1508732945
ISBN-10:1508732949

Publisher: Infinity Press,
421 Signorelli Drive,
Nokomis, FL, 34275

Acknowledgements

I would like to thank Megan who recognized the nucleus of a good story, to Dona Lee who helped us publish the revised edition, to my two excellent Beta readers, Mary Haider and Jim Bentley, to the Detroit Fire Department for allowing me the use of their most honorable name, and last but not least, to my wife, Helen, for giving me the encouragement to start the ball rolling…again.

Dedication:

CAPTAIN LLOYD SMITH

"Thanks for all those wild rides we had together, Cap'n"

On behalf of the Toledo Submariners

Author's Note

In my first edition of Rogue Planet, I had the pleasure of introducing you to Tobermory, and Georgian Bay, considered by many the world capital of freshwater shipwreck diving. It has grown in popularity to include visitations by countless naturalists and explorers as well. But wait, I'm getting ahead of myself. Let's back up a few years.

I was introduced to Tobermory at the beginning of my diving career, when sport diving was in its infancy. As with so many others then, when Jacques Cousteau (underwater explorer) was our mentor, and Lloyd Bridges (Sea Hunt) was our hero, we flocked to Tobermory in droves. But that came later. We were cautious at first. In diving lingo, we were just taking our first baby-steps into deep-water penetration and getting introduced to 'The Martini Law;' for every 33 feet you go down it is like drinking a martini on an empty stomach. Like newborns, some of us learned the hard way when its implications were ignored.

For the first time, none of us had seen the likes of it before—freshwater as clear as a Florida spring; cold as water trapped under ice; water you could drink right out of the Bay, and depths beyond imagining. You didn't have to worry about currents, chemical reactions, visibility or sharks as divers in salt water had to contend with. Most of us were used to muddy lakes and stone quarries with fish no more dangerous than a guppy. We frolicked in depths

not exceeding two or three atmospheres (33-66 ft.).
Finding an inland body of freshwater that you could get lost
in, like Georgian Bay, was like finding a true wreck-diver's
paradise. For a bunch of neophytes like us, it was the
beginning of a beautiful relationship. Shipwrecks, not
camouflaged by barnacles or eaten away by boring sea
worms, many of them intact, with goodies galore, lay ripe
for the picking. Ship's wheels, binnacles, dead-eyes, and
countless other artifacts, were in depths that could still be
reached with compressed air. Anything deeper, we still
used compressed air. In those days, when diving in
Tobermory, we got used to wearing doubles. (72's) Most
wrecks we found were between fifteen and twenty fathoms.
There was no such thing as Trimix in sport diving then. To
avoid decompression sickness, we religiously followed the
U.S. Navy's Decompression Tables to the letter. If you
didn't have a boat, local fishermen chartered out theirs. It
was only when commercial salvagers moved in that the
Canadian government said enough was enough. From that
day forward, all that could be taken out of our Garden of
Eden were pictures. Does that mean there's no thrill left
exploring a shipwreck? That's like saying there's no thrill
left riding a roller coaster more than once. Crawling
through a wooden schooner or an 18th century iron steamer
is an experience you'll never forget. Even today, there are
dozens of virgin shipwrecks lying on the bottom of
Georgian Bay still waiting to have their picture taken.

     The revised version of Rogue Planet you are about
to read digs deeper than the earlier version. In the earlier
version I was remiss at not giving you, the reader, a more
complete background of the coming earth changes and the

reasons behind it. Not only Edgar Cayce but many contactees, who were befriended by extraterrestrials, most notably Howard Menger and George Adamski, heralded the coming of the New Age. Also, God's role in the earth changes and mankind's free will for allowing it to happen will be examined in further detail. As you go along you'll also discover short snippets of information that titillated my sense of logic and reasoning, and maybe it will yours too. The hardest thing about writing a story such as Rogue Planet is determining its genre. Is it fiction or non-fiction? Much of the alien side of it is taken from contactee reports. They say truth is stranger than fiction. Sometimes I had to stop and think. The story and its cast of characters is fiction but based on real people, true events, historical background, and personal observations. Enjoy. The best is yet to be.

Chapter 1

November 28—7:06 P.M.—Bruce Peninsula

As he drove down the desolate highway in his vintage Cadillac Escalade, Philip Deveroux stole a glance at his wife, Linda, for the umpteenth time. She was in the same fetal position as the last time he looked—knees braced against chest, arms locked around ankles, legs and body poised for a spring and release (a self-defense maneuver he had taught her). She stared over her kneecaps with unseeing eyes. She hadn't said a word or even muttered a sound since they had stopped by the roadside in what seemed…God, it seemed like an eternity, he cried in silent anguish. It had only been minutes according to the dashboard clock.

He rocked his head from side to side, trying to unravel the tightened cords in his neck. He felt as if they were about to block the blood circulation to his brain at any minute. In the cool semidarkness of the car's interior, his white knuckles gripped the steering wheel with a vengeance. A deep sense of foreboding stirred in his gut. It was like déjà vu. He had the feeling he and Linda were reliving a bad dream.

Suddenly a flow of hot air was blasting him in the face. Oh great! The air conditioner's thermostat is acting up again. Time hadn't allowed him to get it replaced before leaving home. Phil had little doubt that the torrid heat wave sweeping the country was putting a severe drag on its performance ratings. Using the old trial and error method of jiggling a couple of switches back and forth until something started working, cooler air finally prevailed, at least temporarily. In any case, it was more than what he bargained for. The sudden coldness propelled his thoughts back to when he appreciated even more the frigid atmosphere of a hospital morgue on days when the heat index was going through the roof. Many of his emergency runs were done in life squads where the stench of death, a pungent sweet and sickly smell, was the ultimate price to pay for one of the morgue's cold metal slabs. Unfortunately, knifings and shootings were their primary source of customers. That was typical of any large metropolitan city. When a full moon on a Saturday night was on the calendar, police blotters and E.R. stats proved beyond a doubt that more crazies were loose on the streets. It was equivalent to Happy Hour for the neurotic and criminally insane. Some were just insane.

The lieutenant/paramedic rubbed at his temples to clear away those grisly thoughts. He needed a break from all that his mind was trying to sort out. Phil went back to his old standby, part of a yoga routine he had practiced before. He refocused his thoughts, taking several deep breaths, holding each one a little longer before releasing. He repeated the process until he could feel the culmination of induced oxygen and expelled carbon dioxide rejuvenate his thinking processes. Some called it hyperventilating, a term sometimes used by scuba divers to explain its dangers of blacking out if practiced underwater to conserve air. Right now, it had a secondary purpose. He hoped it might relieve some of the ballooning headache starting to spread its feelers into his brain.

Glancing in the rearview mirror, Phil saw the shadowy outline of a strain-torn face with expressionless eyes and sunken cheeks. It was not a face he was accustomed to seeing staring back at him. It looked like he had just finished battling a major fire and the fire had won its pound of flesh. With renewed concentration, he willed himself to break out of his funky self-analysis. He gave another quick peek at his wife. It was like looking at a caged animal ready to bolt.

It all started when, only a few miles back, he and Linda came face to face with one of life's little surprises— an alien life form. It wasn't what you'd expect from all the books and movies made on the subject, he reflected. The creatures floated through the air like hideous ghosts. He thought about how crazy it would sound to someone who didn't believe in UFOs, or aliens, or anything that suggested extraterrestrials, above all, his friends and colleagues on the fire department. They would laugh at him, and most certainly, the department shrink would tell him he had been hallucinating. But it was as real as the day before when he and Linda discerned a similar shaped UFO in flight over their house. Phil got the feeling it was looking for him. Once it passed over their house, it made a sharp one-eighty and retreated back toward Lake Huron. When Linda questioned his reason for saying that, Phil couldn't come up with an answer. The UFO they had witnessed at the cove was twice the size and unmistakably more threatening, landing just a stone's throw away from where they stood. That in itself can rattle anybody. He wasn't used to being rattled. Throughout his adult life he had always managed to cope with the unexpected, to maintain a tough skin, to show no sign of alarm. This coolness under fire was ingrained in him from his twenty-two years as a lieutenant/paramedic on the Detroit Fire Department.

But things were different now. Linda didn't have the same armor plating he had learned to wear on the Detroit city streets. On the contrary, because of her abiding faith in a world of unchanging laws, her mind would retaliate if something unforeseen came along to shatter that belief. It most certainly did, Phil thought. He was almost positive that was the dilemma her mind was dealing with now. Doctors, he knew, called it catatonic shock, the refusal to face reality. He had seen it happen to accident victims. Now it was happening to his wife. It was as though she had crawled into a shell and would let the rest of the world fend for itself.

"Look kid," said Phil, calling her "kid" since they were married. He was ten years her senior and always insinuated the fact that he would be her karmic debt once he became old and decrepit. He lowered his voice to sound as if he was whispering and swallowing gravel at the same time. He knew how much she abhorred his attempt to imitate the raspy Bogie drawl. But at this stage of the game, he was willing to try anything to garner a reaction from her. He could plainly read the torment on her face, her lips stretched thin. He shrugged his shoulders helplessly. It was like trying to pry open a Louisiana clam. Like the hardy mollusk, who didn't want to open up and be eaten, Linda didn't want to open up and be found. He was starting to worry. There was no telling what demons were locked inside. Perhaps he would try a different tact.

"Try and forget about what you think happened," he said. "Clear your thoughts. Use that old yoga trick I taught you. Everything's back to square one. We haven't spotted any of those creatures since we left the cove..." He paused, his eyes darting surreptitiously to the digital display in the dash. "Over a half-hour ago," he finished with a trace of false bravado. He realized he was more tired than he let on. He was starting to slur his words; his thoughts drifting. His mind was beginning to be torn with crazy thoughts, things that it had trouble grasping—UFOs and strange looking aliens that resembled giant apes. "Chances are they're gone by now," he added for good measure. "It's a million to one shot we'll ever meet up with them again." He was stretching it. Trying to keep the desperation out of his voice wasn't easy.

The tug of his seat belt prevented him from leaning closer, but he could see by the strained look on her face, his lame excuses had little effect on her. She still maintained a defensive position in case her mind posited the notion she was being attacked again. Then, ever so slowly, Linda's arms unwound, letting her legs drop to the floor. She gave Phil a sideways glance that would have frozen a mugger in place. Like a caged animal suddenly freed, her eyes stayed fixated on her husband with a wary stare. The only other form of returning life he saw in her was a hyperactive muscle twitching in her left cheek. But more significantly, her demeanor no longer had that frightened, panic-stricken look. From the moment the UFO touched down at that remote cove, the aliens seemed to know where to find them. It was strangely reminiscent of when Smoke was lost, and Phil knew where the most likely spot would be to find him, the next door neighbor's garbage can.

"I don't believe you, Phil. You know as well as I do that something more bizarre than encountering aliens happened to us back there. Now damn it! Quit trying to bullshit me!" She said it with such vehemence before curling back into her shell that Phil had no ready answer. But her words screamed for acknowledgement. Phil nodded his head, silently relenting to her outburst. She was absolutely right. It had very little to do with just a close encounter with aliens. It had to do with time dilation. Scientists commonly referred to this time-space continuum as the fourth dimension. He had suspected it from the beginning. It was something neither of them would have any inkling of understanding in a million years. All he knew about it was what little he had read of Einstein's Theory of Relativity in some science magazine. According to Einstein, time, like motion, was not absolute. It could be bent, twisted or even made to slow down for a body moving at very high speeds. Einstein speculated that if technology could produce vehicles to move through space beyond the speed of light, space voyagers would virtually become ageless. All human concepts presently involving time and distance would suddenly become obsolete. Within earth's time frame, for example, man would have the ability to galaxy-hop about the universe within the life span of a fly. And what a universe to explore! Four-hundred-billion stars just in the Milky Way alone. A traveler would return home years later at almost the same age as when they had left. But what they would come back to would be a world thousands of years into the future. Phil guessed it was this esoteric world that his wife was trapped in. Phil decided not to try explaining time displacement to Linda. She was already suffering from delusions of what the aliens might of done to them. It was a difficult concession to come to terms with. The bottom line was that he and Linda had been abducted. It was like sweating bullets trying to accept this as fact when it was so foreign to his sense of reality. But since neither of them remembered the circumstances surrounding the evil deed, it was easy to deny it ever happened. The only difference was that there was empirical evidence to the contrary. It did happen. Scientists loved to deny the existence of UFOs by hanging their hat on the empirical part of it. They seemed to forget, however, that astronauts prove Einstein's Theory every time they're launched into space. Even for short distances from earth to the moon and back, upon their return, their time pieces had slowed by several minutes more than their colleagues on earth. Now that the cat was out of the bag, Phil hoped and prayed that their experience had been their first and only debut with time travel. On the other hand, by her reaction, Linda seemed to think they were committed to a lifetime of UFO frequent flyer miles.

But first things first. The supervisor in him kept warning not to jump to conclusions. False alarms from street alarm boxes used to be an all too common occurrence on the fire department. So, could this be the same scenario? The machinations of a clock, for example. A freak set of circumstances that caused a faulty diode or microprocessor to slip or burn out perhaps. Phil once again directed his attention toward the row of lighted buttons lining the dash. Sequestered among them was the clock's digital readout denoting time, day and outside temperature. He would have liked to believe that those false numbers were really false numbers and the cause of his and Linda's anxiety crisis. Some inexplicable malfunction, that's all. Nothing to worry about. But that explanation seemed shallow, a cop-out. His brain kept reminding him that more than just wires and printed circuits were involved here. Dates don't lie, especially when they start ganging up on you. The times on his watch and the car's computer were only seconds apart. That was no surprise, he thought. But he was shocked at what the date readouts were asking him to believe. That troubled him deeply, and struck an even deeper chord with Linda. Somewhere they were missing FOUR whole days! The dates on his watch and the clock matched perfectly. Impossible as it seemed, Monday, November 24th had inexplicably transposed itself to Friday, November 28th. If it wasn't for the timepieces, Phil mused, he and Linda would have never known anything had happened.

Suddenly Phil felt moisture trickle down his backside and pool at his buttocks. He was breaking out in a cold sweat just rehashing in his mind all that had transpired since arriving in the cove. Worst of all was recalling Linda's screams echoing in his ears. It was a nightmarish scene. It had seemed so unreal. The memories of it came rushing back, back to the very beginning...

CHAPTER 2

Philip and Linda lived in one of the tiny backwaters of Detroit, a quiet, unassuming little community called Northville. It was here that they had raised a set of twins, Genny and Brian, and a soot-colored boxer named Smoke. It was a meaningful but, alas, mundane existence, he reflected. Throughout their marriage, he and Linda had become slaves to raising a family, paying their taxes, saving for retirement and keeping up with the daily regimen of suburbanite living. It was a comfortable life, but not very exciting.

Then came the morning of November 24th, when, four days before Thanksgiving, a very peculiar thing happened. It all started innocently enough, Phil recalled—-the morning he awoke disturbed and mystified, as though he had a most unsettling dream and couldn't remember any of it. Even stranger was his impelling urge to dispense with the normal holiday festivities and spend the week at their two-bedroom cabin in Tobermory, a tiny, secluded resort village in southeastern Ontario. The cabin rested directly on the tip of Bruce Peninsula, a spiny finger of land that jutted sixty miles into the very heart of Georgian Bay. It wasn't fancy as getaways go, and its relative distance, about three hundred miles, kept them from going more often. But they considered it their retreat away from home, a welcome break from the sights and smells of a city plagued with overpopulation and a runaway deficit.

Phil recalled the mysterious phone call from their Canadian friends, Steve and Lucienne Shackter, from

Toronto. Serendipity had played a hand when they asked the firefighter and his wife to join them the following weekend in Tobermory. They couldn't have guessed that he and Linda had, by an uncanny coincidence, already marked the rustic tourist stop on their calendar earlier that morning. They welcomed the opportunity from their busy work schedules to extend their trip for a few extra days. They had invited their mutual friend, Captain Smollet, over for Thanksgiving dinner, and they were looking forward to seeing him again. Canada had celebrated their Thanksgiving the month before. The trip looked as if it might prove interesting. Steve had sounded excited, saying he and Lucienne had made a fantastic discovery, but he wouldn't elaborate over the phone. He acted very secretive and evasive when Phil tried to question him about it. But knowing the flair Steve had for the melodramatic, both Phil and Linda decided to play along with him.

Phil and Linda left Northville on Monday morning. They decided to keep their fifteen year old black Lab, Smoke, at home with their neighbor this trip. Phil had rescued her as a puppy from a fire and fought her back to life from smoke inhalation with his own breathing mask. She had suffered from emphysema attacks ever since. Their bags and scuba gear overstuffed the trunk space of their pre-owned Escalade, a somewhat extravagant purchase celebrating his recent birthday. At fifty-five, Phil felt he was not too old to savor some of life's unkempt pleasures before retirement. The car's engine was diesel powered, escaping the sky-rocketing gas prices OPEC was dictating. It was a sturdy car, and affordable, although some nuisances, like the air conditioner, was breaking down at the most inopportune time. But he liked the roominess it afforded. They were scuba divers and liked the convenience of hauling their equipment wherever they traveled. The cold refreshing waters of Georgian Bay promised a welcome respite from the heat. Record breaking temperatures of 100 degrees-plus were being recorded as far north as Baffin Bay, near the Arctic Circle. Alarmists were even talking about the ice cap melting, causing severe flooding worldwide, if the torrid heat continued for much longer.

Phil was no novice to the sport of scuba diving. When he saw the movie Underwater as a youngster, it sparked an undying fascination for the sport. After a four-year hitch in the navy, he joined the Detroit Dolphins, a local dive group. That's when he was introduced to Tobermory and Georgian Bay, one of the largest bodies of fresh water for shipwrecks in the world. That's also when he met Linda. Their professions seemed to blend nicely together. She was a nurse in training, he a rookie firefighter. They both enjoyed scuba diving and sharing the excitement of shipwreck diving. Tobermory had opened up a whole new world to them. It was love at first sight. Now, twenty-one years later, she still retained that exuberance and inner strength he had always admired in her. Whenever he needed her, she had always been there for him...

He blinked a couple times to bring his troubled mind back to the present. He needed her now, desperately. The longer he saw her like this—cold, uncommunicative— made him feel alone and vulnerable. The silence inside the car made the atmosphere even more oppressive. He suddenly wished to be somewhere else, to be in more familiar surroundings, to be with people. He wanted somebody to tell him he wasn't going crazy.

In his mind's eye the serene countenance of Captain Lloyd Smollet and the free-spirited faces of Steve and Lucienne popped into view. Lucienne was blind, following a skiing accident in high school. Her optic nerve had been irreparably damaged, but it didn't seem to have affected her ebullient nature and rosy outlook on life. She was also psychic. The accident had somehow activated a sixth sense in her brain. As a result, she had displayed extraordinary powers of ESP ever since. He and Linda had met them on one of the club meets to Tobermory one summer. Over the years they had become close friends.

Captain Smollet was their charter boat skipper. He had befriended the lot of them with his ukulele and hearty renditions of Scottish folk songs, an odd cultural combination that Phil found amusing. That was in the early days, when Tobermory was just a brief stopover for travelers taking the ferry boat M.S. Chi-Cheemaun across to South Baymouth on Mannitoulin Island. In earlier days it was the Norisle and Norgoma, that shuttled people and their cars across Georgian Bay. Phil was saddened by the fact that the role those pioneers played in Tobermory's rich past was forever lost in the mist of time. He could remember the coal piles waiting for them on the dock at the end of a day's run. One may have forgotten all that, but for the crews who worked on the old coal burning carriers, their memories live on.

Over the years the sleepy little hamlet grew, soon becoming a haven for divers from all over the world.

Every summer, an estimated eight thousand of them inundated the town and the crystal-clear waters off its rocky beaches, searching for shipwrecks. The area abounded with sunken hulks, nineteen known ones listed on the local charts, mostly dating in the nineteenth century. Many still lie waiting to be found, Phil speculated. Like the pot of gold at the end of a rainbow, the all-elusive virgin shipwreck lures many of them back.

This is what Phil suspected lay behind his friend's mysterious phone call. Steve even volunteered to bring the Tri-mix, an expensive breathing gas, which promised a deep dive was in the offing. He and Lucienne had probably stumbled across a virgin shipwreck and, like true collaborators, wanted Phil and Linda in on the spoils.

Abruptly he veered the steering wheel sharply to avoid a large pothole, but it was too late. He managed to just catch the edge of it, making the car sway erratically before he was able to straighten it out. Out of the corner of his eye he watched to see Linda's response to the sudden jarring. Nothing. She hadn't even flinched. He thought perhaps his Bogie impersonation, along with the jarring, might have started a chain reaction, but apparently not.

As the car eased into a gradual curve, the village of Lion's Head hove into view. The street lights exuded a warm glow of welcome. The town square, with its traditional statue of a fallen war hero standing guard, looked homey and friendly. But he noticed the sidewalks deserted, the shop windows darkened. There wasn't anyone around. For all he knew, everybody could have been dead. He paused, afraid his imagination was starting to get the better of him. Then it dawned on him. It was off season. All these little towns on the peninsula rolled up their sidewalks at dusk. But still, it didn't make him feel any better knowing he and Linda were the only ones around.

At the main intersection, he turned onto Ferndale Road, which would take them to Route 6, the main artery to Tobermory. He had memorized from earlier trips how much further they had to go from that point. "Only thirty miles to go, kid. We'll be there in less than a half hour." He said it almost in a whisper, not realizing he had an audience. Suddenly he felt the presence of a pair of eyes scanning him. A bolt of excitement quickened his blood. She'd heard. After all, he mused, it was an encouraging sign. No matter, he didn't want to push his luck. He stayed silent, concentrating on the road ahead. The hum of the tires was his only feedback. He felt confident that once she got to the cabin, among familiar surroundings, all this foolishness of abductions and time warps would be nothing but a bad memory.

The Cadillac's high-performance engine seemed to take on a more frenzied note now that they were on the final leg of their journey. Picking up speed as he negotiated a tight S-curve, the tires murmured a frenzied note when the steel-belted radials bit deeper into the asphalt. The hyphenated median strip slowly merged into an indistinct blur. Telephone poles embedded in buckets of stone lining the berm began to flash by like a ghostly picket fence. His foot felt heavy on the accelerator. Quietly, almost imperceptibly, the car was picking up speed. Phil sensed he was letting his psyche gain control of an emotional dam ready to burst. All his pent-up fears and doubts were spilling over, trying to find release. He tried subconsciously to suppress the feeling, but it was hopeless. His mental toughness was slowly giving way. Suddenly, the screams, followed by the vision of those panic-stricken moments flooded into his brain like a tidal wave…

CHAPTER 3

November 24—5:37 P.M.—Horseshoe Cove

"This looks like a great place to have a picnic, Phil!" Linda exclaimed excitedly. Let's go down and get a closer look."

"Sounds good to me," Phil replied. For the past half hour they had been following the old coastal highway which circuited the escarpment of Bruce Peninsula. Off to their right, sparkling invitingly beneath the setting sun, was Georgian Bay in all its glory. They were just north of Colpoy's Bay when Linda spotted what they were looking for, an old logging trail leading down to one of the many coves and inlets dotting the coastline. Phil judged this one to be a little larger than most. After a quick check, he realized once he committed the SUV to the steep decline, there would be no turning back. The road's humped back and deep ruts only reinforced his fears of tearing out the car's muffler and perhaps an oil pan if he wasn't careful. And getting stranded in the middle of nowhere was the last thing he wanted. By the tangle of overgrowth covering the entrance, it looked as if they were its first trailblazers in years. But they both agreed that hiking to the beach would be a backbreaker with all the picnic paraphernalia they would have to carry. So they settled for Plan B. With the higher undercarriage on the Escalade, it shouldn't be a problem, Phil decided. Viewed from atop the ridge, all the coves pretty much looked alike. It was only when standing at the bottom one hundred feet down did one realize how isolated you were from civilization. As he and Linda stepped out of the car, besides getting blasted with one hundred degree heat, this particular cove probably didn't look any different than it did ten thousand years ago—a rugged, desolate gorge of primeval beauty with a spattering of pinewood and fir tenaciously clinging to its bluffs. It was breathtaking. The solid wall of perpendicular rock loomed over them like a giant fortress. It ballooned outward in a horseshoe pattern for several hundred yards before breaking off into a narrow gap at its farthest point. Through the opening they got an excellent view of blazing sun rays spreading their own exotic shades of orange and yellows across the horizon. Seagulls wheeled and soared among the air currents, screeching hungrily for a free handout as they saw them coming. Phil parked the car in the shade of a small stand of Eastern White Pine adjoining the beach. The beach itself was only a thin strip of shale rock with a few bigger slabs scattered about. Across the road, which buttressed the trees, was a heavy thatch of fir, birch and spruce camouflaging what appeared to be a large clearing.

Phil and Linda found a reasonably flat rock jutting out into the water to lay their blanket on. Away from any obstructions, they would have first crack at any breeze blowing in off the bay, Phil thought. But they needn't have bothered. There wasn't a breath of air stirring. In no time he and Linda were drenched with perspiration. In this heat, it didn't take much exertion to get uncomfortably sticky. Phil was almost tempted to suggest taking a dip before eating, but impending nightfall stopped him short. He didn't feel like trying to find his way out of this place after dark.

They broke out the sandwiches, knowing this could well be their final meal for the night. The 'Bruce' as it was affectionately called by the locals, sported a variety of restaurants, but this late in the season, they would be hard pressed to find one open. Waiting to reach Tobermory was not a viable option either. Their cabin larder was about the equivalent of a prospector's shack: a short supply of beer and a day-old newspaper. On the other hand, going thirsty was not their main concern. The bacteria-free water of Georgian Bay provided a huge drinking reservoir. But even that luxury was slowly being despoiled by human encroachment, the ecologists warned. It wouldn't be long before the entire ecosystem of the Great Lakes was nothing more than an interconnected cesspool.

The sun's rim was just tipping the horizon when Phil heard something that didn't belong in this peaceful setting. At first he thought he was imagining it. It sounded almost like a high-pitched whine, but it was so feint he disregarded it almost immediately. Then, a minute later, he unmistakably heard it again. Linda perked her head up this time.

"Phil, what's that sound?" She looked toward the trees but, except for the car half-shrouded in advancing shadows, there was nothing moving.

"It reminds me of a turbine," she continued.

Phil couldn't answer. The muscles in his throat had suddenly constricted whatever sound was trying to come out. He had leisurely turned in the opposite direction just in time to see the object before it ducked behind the wall of rock encircling the lagoon. A second later it reappeared and he could see it was approaching the inlet. Whatever it was, it was big, gliding in over the water at a ponderous pace about a thousand yards distant. It resembled a round, silvery ball about the size of a silver dollar held at arm's length. The first thing Phil thought of was a helicopter, but that didn't make sense.

You could hear the whump-whump-whump of a helicopter from a mile away. Nor was it a balloon. It was going too fast. Something just didn't seem right about it, like it was being guided toward a specific destination by unseen hands. Intelligently controlled, Phil quickly decided. He instinctively dropped to the hard rock, pulling Linda down with him.

Glittering in the waning sunlight like a jeweled mote, the falling object quickly swelled in size. They could now discern it to be more elliptical in shape. And from its sloping trajectory, it looked as if it were going to pass directly over their heads.

"Oh, my god," Linda gasped. Her face paled. She looked at Phil as if she couldn't believe what she was seeing. They were both hunched down, trying to be as inconspicuous as possible. By this time Phil admitted to himself it was neither an airplane or a balloon. There was only one other explanation, and yet he couldn't bring his sense of reality to accept it.. As it kept getting closer, they could make out a convex dome crowning its top, surrounded by a double row of window-like openings. The lower half of the object was somewhat flatter, with what appeared to be luminous ionization of air around the craft.

A ring of white light was holding steady under its bottom, becoming brighter the closer the craft approached them. It left the impression to Phil that it was on automatic pilot. Its distance fell exponentially as it slowed down to the speed of a weather balloon in flight. The smooth, polished exterior of the main body looked metallic. The diminishing rays of the sun bounced off its surface like a kettle, giving it the color of burnished bronze.

A hard knot had formed in the pit of Phil's stomach. He finally could believe what he was seeing without qualms. He had seen many pictures of them in books and magazines and had devoutly followed their antics for years. Ever since he originally saw one in Rhodes, Greece while in the navy did he ever doubt they were real. The UFO sighting over their house was precisely that, unidentified. Not today. "That, my dear," he whispered excitedly in her ear, "is a real, live flying saucer!"

Linda didn't answer. The awestruck look on her face said it all.

By this time the spacecraft was almost on top of them. It was absolutely enormous. Phil estimated that it was at least four hundred feet in diameter, roughly the size of a baseball field. And there wasn't a sound! It was as if he and Linda had been suddenly encased in a vacuum. A glowing incandescence blazed out from beneath a large opening in its belly, showering them with the brilliance of a supernova. It was blinding, like gazing into the sun!

It moved past them without any wavering or hesitation whatsoever. Strange, something that big could fly so close and not make a sound, Phil thought. It was as though the air around it was empty and void. The normal air humans lived and breathed was no longer. The ship continued to slowly descend as if the occupants, if there were any, knew exactly where they were going. Sure enough, once the spacecraft reached the clearing behind them, it poised like some ungainly bird hovering on a powerful updraft for just a split second before starting its descent. A minute later they lost sight of it as it dropped below the tree line.

Even after several seconds had passed, Phil and Linda were still rooted in place from the aftershock. Phil felt he was living a chapter out of Rod Serling's Twilight Zone. But quickly the numbness wore off and his unbounded curiosity took over. "Come on," he whispered loudly.

Hand in hand, they scrambled across the road and into the trees. The underbrush was thick, momentarily stopping them in their tracks. Dropping quickly to their hands and knees, they half-ran, half-crawled through the thicket, oblivious to any prickly thorns and brambles along the way. By the time they reached the clearing, they were bathed in sweat.

They arrived just in time to see the giant craft eject four spindly legs from its undercarriage as if they were being excreted from a mechanical spider. After they sank a few inches in the soft soil, the rest of the machine seemed to settle one side at a time, as though the struts were riding on independent stabilizers. When all movement ceased, the flashing lights suddenly blinked out.

An ominous silence followed. The air became deathly still. Nothing moved. Phil was afraid to even breathe. The only sound was the ear-splitting pounding of his heart as adrenaline raced through his veins. Surely the aliens will be able to hear it, Phil reasoned. Aliens! What an unearthly sounding word! And yet, for all intents and purposes, that's what they were, beings from another world. He and Linda were actually gazing upon their interplanetary spacecraft. It must have come from a place so different from earth, Phil opined, it was beyond his imagination to even visualize.

Somewhere in the back of his mind he had read that many scientists believed UFOs were interdimensional— perhaps from some interpenetrating universe. They could materialize and dematerialize at will. Thousands of witnesses of these mysterious machines have said the same thing, Phil recalled. They can suddenly pop up out of nowhere, and disappear just as quickly. Maybe so, the Detroit firefighter exclaimed to himself, but this one sure stayed solid enough the whole time he and Linda had it in sight. It was now just sitting the length of a hose line away (50 ft.) from him. Why, he could almost reach out and touch it!

"Do...do you think they know we're here?" Linda stammered.

"I don't know," Phil managed to reply. "If they didn't see us as they came in, I'd say we were awful lucky."

Lucky or not, for the moment he couldn't keep his eyes off the craft's sheer magnitude. It was almost overwhelming. Being so close, his eyes were taking in more data than what his brain could assimilate at one time. He should have been more cautious, staying as long as they were. He couldn't imagine the occupants hadn't seen them on the beach, trying to hide. Phil had read so many stories of UFO's abducting people or zapping them with ray guns, it was almost cliché. But for some reason, he wasn't frightened. Instead, he could sense some awesome force at play here, some supereminence infiltrating his awareness. Something was trying to tell him that behind that façade facing him was a world of infiniteness so great, to grasp even an iota of its power meant being one step closer to immortality.

Linda's nervous prodding at his ribs cut brusquely into his thoughts.

"I'm getting scared, Phil. Let's go!"

"Let's wait just one more minute," Phil pleaded. "This might be our only chance to learn what this saucer looks like inside" Hungrily, his eyes kept searching for clues. He was looking for hatches or doorways or anything that looked remotely like an entryway, but he couldn't detect any. Nor were there any protuberances, such as fins or stabilizers, to mar the craft's sleek symmetry. From what he could determine, seams or cracks were nonexistent. Aerodynamically, its streamlining looked flawless. Suddenly, Phil came to a sobering conclusion. This machine was made to cut through atmospheres at speeds mere mortals could only dream of. Whoever built it had to be hundreds, maybe thousands, of years ahead of Earth technology. It made him feel in comparison what a flea feels like next to an elephant.

The tall birch and spruce trees surrounding the clearing were starting to create an ominous effect, making the waxing shadows even darker around the spacecraft. He had to see more! They were too close to get an overall perspective. On top of the cove would be the ideal spot, he decided. It would be dark soon. They had to hurry!

He nudged Linda on the shoulder. "Let's go!"

Using the woods for camouflage, they began skirting the edge of the clearing. Without thinking, Phil stood upright to peek over the edge of a tall azalea. He could now see a row of curved inlaid windows perforating the hull. They were about three-foot square and seemed to gird the entire top portion of the disc. An ethereal bluish glow was shining from several of them, casting an air of unearthly presence

"Get down, Phil!" Linda said aloud, grabbing for his sleeve simultaneously.

"There's windows!" he cried excitedly. "And there's lights behind them!" There has to be somebody inside, Phil rationalized to himself, unless the ship was remotely controlled. He ruled that out almost immediately. Why would an automated system need windows? A crazy notion suddenly occurred to him. Maybe he could communicate with them. He felt no danger signals coming from within the spacecraft. Sometimes he had those same feelings when accompanying police as first responders. Keeping your reception channels open often helped to communicate your peaceful intentions. He stepped a foot forward into the clearing when suddenly he felt a frantic tugging pulling him down.

"What are you doing? Are you crazy?" Linda hissed. "What if they see you?" Curiously, that had been his intention, irrational as it sounded. Although a fleeting scene of Martians disintegrating everything in their path with lasers and heat rays had crossed his mind earlier, the image had soon faded.

"If they see us, maybe…"

Linda's look of terror stopped Phil in mid-sentence. Her eyes were almost popping out of her head. He found himself instinctively cringing as he reluctantly followed her gaze.

As if appearing by magic, a pair of strange-looking creatures had suddenly emerged from a cylindrical shaft of bluish-white light that had just blinked on beneath the center of the spacecraft. Once the aliens cleared the deeper shadows of the spacecraft, Phil and Linda were able to get a better view of them. They presented a most grotesque sight. Both were tall, hairy, disproportionately shaped, with long gangling arms and legs, short, squat bodies, and small heads. They looked like a cross between a orangutan and a gorilla and had the faces of bearded monkeys. They were moving in tandem like a pair of automatons. What was most incredible, they were riding on some kind of invisible beam. The more they moved about, as if orienting themselves to their new environment, the more it appeared to Phil they were being intelligently controlled from inside the ship. When one of them turned and looked directly at him and Linda peering from behind a cache of fallen white pine, his heart stopped. The other robot looked in their direction also, its arm extended in a supplicating manner. Uniformly, as if programmed to follow certain commands, they both started floating toward the frightened couple.

What came next was a series of blurred impressions and garbled screams as Linda was the first to react. It was a combination of pure terror and panic.

"Let's get out of here! Hurreeee!" Linda screamed hysterically, grabbing Phil's arm. She began back-pedaling furiously, stumbling and falling in the process. He let her drag him along, although he was surprised at the intensity of her theatrics. After all, couldn't she hear the voice talking to him? It wasn't exactly reciting words as much as it was a succession of thoughts and images imploding inside his brain. It kept repeating the same thing. 'Do not be afraid…We are your friends…Do not be afraid.'

Phil repeated the message to his wife, but she wouldn't have any part of it. Her replies of: 'are you CRAZY?' to: 'you must be NUTS!' were understandable to him under the circumstances.

Like a disinterested bystander, it seemed he was watching a grim melodrama unfolding around him, and he couldn't have cared less. When he finally refused to budge altogether, she began screaming in his ear, pulling and tugging at him in a wild-eyed frenzy. In desperation she kicked him in the shins. The pain snapped Phil out of his hanging back long enough for him to keep up with her on their last mad dash to the car. By the time they reached it, they were both gasping for breath. It was as if the oxygen had just been sucked out of the air. Having the unenviable position of sitting in the driver's seat, it was Phil's responsibility to get them out of there. The ignition key was in the ignition where he had left it.

"GO! GO!" Linda screeched, pounding on the dash for effect. She was on the verge of sheer panic. Tears were streaming down her face.

Phil reached down on the steering column and, after a maddening few seconds of fumbling with the ignition key, managed to get his fingers untangled. He turned the key. Nothing! With tortuous deliberateness he studied the floor console. He had the gearshift indicator in 'park.' Everything looked okay. He tried again. Still nothing. The solenoid wasn't even clicking over. It was if the battery had gone completely dead.

Again, a voice interrupted his train of thought. It was now a continuous mélange pounding in his brain. 'Do not be afraid. We are friends.'

"Please, Phil! Hurry!" Linda cried imploringly.

Phil gave Linda one of those foolish "it ain't my fault" looks. She must have thought her husband was joking. She lashed out with a salvo of epithets that would have shamed a drunken sailor. As if possessed by the devil, she shoved his hand aside and began turning the switch herself. Meanwhile, the robots had been steadily gaining on them. By the time she realized the truth, it was too late. She looked up and there they were, one on each side of the car. Bizarre looking creatures! Their hideous eyes glowered at them like hot glowing coals.

At that point, Phil snapped out of his fascination with hearing telepathic voices. It was as if he had just been jolted with a cattle prod. A cold chill swept through him. Oh, my god! This was really happening!

The creature at Linda's side raised its arm as if in greeting. But in its claw-like appendage Phil saw something that froze his blood. What in God's name was it? It looked like some kind of fluorescent wand! A livid brilliance suddenly filled the car. He heard Linda's scream cut short by the searing white light. Then everything went blank.

CHAPTER 4

November 28—6:28 P.M.

When Phil regained consciousness, the apelike creatures had mysteriously disappeared. He shook his head to clear the cobwebs, at the same time giving Linda a quick check. She seemed to be sleeping peacefully enough, he thought. Her steady breathing, with low guttural sounds mixed in, sounded like a person sleeping it off.

Cautiously, he peered outside. An ephemeral quiet had settled over the landscape. In the early night sky, a host of stars were shedding a magnificent luminary display against the black velvet. Occasionally, a shooting star could be seen streaking across the vastness of space. A full moon was on display. Through a slight break in the trees he was able to see a considerable distance over the lagoon. The surrounding cliffs gave the illusion that the whole scene was contained inside a fishbowl. It looked calm and peaceful for the moment, he confessed. But as the seconds ticked by, he was getting the distinct impression things were not the same. He and Linda were too vulnerable. At any moment those apes could return. Behind them, even the silent woods exuded an air of mystery and potential danger. He couldn't shake the uncomfortable feeling that something or someone was still lurking in the shadows.

This time the car started without effort. Phil appreciated the quiet of the big diesel as he eased the aging Escalade back onto the main trail. He snapped on the headlights, and the powerful halogens instantly illuminated the darkness with two converging beams of yellow-white brightness. Without so much as a backward glance, Phil jammed the gearshift lever in drive and steadily, but firmly, pressed the accelerator to the floor. The serene landscape instantly vanished in a billowing cloud of dirt and gravel.

After some tricky maneuvering, he managed to manhandle his way back on the main highway without too much bumping and scraping. Speeding into the darkness, he kept the speedometer needle at 70 mph on the narrow road. Too fast! Too fast! This road was made for slow heavy haulers, like log-carriers, Phil chided himself, not a speeding greyhound who couldn't see what was coming around the next bend. He cut his speed in half.

Several miles later, he began having second thoughts. This was crazy, he thought. Out here in the open country, they were nothing but sitting ducks. The night sky overhead was a perfect blind for the aliens. They could blend in easily among the stars. He and Linda would be better off on foot hightailing it through the dense patches of woods skimming by occasionally on either side of the road. Better cover. However, not a viable option at this stage, he opined. They had to search for a better hiding place. Now!

Up ahead Phil spotted a tall stand of evergreens next to a picnic area, with wooden tables and stone barbeque pits stationed around. Perfect, he said to himself. He pulled over under a dark conifer, dousing the headlights and shoving the gear shift lever into park all in one smooth motion. It was still so hot out that he was forced to leave the engine running to give juice to the air conditioner. Tension slowly dissipated from his body as he powered his bucket seat back, leaned back against the rich mahogany leather, and closed his eyes.

But his brain refused to let him rest. It was bursting with a hundred and one questions. He sat up, eyes wide open, while his senses tuned to the vibrations of the darkness outside. What if those creatures were sitting over the next rise waiting for them? Or were they just a harbinger of more to come?

Phil heard a rustling next to him. Startled, his eyes squinted automatically in a conditioned reflex. Linda was stirring.

"What happ…"

"Shhhh," Phil hushed her. He left her half-spoken utterance hang in the stillness.

"We're out of the cove and back on the main road," he whispered. "I think everything's okay now. I'm going outside to check." He opened the door and slipped out into the blackness. It was like stepping into an oven. Sweat beads started to form on his forehead ten feet away from the car.

Phil sneaked out from beneath the drooping branches of several tall fir mixed in with evergreens. Under their protective canopy, he felt safe from prying eyes. He scanned the bright, starry sky with apprehension. The moon was in the process of waxing to full, which didn't help curb his uneasiness. Hanging over the eastern edge of the world like a giant solar reflector, at any other time he would have marveled at the beauty of it all. The countryside was bathed in the moon's melted colors of a Monet landscape. As it was, he cursed under his breath at the illumination it provided.

Phil found a shallow depression running parallel with the road. He crouched in it for an interminable five minutes, waiting for something to happen. At any moment he was expecting one of those tiny specks of light dotting the heavens to come hurtling down, morphing into a giant UFO. As it turned out, his fears proved groundless. The mournful, strident sounds of the crickets and cicadas seemed to make everything normal and in balance again. Even the harsh screech of a wood owl made him feel at ease.

As he was getting back into the car, the automatic voice recorder of the clock, was just announcing the time, date, and temperature in a metallic monotone. He listened to it abstractedly before a red flag popped up in the back of his brain.

He pushed a lighted button on the console to have the message repeated. "Good evening. The time, 6:56 P.M. The date, November 28th. Outside temperature, 96 degrees Fahrenheit."

Phil could have sworn he heard November 28th as the day's date. Even Linda's ears perked up when she heard it. But it couldn't be! They had left that morning, the 24th.

"Check the date calendar on your watch, Phil," Linda said anxiously.

Yes, of course, Phil nodding his head in agreement. Both instruments can't be wrong. He pushed a minuscule button on the left side of his watch to light up the face. There, in tiny black numerals, was the answer.

Linda leaned over his shoulder to read it too. Both of them stared at the date in disbelief.

"It...it reads the 28th! But that can't be, Phil! I don't believe it!"

Fear began creeping over her face. Her lips twisted into a pained expression of shock. Phil could just about read what she was thinking. He was starting to think some weird thoughts himself. The only answer he could come up with on short notice didn't make sense. He and Linda had been teleported through time somehow. It was best to keep the most obvious to himself, he decided, and concentrate instead on damage control, coming up with a more plausible explanation. The trouble was, he couldn't think of any offhand.

"It's gotta be a malfunction," he said with false conviction in his voice. "My watch is screwed up. So is the clock's. Maybe we went through some kind of force field when the saucer passed over us. Who knows? Don't go reading anything more into it, okay?"

But his warning came too late, or maybe the way he spoke wasn't convincing enough. He promised himself he would try harder, keeping her mind on alien contact rather than an abduction scenario. That would be easier to live with, he thought. So far, it wasn't working. Linda's whole body began shaking as she withdrew into her own corner of the seat.

"Oh my god!" She mumbled. "What happened to us, Phil? What happened?" Her voice was trembling, having risen to a high falsetto. "What did they do to us?"

"Honey, they didn't do anything to us! Nothing happened," Phil retorted. He was amazed at how easily he could fabricate the truth. It was most certain from all he had read of alien abductions that he and his wife had been examined and maybe even inserted with some kind of probe. He reached over to touch her arm, to reassure her, but she shrunk back from him, her eyes wide with fear. Slowly, cautiously, he touched her hand. It was as cold as ice. He had seen rape victims react the same way. She began to cry, whimpering at first, then changing to deep, mournful sobs. It was the cry of a lost child reaching for help.

Phil started the SUV and pulled it back onto the narrow asphalt. He drove in a daze, his mind in a turmoil. He was doing his best to keep everything in perspective. The same question kept popping up in his subconscious. How could you give up four days of your life and not know a damn thing about it? He didn't feel any different, yet something kept nagging him. Was there something more to this anomaly than met the eye? What did the aliens have to gain by their abduction, and then, four days later, leave them in limbo? Perhaps the answers lay waiting in Tobermory, Phil surmised. Only time would tell.

November 28th—7:48 P.M.

Topping a steep ridge, the Escalade swooped down on a familiar landmark, Sutter's Campground. It was closed for the season, but its darkened florescent sign meant only four miles to go. He gradually eased up on the accelerator. Coming up on the right was Cully's Miniature Golf Course. It was no putt-putt; everything in it was handmade, but put together with a rustic charm all its own. Although it looked like it had been unkempt for years, it revived a long-ago memory that brought a quick smile to his lips. He remembered the time Linda and the twins were attacked by a swarm of bees at Cully's one hot summery night. His smile bordered on a chuckle and then a laugh at what transpired next. For some reason, he was immune to the bees' attack. Maybe his after shave lotion acted as a repellent. The others weren't so lucky. What a sight! While he had stood laughing his head off, Linda, Genny and Brian went running away shrieking and flailing their arms like The Three Stooges.

Phil was still reminiscing when he felt a gentle nudge on his arm. He glanced over to see Linda had unfurled herself from her fetus-like position and was giving him a weak smile. Her refined features looked delicate and waxen in the dim light. She usually wore her hair shoulder length, but for the trip she had styled it in a French twist. Some of the ends had worked loose and were hanging down in straggly columns, but that didn't matter. She was as attractive as ever, Phil thought. He had to admit, at forty-five, she still hadn't lost any of her sex appeal.

"You look like hell, Humphrey." The first words out of her mouth weren't exactly appealing to his ego but he was grateful she was starting to get back to reality. She had involuntarily dug her fingers around his arm, acknowledging her presence. He knew how much courage it was taking her to break out of her shell.

"I feel like hell too," Phil answered back in his Bogie voice. "Just the same, here's looking at you kid. Glad to see you back." He held up an invisible glass, toasting her return. He began to sing an old Caribbean tune he remembered from his travels in the navy, grinning foolishly in the process. He even tried to put a Jamaican twang in his voice for effect as he sang the lyrics. Unlike his Bogie impersonation, she responded in a strained laugh, at the same time releasing some of the tightness to his choked arm. Her eyes flashed with renewed spark as she softly lip-synced the words with him. When she finally snuggled closer to him at the finish of the little tune, he knew the worst was over. He wasn't used to saying it, but he silently said it anyway. Thank You, God.

Over the next rise a large black sign with the name TOBERMORY embossed in bold white lettering leaped into view.

CHAPTER 5

November 29th—6:30 A.M.

Phil woke up lazily smelling the fragrance of jack pine and cedar. Sweet-smelling traces of rose-purple and white Queen Lady Slipper were also in the air. Terns sang like minstrels outside his open-screened bedroom window. The atmosphere was almost that of a tropical garden, he mused. The prolonged summer had kept the blossoms open and the trees from shedding their leaves. The luxuriant smell was a soothing tonic that gently caressed his senses while his mind teetered between a dreamlike state of wakefulness and sleep. He managed to give a one-eyed peek at the dawn light streaking through the Venetian blinds. Compared to a nerve wracking night of looking over his shoulder every minute, it was like waking up to a new beginning in life. He sighed in resignation. He had just been dragged through an emotional meat grinder the night before and could have soaked up the tranquility of the morning even more. But, it was not to be. Wakefulness had inevitably gained control of his bladder

He rolled out of bed, urinated, showered, shaved, brushed his teeth and got dressed, all without arousing a peep out of Linda. She being an inveterate early riser, beating her out of bed was no small feat, he thought.

Standing in front of the cabin overlooking Georgian Bay, breathing in deep gulps of unsullied air, Phil couldn't help but be reminded of the many pleasant memories he and Linda had shared there with the twins. Genny and

Brian should be with Linda's widowed sister in California right now, he reflected, taking a break from their studies at Berkeley and trying to digest the copious Thanksgiving turkey dinner Kay would have baked for them.

Phillip and Linda's cabin was strategically located on an acre of prime real estate at the very peak of what used to be called, the Saugeen Peninsula. In the same breath Tobermory was then called Collins Inlet. But that was years ago, Phil mused, when the cabin passed from the hands of an old sailor/fisherman named Orrie Vail. He claimed he was the original discoverer of the famed ship, Griffin, the first ship to sail the Great Lakes. When he died, the cabin stayed empty and in disrepair before Phil and Linda found its desirability as a hideaway. They bought it fairly cheap then, before entrepreneurs and investors also invested, providing tourists with a rich variety of ways to enjoy the grandeur and uniqueness of Tobermory. New motels and restaurants sprang up quickly to accommodate the influx of scuba divers and naturalists flooding Little Tub, the main harbor. Charters to the shipwrecks, sunset cruises in glass-bottom boats, forays to Flower Pot Island, and deep-sea fishing were some of the more popular items on the agenda. It was like watching a boom town being resurrected from the days of the Old West, Phil recalled.

But this boom town also attracted scavengers and profiteers. Many shipwrecks had been blown out of the water simply for their scrap metal value. It wasn't until the Canadian government stepped in and inaugurated the Georgian Bay Marine National Park that the carnage stopped. Later came the Fathom Five National Marine Park, established in 1987. It specifically protects and watches over shipwrecks, islands, and light stations north and east of Tobermory.

As Phil gazed across Cape Hurd Channel, the sun was just starting its laborious climb over the outer islands. In a few minutes, the early morning haze would disappear and the full fury of the sun's energy would break through. And with it, merciless heat! Even more disconcerting, Phil mused, was the thought of being blasted with mega doses of ultraviolet rays. Every year the ozone layer was being depleted at a faster rate by the tons of toxic gases being spewed into the atmosphere. Because of the breakdown in the earth's protective shield, the number of melanoma cases throughout the world was increasing at an alarming rate.

It dawned on him that he had forgotten to apply any sun block before leaving the cabin. Since a boy, his immune system was in constant battle with skin cancer. It almost prevented him from becoming a firefighter. Linda was always on his case for forgetting to use the #1 skin protector—sun avoidance. He started to retrace his steps, then stopped. Oh, to hell with it, he mumbled to himself. The sun was just breaking the horizon. He shouldn't have to worry about it yet, he thought.

Phil could hear the faint gurgle of water lapping between rocks as he worked his way barefoot down the rocky shoreline. As he stepped into the small tidewater pools warmed by yesterday's sun, it felt as if he were stepping into bathwater. He played hopscotch over several of the larger pieces of limestone slabs that looked as if they had been riddled by a machine gun. He stepped gingerly onto one particular Swiss-cheesed specimen jutting its nose into the water. From there he could see for several leagues in a northwesterly direction such rock-studded refuges as Cove, Peters, Echo, Harbor, and North and South Otter Islands. Under a cloudless blue veil, and without any hint of a breeze to ruffle its surface, the water in-between lay unblemished and as smooth and flat as a lead-gray carpet. The undisturbed serenity of sea and sky held a magic quality all its own, he thought.

Off in the distance to his right, an aggregate of larger green-topped islands ringed the main channel, the main ferry route to Manitoulin Island. Most every spit of land or jumble of rocks in between was a grave marker for some hapless ship, Phil suspected. November was historically a bad month for the Great Lakes. That's when the nor'easterlies began to blow, driving gale force winds and blinding snowstorms into hapless victims trying to find sanctuary. Ships that got lost in the fog or were swept ashore in a storm invariably had their bottoms ripped open by rocks lying in shoals like dragon's teeth.

Farthest to his right, the scaly cliffs of Flower Pot Island, with its reputation for having the legendary flower pots, also could boast having some of the escarpments rarest orchids growing in its rich soil. The island, pocked with caves and crevices that would tease the most avid spelunker, was just making an appearance under the tawdry rays of a dawning sun. From where Phil stood, the large and small flower pots, 50 foot and 30 foot respectively, were hidden from view on the other side of the 300 acre island. He needn't have to be reminded, however, that these scenic wonders had become top tourist attractions—

natural rock formations, and towering stone monuments—intricately carved by countless eons of wind and waves.

Ojibwa Indians of the region had a more apt title for the flower pots—Devil's Pulpits. Captain Smollet said the name stemmed from an old Indian legend. Whenever a storm was brewing, dancing lights could be seen playing over the flower pots, supposedly a warning signal from the evil spirits to stay away. The island was taboo to the Indians; they wouldn't set foot anywhere near it.

Phil grinned. The good captain swore on his wife's grave he always saw the lights whenever storm clouds gathered on the horizon. Phil remembered the castigating look the captain had once given him when Phil had scoffed at the idea and suggested the lights were a natural phenomenon.

"No sir-ee, laddie," the captain had emphatically replied. "Them there lights are real all right. Just you wait and see."

The memory of the scene quickly faded as Phil let the lush smells of the woods carry him back to the present. The clean scent of juniper and pine tar hung heavy in his nostrils. It felt wonderful just to be able to clear out his lungs again, he mused. There weren't too many places left in the world where you could breathe air that hadn't been belched out of a chimney or expelled through an exhaust pipe.

As Phil began backtracking, he absently swung his gaze back across the channel. Something moved. It could have been anything, he figured; a rodent or a bird along a narrow spit of land called Russell Island. Although it was merely a couple of hundred yards long, and sported only a handful of balsam fir and scrub pine, the two 100-foot deep wrecks, the James C. King and the W.L. Wetmore off its north shore guaranteed it a permanent marker on diver's charts.

There! He saw it again. Ripples in the water this time! A fish! It must had been a pretty good size for his eyes to spot ripples from this distance, he figured.

Stepping cautiously, more out of curiosity than anything else, Phil kept his eyes peeled on Russell's narrow 100-yard gap that separated the island from the mainland. Russell Island and further south, Devils Island, symbolized an imaginary line of demarcation between Georgian Bay and Lake Huron. Except for a few summer residents, both islands, he knew, were pretty much deserted.

He guessed what he saw had to have been a sturgeon, one of the largest fish in the Great Lakes, foraging for food. They liked to stay in deep water but for some reason, this guy must have had to look for his dinner nearer the surface, Phil surmised. Who knows how this heat wave was affecting the underwater food chain, he asked himself. The direction the fish took indicated that, more than likely, it was heading toward a deep water channel that ran parallel with Devils Island.

Suddenly, a pair of soft, warm arms enveloped him from behind. It startled him momentarily. A fragrant, blonde head brushed against his cheek.

"Oh, darling, It's so peaceful here. Let's just stay here forever."

The sound of Linda's voice had a subdued quality to it. She was always enraptured by the exotic appeal of Georgian Bay, especially at dawn and dusk. The sun's rays highlighted each and every island like emeralds displayed on a blue backcloth. It was a lot different than the flat wheat and barley fields of Indiana where she was raised, she once admitted. Any trace of nerves from the night before seemed to have vanished. The mind has a way of protecting itself by engaging its own defense mechanism, he discovered. Phil turned around to look into her blue-green eyes. Linda was standing on tip-toe, stretching her five-foot, five-inch frame so that her gaze was even with his. He always accused her of being able to turn on the sultry look of a Marilyn Monroe whenever she cared to excite him. He thought his wife was doing so now. Her suntanned, unblemished face, except for the tiniest of crow's feet crinkling her eyes, held a sensual smile that belied her previous night's terror. She had let her hair fall down to her shoulders to give it the final touch. To Phil, she looked ravishingly beautiful.

"You shouldn't sneak up on a guy like that," he chided jokingly. "I might mistake you for somebody who's looking for trouble." He reached over to grab her but she was able to slip away. Her voice suddenly became serious. "There's no sense kidding ourselves, Phil. Something happened to us out there last night."

"I know, but you can't dwell on it; otherwise, you'll drive yourself crazy."

"Maybe we should go tell the police."

"Why? What can they do? It's better we just try and forget it. Nobody will believe us anyway."

Linda shrugged. As far as Phil was concerned, it was a one-time, only time happening in their lives that had to be expunged out of their systems as soon as possible. It was like a cancer that had to be cut out before it metastasized and took over your very soul. It was what was left unsaid between them that disturbed him the most. If they had been abducted, and that seemed to be a foregone conclusion, visions of being sexually molested stood out the most.

From everything Phil had read about them, the aliens were obsessed with human reproduction. Many books had been written of the abducted having to endure tortuous examinations which included implantations of embryos in females, or extraction of sperm from males. In giant mother ships, onboard space nurseries were continually being reported after witnesses claimed to have seen row upon row of hybrid fetuses lined up like honeycombs.

Linda knew her husband well enough to know the subject of abductions disturbed him as much as it did her. She wasn't totally ignorant of the alien's proclivities either. Only he was able to bury it in his psyche better than her. "Are you hungry?" she asked.

"Uh-uh."

Her lips cracked into a devilish grin. "If we go for a dive before breakfast, maybe we can work up an appetite for later."

Phil nodded. The definitive word was 'later.' A quick morning plunge before Steve and Lucienne showed up didn't sound like a bad idea either. Besides, the exercise would help break the mood.

"You took the words right out of my mouth, kid." He grabbed her from behind and gave her a gentle bear hug. "But we'd better hurry before I remember what a dirty old man I am." She laughed. It was good to hear her laughing again, he thought. The sound mingled nicely with the lilting cry of a loon far off in the distance.

CHAPTER 6

November 29—-7:33 A.M....Dog Patch

Phil and Linda had just finished hauling their scuba gear to a pear-shaped rock sticking out into the water like a splayed finger. They were within a stone's throw of their cabin, so it was an easy carry. Out in the channel, one hundred and fifty feet away, floated a cylindrical-shaped buoy which marked their destination, a sunken barge 120 feet below the surface. Phil had placed the buoy there years before in order to show other divers not familiar with the area where to find the wreck. It was a wreck in name only, but still interesting to dive on, he figured. Most shipwrecks in the Tobermory area were wooden schooners that sunk in the 1800's before up-to-date navigational aids were used. The best available aids at the time were strategically placed lighthouses to warn of rocky shores and blinding fog. When steam was introduced, sailing ships became a thing of the past and were mostly converted to hauling cargo. They were then considered barges with their masts still intact but empty of sails on their yardarms. Instead they were towed by the new iron boxes that burned coal, bypassing forever the wind that eventually spelled their doom.

This part of Cape Hurd Channel was called Dog Patch. Phil never found out why it was called that, and as for the name of the barge, he never found anyone who cared. Changes of ownership were quite frequent in those days, and so were the names of sailing vessels plying their trade. It could be quite confusing. All Captain Smollet could tell him about the relic was that it sank in the Bentley Gale of 1886 with a cargo of lumber. The lumber had long since been salvaged, and all that remained was a dilapidated old derelict. When a vessel sinks, however, it brings on its own notoriety. Phil once was told by someone that they thought a shipwreck was no longer of any use to anyone, that it was a myth to think they were anything more than that.

"Retirees are not a myth," Phil emphatically stated back in reply. He never met a retiree yet who didn't relish leaving the drudgery of a lifetime of work behind. It soon became a forgotten footnote in their life's last chapter. Retirement meant a new life and a new role to play in it. He went on to say that a ship is basically in the same position, a workhorse all its life, whether for work or play, always having to obey the commands of its captain. But when it founders, it is officially designated in the marine register as a shipwreck and its status automatically changes to 'retired.' Whether it be an ore carrier, a freighter or a simple barge, its sinking is no less important than the Titanic, its history just as interesting in some respects than others, as they eternally lay on the bottom of some ocean, lake or bay, and pose for divers. I bet a lot more pictures are taken of them now than when they were floating on the surface, he would always say. He never got an argument back.

Phil and Linda began suiting up in their 3/4-inch neoprene rubber wet suits. Only a few words were exchanged between them. The solitude of the early morning seemed to have a calming effect on their nerves, as well as their spirits, keeping them in a meditative mood.

Normally they used cryogenic, or liquid air, a relatively new concept in sport diving. It was based principally on evaporation instead of compressed air. The ambient temperature surrounding a diver's tank was always warmer than the liquid inside, which caused evaporation and the continual release of breathable air through a standard regulator. The nice thing about it was the fact you never needed much frozen liquid as you did compressed air to stay within a sport divers realm of 130 ft. (5 atmospheres) without decompression. The bad thing about it was liquid air still contained nitrogen, which was poisonous to divers the longer and deeper you spent underwater. It was much cheaper than Tri-mix, an electronically regulated mixed-gas system of oxygen, helium and nitrogen, which was in secret use by the Nazis during the Second World War. Combined with titanium tanks and computerized systems of the 21st century, it has allowed divers to go longer and deeper than ever before. Today's dive was considered a bounce dive, requiring just enough cryogenics to limit their bottom time to one hour at a depth not to exceed 200 feet without decompression. It was a far cry from earlier days. Decompression Tables were a thing of the past. Everything was now run through a computer. A consummate stickler for safety, Phil still liked to double-check the figures by hand. If fed bogus information, even computers are not infallible. He vowed that would never happen on his watch.

A large slice of the sun was now visible over the treetops as Phil and Linda hurried up donning the rest of their gear. It was a very hot and sweaty job. They could feel the temperature building up inside their wet suits, as if someone were turning up a thermostat. The suits, like rubberized saunas, prevented their body heat from escaping. Once their tanks were on and their regulators in place, their life vests adjusted, (they favored the old-fashioned Mae-West type) Phil and Linda proceeded to wobble into the water like two overweight penguins. They waded in waist-deep, pausing just long enough to slip on their fins and masks before giving each other the thumbs-up sign, indicating their readiness.

Once submerged, they instinctively braced themselves for the ice-cold temperature to come. Although their wet suits were electrically heated by two-pound battery packs strapped to self-adjusting weight belts, they still had to endure a brief period of cold water conditioning. It was a necessary evil when diving in Georgian Bay. The deeper you went, the colder it got. The law of physics. Once you passed the thermocline, if there was one, it was not unusual to reach temperatures hovering just above the freezing mark. Nevertheless, the trapped, heated water in your wet suit, regardless of whether it came from body heat or battery pack, acted as perfect insulation, warming their bodies to the temperature of toast within seconds.

There was always a debate among scuba divers of the pros and cons of wet suits versus dry suits when deep diving on shipwrecks in Georgian Bay. With dry suits, you had all the comforts of home, Phil reasoned. Except for hands and face, you never had to encase your torso in a cocoon of numbing cold. Not until you got an unexpected tear in your suit, that is. Phil lost count of the number of times he tore his wet suit when crawling through deep-water shipwrecks such as the James C. King, the Forest City or the Marion L. Breck. All shipwrecks, no matter how deep they are, are lethal deathtraps to the unprepared. Divers have to contend with sharp, hidden protuberances of all kinds as they swim, and sometimes crawl, through narrow passages. Also, avoiding broken and twisted planking that has been ripped apart, leaving jagged splinters that resembled spears; or snapped off engine parts, edges like razor blades, with a notorious reputation of slicing through flesh like a knife through butter; or split cables that can brush raw an arm or leg without effort; and hundreds of scattered iron spikes throughout the wreck sticking up out of nowhere to snag an unwary diver, were par for the course. After some dives he and Linda would be up half the night patching their suits, getting ready for the next day's dive. At the depths they were diving, between one hundred to one hundred and fifty feet, (divers tend to add an extra atmosphere or two the more experience they gained in deep water) if they were wearing dry suits, the slightest rip in them would have caused a horrible, freezing dilemma. The odds of survival was like playing Russian Roulette. A rip in a wet suit remains localized and you live to fight another day.

Water weighs 8.3 pounds a gallon. Firefighters know that fact. Smart divers do too, Phil acknowledged. And, then again, some divers don't. It all has to do with how lucky you think you are if you don't follow the rules of self-preservation. Rules of logic, so to speak. You've got to ask yourself these questions. How many pounds of water would a diver's clothes absorb if their dry suit sustained a rip? Would depth be a factor? You would certainly think so if you were down five atmospheres, (132 ft.) for example, and all of a sudden your body was subjected to a 40 degree drop in temperature. Do you think a buoyancy compensator would get you to the surface, even after dropping your weights? Even if it did, how do you regulate your rate of ascent? Shooting up without stopping for decompression could easily give you the bends. Also, the pressure would be magnified, squeezing whatever warm insulation you were enjoying, down to zero. Next, the long ascent back to the surface with X amount of gallons flooding your suit, the cold water freezing your senses, would make it extremely difficult. How much more energy would your body require to neutralize the extra weight? It would be like carrying an anchor on your back. How exhaustive would it be to reach the surface with all that happening to you with a shocked body and a befuddled brain. Assuming you reached the surface in time before your heart gave out, that is. The question and answer session was conducted by Phil to the training class when he was practicing for certification as a scuba instructor one year. He had dreams of teaching firefighters to become part of an underwater search and recovery team. His teacher, when asked his opinion on the subject of what suit was safest for diving on deep water shipwrecks, gave the most logical answer. Phil never forgot it. "It's a lot cheaper buying a can of neoprene cement to patch up a wetsuit than it was paying for a funeral."

Because of the coldness, shipwrecks in Georgian Bay were preserved many years longer than ones found in warmer salt seas. In the world's oceans, wooden objects were rapidly devoured by boring sea worms or concealed by crustaceans and sea weeds. Fresh water sites didn't have those drawbacks. About the only problem Phil and Linda ever faced was finding wrecks intact enough to explore before ice or scavengers got to them first. The solution was to break out the charts and look for out of favor wrecks that were either in sheltered coves or deeper waters. For that you needed a boat, side-scan sonar and finances to sustain an exploratory trip to remote sites. That criteria fit their Canadian friends who were just now flying in to join them.

After being land-bound for weeks on end, experiencing the exhilarating thrill of weightlessness was always a heady sensation when Phil and Linda returned to the underwater world. Unshackled from the burdensome weight of a surface atmosphere, they adapted quickly as Phil effortlessly soared over a wide assortment of rocks and boulders, with Linda in close pursuit. Some had odd configurations that reminded him of a child's scattering of wooden blocks. Together they stopped to pinch their nostrils and blow to equalize the pressure in their ears before continuing their descent.

Catapulting over a particular large slab, they suddenly found themselves hovering over a sharp drop-off. It was as if they were looking down into a fog-shrouded graveyard, the rocks fading like hazy tombstones into the depths below. This, they knew, was where the underwater slope of the mainland went perpendicular in its dizzying plunge to the bottom. With hardly an interruption to their rhythmic kicking, they catapulted like gymnasts over the void, increasing their pace slightly to reach the bottom in three or four more strokes. They were soaring like hang-gliders reaching for the clouds, free as birds. It was exhilarating. Phil imagined that he and Linda must have looked like monstrous predators to the dozens of tiny crayfish scurrying for the safety of their holes. Suddenly, the slope bottomed out into a flat, featureless plain. Out of habit, Phil took a quick glance at his depth gauge. One hundred, twenty feet. When a ghostly outline of a large, wooden object appeared in front of them, he knew they were dead on target.

With a lazy scissors-kick, they approached the wreck from its starboard quarter. Visibility this time of year was no different than any other time of year, excellent. Optimum range. Not as clear as a Florida spring perhaps, Phil thought, but as long as you stayed a foot or two off the bottom, a diver was able to view the wreck in its entirety. It was about 230 feet long, lying on its port side, mute and forlorn like a dead whale. Pieces of timber lay scattered about, a silent testimonial to nature's supremacy. When hit by the gale, the barge was being used strictly for transporting raw materials. The masts were still attached, but no sign of machinery, which led Phil to believe it had not been converted to coal.

From the beginning of his sojourn through the Great Lakes, Phil found that all shipwrecks, no matter where their final resting place lay, are layered with varying degrees of mud and silt. This relic from the past was no exception, he discovered. Once agitated, the sediment billowed out like an obsidian cloud, obliterating whatever visibility you had. Since Phil's and Linda's jet fins had great thrusting power, and could upset the balance easily, they kept a watchful distance as they circled the wreck. They surveyed the crushed hull and broken timbers with dispassionate interest. After all, this must have been at least the umpteenth time they dove on it, usually for the same reasons, Phil opined, to stretch their legs and get reacquainted with their gear. It was usually a dull dive. Nothing to retrieve, even if you could. It was pretty much stripped. In days past, salvaging dead eyes, bells, whistles and ship's wheels were prime trophies to take home and hang on your mantel. Now, just the thrill of diving on such dead wrecks, taking nothing but pictures, was a special challenge. Using a little imagination, they could almost visualize the death struggle the old carrier waged before the viciousness of wind and waves battered her into submission.

They were about halfway around the wreck, working their way toward the bow, when Phil began to feel a prickling sensation at the back of his neck. The hairs were sticking up under his hood like the bristles on a hairbrush. Ever since childhood, the sensory receptors inside his brain had developed a high sensitivity level when it came to danger. He used to joke about it by saying Robby the Robot (from Lost in Space) was in his head. It stood him in good stead fighting fires. It was almost as if some inner faculty were still telling Robby to warn his master when there was...'DANGER, WILL ROBINSON...DANGER!' present. Through trial and error, he had learned to listen to the robot's subtle warnings without question.

By the time Phil and Linda reached the bow, Phil had developed a case of cold chills. He motioned Linda to stop. Warily, he began to scan the area in a slow, methodical search. Most divers understood that wearing a face mask is a lot like peering through the short end of a tunnel. A full facepiece was better but made it harder to buddy-breathe. It restricts your peripheral vision almost to the point of wearing blinders. A full facepiece was better but made it harder to buddy-breathe. A long minute passed before Phil was satisfied. The bottom of the channel was pretty much flat with only an occasional boulder to disturb the emptiness. There were no fish to speak of. He had no idea what he expected to find, but he was sure something was out there that shouldn't have been. There was nothing. And yet, the feeling persisted.

He questioned Linda with a pair of forked fingers pointing at her eyes, then sweeping them over the landscape. She answered his query almost immediately with an emphatic nod. He peered closely into her eyes. He could tell by their owlish expression that she was frightened. She must have been getting the same vibes he was. He jerked his thumb upward. It was the universal diver's signal to surface at once.

It was only after their heads had broken the surface and they were safely back on shore that Phil felt less vulnerable. But the feeling of danger was stronger than ever.

"Did you feel it too?" Linda's voice had taken on a squeaky higher octave.

"Yeah, I sure did," Phil answered reflectively. "It almost felt as if someone was looking over my shoulder."

He took a long, hard look back at Russell Island. Could it have been other divers in the area they were sensing? Or could those creatures from the cove be back? He began to have second thoughts about not asking for help. Maybe it was time for he and Linda to find out what the hell was going on around here.

CHAPTER 7

November 29—9:05A.M.....O.P.P. Station

The Ontario Provincial Police Post was located directly on the main highway leading into Tobermory. It was a modern-looking one-story cement block structure with a tall radio tower mounted off to the side. Phil spotted a small barn inside the tree-line where it sat next to the parking lot. There were two horse stalls enclosed , one occupied by a big, black gelding. Two police cruisers with O.P.P. stamped on their sides were parked in the lot as Phil and Linda walked through the front door.

A solidly built man about thirty years old, with military bearing and police sergeant stripes, was sitting at a desk behind a front counter. Cool air was blowing through an overhead vent, keeping the room comfortable. He looked up as Phil approached.

"What can I do for you folks?" he asked courteously. He spoke heavily in a French-Canadian accent, and his voice had somewhat of a lilt to it. He impressed Phil as having happier days, and this wasn't one of them. He had stopped pecking away on an ancient computer keyboard to gaze at Phil and Linda through heavy, bushy eyebrows highlighting a thatch of red hair and a freckled face. Although he sported a thick mustache, it was neatly trimmed with just enough blending of dyes to match his hair. His eyes, sunk in dark, hollow pits, made

Phil think the sergeant hadn't had a good night's sleep in weeks.

"We're here to file a report on sighting a U.F.O," Phil answered. He and Linda had decided to dispense with the missing time portion of their account. After all, reciting a UFO encounter was hard enough for anyone to swallow at one sitting. The sergeant's eyebrows went up a notch, but he didn't seem to be overly excited at Phil's announcement.

"Okay," he replied noncommittally. He reached into a drawer and pulled out a form. "C'mon over here and pull up a seat." He motioned to two slat-back chairs in front of his desk. Then he scrolled through the computer until he found what he was looking for. He then copied some information off the form onto the computer. Phil thought the dexterity he did all that without pause showed he had practiced it before. A small bronze plaque, with the name J. Putnam embossed in black lettering, was prominently displayed on the front of the desk.

As they sat down, Phil noticed an ashtray full of cigarette butts. Lying next to it was a half-eaten egg sandwich, a thermos and a steaming cup of black coffee. It looked like coal tar, but it smelled good and made Phil remember that they hadn't eaten breakfast yet.

Phil did most of the talking as the deputy filled in the form. He interrupted occasionally to question a point or two, but for the most part he let Phil talk without interfering. Phil even mentioned, in passing, he and Linda's dive in Dog Patch. He emphasized the strong feelings they had of imminent danger down below, but Sergeant Putnam gave them the impression that he had heard it all before. Out of curiosity, Phil questioned him about it. "Have you had similar UFO sightings like ours? Perhaps someone else saw the same thing."

The police sergeant looked at him with a blank stare, as if Phil had caught him unprepared. His lips twitched, making his mustache quiver as though some puppeteer was pulling strings. It was obvious to Phil the man was desperately in search of finding an answer that wouldn't sound stupid. Finally he gave a reluctant nod. He paused to light a cigarette, politely offered one to each of them with shaky fingers, and with a slight fidgeting in his seat, began to speak as if he had resigned himself to this moment.

"My office has been swamped with calls from local farmers the past several weeks. UFO's have been landing and taking off in their fields, scaring the hell out of 'em. That must be where these hairy bipeds you described are coming from, too. They seem to be poppin' up all over the place." He stopped to take a long drag from his cigarette.

"Are you sure they were levitating," he continued, as a fresh blanket of smoke issued from his mouth, "and shot some kind of anesthetizing beam at you that made you groggy?" The sergeant stretched his long, lanky legs out from behind his desk and directed his scrutiny at Linda. By his stare, Phil had the feeling he was trying to intimidate her. Why would he do that?

"Yes, it was absolutely terrifying ," Linda retorted defensively. "I'll never forget them as long as I live! They were hideous monsters!" She shuddered. Her fists clenched. Phil was afraid for a second his wife was going to call the sergeant to task for doubting her word.

"Isn't it kinda strange," Phil broke in, "that all of a sudden the countryside is being inundated with flying saucers? I mean, what about the rest of Canada? What do the news reports have to say about it? And your government? Do they know what's going on up here?"

A look of frustration suddenly covered Sergeant Putnam's face. His brow furrowed into a thousand tiny creases. "I wish I knew, Mr. Deveroux, but a strange interference signal has drowned out everybody's radio and TV reception, including mine. Every internal combustion engine this side of Lion's Head is knocked out, too. By the way, how'd you get here?"

"Car," Phil answered. "I got diesel," anticipating the sergeant's next query.

He nodded, seemingly knowing ahead of time what the answer would be. "About the only way in by highway is by diesel nowadays," he interjected. "I had to get old Nellie out of the barn so I could get around," motioning to the horse stalls next door. "What with the hunting season an' everything, Chet's Marina out at Dunk Point is about the only other way in by boat. Of course, you could fly in. If everything else fails, you can hike in," he added, giving a mirthless grin. "As for your second question, I have no way of knowing what the government is doing about it. I can't even get a long-distance call through." He stamped out his half-finished cigarette in the ashtray in a gesture of disgust.

"What about short-wave?" Phil remembered the tower he saw as he and Linda entered the building.

"That, too. All I get is static," he rejoined, nodding his head toward the back room. "Set's back there. You're welcome to take a try yourself if you know of any tricks to cut through the noise."

At first Phil couldn't believe what he was hearing. All outside communication was knocked out! "Sorry, sergeant. That's not my area of expertise. Perhaps our friends from Toronto can help you. Steve's picking up his boat at the marina there at Dunk Point later today. He's probably got short-wave on his boat. And then again, he's got his own plane. He could fly you out to get help." Because of the prolonged boating season, Phil knew Steve had kept his boat out of storage until the heat wave passed.

Sergeant Putnam's whole body jerked to attention. "Well, that would be mighty kind of him, Mister Deveroux, to do that. I just might take him up on the offer. If you could, have him come by the office when he gets the chance. I sure would appreciate it."

Phil nodded his intention.

"How long has this been going on, sir?" Linda piped up.

The sergeant seemed to have a little more respect for Linda when he inspected her again.

His tone of voice dropped two decibels, becoming more civil, when he answered her question this time. He gave a casual glance at a wall calendar. "A fortnight ago when it all started, Mrs. Deveroux, although it seems longer than that."

"What do you make of it?" she continued to press. "What could cause such a massive power outage?"

"To tell you the truth, ma'am, I don't rightly know. I'm not a scientist, but I've heard solar flares may have something to do with it."

"Baloney!" Phil cried to himself. He also had a short-wave radio at home that he played with occasionally. Solar flares can interrupt radio waves for hourly periods of time, but not for two weeks running. Putnam's answer was just too glib to suit the rationale of it all. UFO landings, alien sightings, power failures. It was all leading to something Sergeant Putnam was afraid to admit, Phil thought. He always could tell when somebody was straight out lying or to a lesser degree, fudging the truth. He had enough practice listening to drug users denying their habit or young mothers who had just flushed their aborted fetus down a toilet, not to recognize the deadpan look of falsehood in their eyes. Putnam had that same look.

Phil gave him a skewed look. It wasn't like him to interfere with or question the law. On the fire department, he lot-of-times had to respond to emergency runs involving altercations. Usually patching up a few busted heads was all that was required. Sometimes he and his crew had to assist the police maintain order until backup arrived. In this case, it was none of his, nor Linda's, business to keep drilling the good sergeant Sgt. Putnam certainly didn't need backup from a couple foreigners. It was time to leave. By now, the deputy's forehead was starting to bead with perspiration. He was definitely uneasy about something, Phil thought. It looked like he had wanted to elaborate on his last statement but at the last minute decided against it. Instead he elected to dab his forehead with a crumpled handkerchief that had magically appeared out of a rear pocket. Let's leave the poor guy alone, Phil decided.

He abruptly got up off the chair, surprising Linda with her husband's suddenness. "Time to go sergeant. We have lots to do before our friends arrive. If you don't have any further questions for us, we'll take our leave."

The deputy followed them as they headed toward the front door. "I appreciate you folks taking the time to report this," he said. "I'll type it up and send it E-mail, as soon as our satellite's working, to our regional office promptly. I'm sure someone from the Ministry will eventually be contacting you on this." He reached out his hand. "In the meantime, don't you worry. I'm sure there's a reasonable explanation for all of this."

Reasonable explanation my foot, Phil fumed. He wasn't satisfied with pat answers that were nothing more than a cover-up, but he returned the handshake in good faith anyway. Even if there was a reasonable explanation for all of this, the authorities wouldn't admit it. Phil was getting the distinct impression it was more of a bureaucratic decision to stonewall whatever was going on around here. Putnam was no more than a go-between.

"If you have any further questions on the matter, don't hesitate to call on me," was his final appeal. Briskly he spun on his heels, ready to go back to his upside down world, when suddenly he felt a soft touch on his arm.

"As a matter of fact, officer, I do have one more question," Phil replied. "Could you please tell me what day of the week this is?" The sergeant looked at him curiously, as if he thought Phil was pulling his leg.

"Why, today is Saturday. Why do you ask?"

Phil could almost hear Linda squirm behind him.

"Oh, it's nothing really. Just wondering. We somehow got our days crossed on the way up, that's all. As I mentioned, we're expecting friends joining us later today.

If by chance they come looking for us, tell them we're with Captain Smollet."

"First we're getting something to eat," Linda buzzed in her husband's ear. "I'm famished."

"Oh, is the captain expecting you?"

"Yes, sir. I called yester…er, I mean last week to tell him we were coming to celebrate our turkey day with him." He and Linda knew that Captain Smollet, being a widower, would enjoy the company.

The deputy did a double take. That must have really confused him, Phil thought. America celebrated their Thanksgiving two days ago. He probably couldn't help but think we were notorious procrastinators.

"Huh…I see. Looks like you're a little late."

"Yeah, something came up," Phil shot back before Linda could respond. To the police it may have sounded a little confusing, but, without preamble, the missing time was a cross he and Linda would have to bear. Their report would have to stand the way it was.

"Well," he said, cracking his lips into a crooked smile, "I do believe you have a point there, heh? Take care and have a good stay. I'll tell your friends where you are if they happen by. If you meet up with them first, please have, what's his name, Steve?" turning toward Phil for acknowledgement, "visit me at his first convenience." And with that final statement he turned and retreated into his office. They caught him lighting another cigarette just as he was disappearing behind the counter in a haze of blue smoke.

Phil and Linda stood in the parking lot for several seconds trying to digest what had just transpired. It seemed

Tobermory was in the grip of a siege of something more than just alien, he thought. Some other motive was at work here. Finally Linda broke the silence. "Let's go eat."

Phil wrapped his arm around her and gave her an emphatic squeeze.

"Now that's the second-best idea I've heard all morning, kid."

Linda looked up. She was putting as much innocence into her questioning eyes as she could muster. "What's the first?" she asked, fluttering her eyelids.

"I'll give you only one guess," he answered with a wolfish grin.

CHAPTER 8

November 29——-Space

The sun glinted off an armada of metallic objects as they hovered silently above the cloud-shrouded planet. In between the clouds revealed the planet to be a water planet, the source of life in the universe. This was a highly desirable asset to certain entities in the fleet as they patiently laid out their plans. Colonization was very important for the preservation of the species. The dimensions of the spacecrafts varied greatly in breadth and scope and their numbers ranged in the thousands. Their enormous height hid their presence from watchful eyes below. They continually monitored the slight rumblings beneath the crust of the planet which the inhabitants called Earth. The giant sphere inexorably spun on a rotational imbalance which would eventually spell its doom. The inhabitants were unaware of their planet's fate.

The occupants of these interstellar vehicles were of mixed worlds and their appearances had striking dissimilarities. In earthly standards, some came over vast distances marked in decades; others, in the blink of an eye, but no boundaries divided their purpose of mind. Theirs was a duty of obeying Universal Law. Saving those who were 'the chosen' was their paramount directive. But there were entities espousing an oppressive agenda as well. There was no remorse, no pity in their behavior, their thoughts, as they made preparations for the mass exodus about to take place. It was only a matter of time, and time was inconsequential to them. Already scout ships were leaving their vast network of underwater bases with humans collected from all five races of the rogue planet. Some underwater bases were in the last stages of abandonment with DNA samples of indigenous plants and animals; others had already left in mother ships with massive laboratories of genetically engineered human cargos. In time, temperature gradients inside the planet would reach intolerable limits. In time, the cleansing would begin in earnest...

In deep space, beyond time, there are worldly dimensions unknown to earthly mortals. These dimensions (houses), written as such in the Books of Learning (Ancient Manuscripts), are inhabited by sentient beings whose existence are on a higher plane of consciousness. These are entities closest to the Source (Creator). They came to the earth in human form, and were the Elders; the original demigods whom the Homo sapiens worshipped and glorified in millennia past. Theirs was a mission of enlightenment, not subjugation or deception. These were intergalactic teachers who subscribed to the Divine Plan of the Creator. What was written in the prophecies would come to pass, following the tenets of Universal Law. It dictated Gaea, Mother Earth, to begin the cleansing process of vile and contaminates it had endured for millennia. It had done so five times before in its four-and-a-half billion year history. It was preparing to do so again. The pollution of its resources, its lifeblood, was again threatened by mankind's intransigence. In accordance with Universal

Law, to eliminate karmic debt was to enlighten the consciousness of its progenitors. The race of Adam, from the beginning, was given the gift of free will by the Creator to follow its path to redemption. Instead, mankind used his free will to follow the path of apathy and negligence, ignoring earth's danger signals of world-wide climate changes, polar ice deterioration and erratic weather disturbances until it was too late. No longer could mankind control his fate or that of his planet. The cleansing process meant human extinction and a new cycle of human consciousness. But, as in previous cataclysms, there would be survivors. And, as history has recorded, beings would return as teachers to show Homo sapiens the way back. Universal Law is paramount and cannot be changed, altered, or absolved. The earth's axial tilt toward the sun had already begun, increasing the global temperature which, if left unchecked, would trigger catastrophic consequences. Man's free will was now at a crossroads.

CHAPTER 9

November 29—10:41 A.M....Land's End

Captain Smollet's two-story clapboard house was built at the turn of the century on the highest northern point of Bruce Peninsula. It offered a commanding view of both Georgian Bay and the surrounding islands. People around there called the site "Land's End." It was an appropriate name for it, Phil thought. You couldn't go any further north without falling over a fifty-foot cliff into Little Tub Harbor. Along with its larger counterpart, Big Tub Harbor, each cut perpendicular out of limestone by an ancient glacier, they served as natural havens for any ship seeking safe anchorage.

Phil once thought if the captain ever decided to cash in on his location, all he had to do was build a viewing stand in his back yard, mount a telescope, and charge admission. But the captain seemed to do quite well just shuttling sightseers to and from Flower Pot Island every year in his homemade guide-boat. During the off-season, he whittled amulets and carved fashionable pieces of cedar furniture, which he sold to a host of mail-order clientele from places as far away as New Zealand and Timbuktu.

Phil sometimes envied the captain's simple lifestyle. The captain had been living that way ever since his wife, Cora, died of cancer some twenty-odd years before, and he always seemed happy with his lot. She had been cut from the same mold as her husband: tough and resilient on the inside, gentle and mild mannered on the outside. They were traits pioneers were made of.

Phil parked the Escalade where the macadam abutted a narrow dirt trail that led the visitor up to the captain's front porch. He and Linda had just finished eating at Bea's Kitchen, a homey little place off the beaten path, that catered to locals, mostly. It was the last holdout before hunting season ended. Phil was mildly surprised to find the place almost empty. But then, he remembered, Tobermory was mysteriously cut off from the outside world by some ill-understood force. It would take an energy field of gigantic magnitude, he figured, to black out everything in town. It was too weird to even contemplate, and for the time being, he shut it out of his mind.

Hand in hand, they followed a winding path that skirted the outer lip of the promontory. Pitch Pine and Balsam Fir trees obscured the water for much of the way, but an occasional break brought the harbor into view. It was a barren scene compared to what he was used to seeing: a fleet of yachts jostling for mooring space along the docks. Because of the extended heat wave, you would have assumed many of the summer crowd would still be hanging around, Phil thought, but that was not the case. Other than a lone harbor patrol boat tied to one of the docks, the place was empty. Ticket booths, normally lined with customers for the glass-bottomed boats, which took tourists out to the more shallow wrecks, stood like abandoned way stations. The mammoth concrete wharf that berthed the two giant car ferries looked desolate next to the once-bustling passenger terminal. But the most noticeable feature of all was the lack of activity. No shoppers, no tourists. The public parking lot was empty. No kids running around. It created an eerie atmosphere. The place was absolutely devoid of people.

"Strange there aren't any people around," Linda remarked absently. "You'd think there was a plague going on."

"You wouldn't know it by talking to Sergeant Putnam. Sergeant Preston could probably have given us more information than he did," Phil shot back with a cynical smile. Linda knew her husband was referring to an old TV show about the Royal Canadian Mounted Police, Sergeant Preston of the Yukon and his dog, King. Too old for her taste, she thought.

"You're dating yourself, dear."

"Yeah, Yeah."

They passed by the rickety old wooden staircase that led down to the water. That's where the captain kept his thirty-five foot, steel-hulled boat, the Genny. She was partly hidden from view by three other captain's charter boats rafting off her. Strange, he thought. Why would those boats be here when they had their own mooring docks to tie up at?

Phil could still see her flared lines with the flamboyant caricature of a turtle painted on the funnel. Genny, years ago, suggested that the turtle would make a fine insignia, since the vessel wasn't much faster than a turtle anyway. The captain must have liked the idea, although he must have thought in his own mind that his boat, with a 250-horse-Cummins diesel powered engine, could chug along at a respectful twelve knots without much trouble. Not bad for a turtle. On Phil's next visit, lo and behold, a green turtle with a toothless grin, adorned the once unsightly smokestack, and beneath the painting, in honor of its creator, was the name, Genny.

Before Phil and Linda started bringing their own boat, a twenty-one foot Sea Ray, up to Tobermory, they spent a lot of time sailing with the captain. That was when he showed them the "back lot" of Tobermory, the secluded coves and inlets where ordinary tourists never ventured. They discovered a land of tranquil beauty, of undisturbed timber and an abundance of exotic plants, shrubs and flowers. The captain even showed them the precious Alaska Orchid after he and Linda promised never to reveal its location. Apparently tourists had no conception of its rarity and would have picked it without a second thought. Together, they went exploring the infinite variety of the Niagara Escarpment made up of Rockport dolomite manifested in its chinks, fissures, gullies and valleys. In its underwater caves and massive bulwarks, Phil and Linda found a naturalist's paradise. It was the last place in the world they would have expected any visitors from outer space.

Rounding a small rock outcrop, the couple came upon a dilapidated accumulation of timber and nails that loosely resembled a wooden shack, surrounded by a thatch of white and yellow birch. Sandwiched in between two of the trees was a satellite dish, which seemed out of place in the idyllic setting, but they knew the captain was a fanatical soap opera buff. It would have been like chopping off his right arm to sever his only link with the everyday scandals of The Young and the Restless, and General Hospital.

They peeked into the tiny enclosure which Captain Smollet used as his woodworking shop. The rich aroma of pipe tobacco and the lingering traces of freshly hewn wood hung pungently in the air. "Hellooo there!" Phil called out. "Anybody home?"

"Well, I'll be…" boomed a husky voice. It came from behind a large, pear-shaped, pine-knotted table lying half-finished on its side. As it was rolled aside by an invisible force, Phil and Linda saw Captain Smollet sitting on a small stool. A hammer and chisel were all but hidden in his huge hands. His faithful dog, Sandy, a buff-colored cocker spaniel, was lying asleep at his feet. The captain sprightly bounced up as they approached.

"I was startin' to worry, bonnies. I was expectin' ye four days ago!"

Sandy woke up and came sidling over to them, his tail wagging a friendly greeting.

"It's a long story, Cap'n" Phil answered apologetically, leaning down to scratch Sandy's furry head.

"Well, come now. Let's go on inside the house and you can tell me about it over a pot of fresh tea. "It's startin' to get too warm out here now that the sun's out." Phil nodded in agreement. Once the sun's rays burst through the morning haze, the temperature had climbed dramatically. He gathered both of them in his burly arms and squeezed them affectionately in a bear-like grip. They winced under the pressure. Though the captain was seventy-eight years old, you could never tell it by gripping one of his massive paws, Phil gathered. Smollet was as strong as an ox and built like one, too. His shock of white hair contrasted starkly with his dark, weather-beaten features.

They all sat around the kitchen table sipping tea, the sun filling the room with a golden glow as it slanted directly through the unshaded window over the sink. The living room in an adjacent room had a window air conditioner. Phil had his doubts it would be able to overcome the terrific heat of the afternoon sun beating down on them. The weather forecast on the car's satellite radio called for higher temperatures in the Northern Hemisphere, and climbing still higher the following week. God only knew what the temperature would be like in the Southern Hemisphere with countries situated closer to the equator, he wondered. The heat was the kind found in deserts. It sucks the moisture right out of your body and makes your skin shrivel up like a prune. Emergency measures were already being taken by every nation to replenish their water supplies. Encouraging pharmaceutical companies to increase their ratings on sun block protection was another priority. Melanoma cases were becoming a pandemic. Gathering enough scientists to determine the why and wherefore of their dilemma, and then, finding a way to stop it was the biggest challenge administrators faced. There was no precedent as to what was happening, let alone finding a solution. All the best geophysicists in the world couldn't figure out why, all of a sudden, the earth decided to increase its axial tilt as it sped around the sun. For the past decade, pollution had increased a hundredfold. Was it because small banana republics, with terrorists funding, began polluting the air big time with their use of nuclear weapons? Or perhaps it's because of an increase of major oil spills of millions of gallons of oil into the oceans by collisions of oil tankers or leaking pipe lines? Maybe atomic power plants leaking radiation into the air, or nuclear waste being dumped into the seas were more reasons for the earth to retaliate. Meanwhile, burgeoning populations around the world continued to generate ceaseless consumption of the world's rain forests for more development.

'Nonsense!' screamed one of the headlines in the Toronto Star newspaper. Captain Smollet held out another headline he had copied from the Internet: 'Don't Blame Us!'

"Call The Kettle Black!" Phil exclaimed. "Mother Earth decided enough was enough."

"It could be, lad," interjected the captain. "I know for a fact, all the animals seemed to have disappeared around here. I've found hide nor hair of em. Mighty strange."

"So is the story we got for you, skipper."

Phil and Linda commenced to relate their story to the old seafarer with as much aplomb as they did with Sergeant Putnam. This time they included the missing four days. The captain listened intently to their description of events leading up to the moment they surfaced after their dive. But something was missing, Phil opined. For want of a better word, 'closure'. He wanted to hear the captain say everything would be okay. Captain Smollet's square-jawed, bristly face looked interested enough in their story, but his steel gray eyes weren't seeing them. They had that impassive, unfocused look of someone who was a million miles away, reliving the past.

"...So that's why we decided to talk to the police, Cap'n," said Phil. "But what got me, he didn't seem too concerned about the whole thing. He seemed to have that wait-and-see attitude. Besides, I got the impression he wasn't telling us the whole truth."

"Yeah. And he was acting awfully fidgety. I never saw a man smoke cigarettes as fast as he did. I think we were making him nervous," Linda piped in shrewdly.

The old man gazed at Linda with a dour expression on his face.

"Don't be too harsh with poor Joe, lass. He lost his partner two...three weeks past and he hasn't been the same since. I guess that's when he started smoking again. He's had a lot of questions asked of him of late which he don't have the answers for. I'm afraid he doesn't have any more idea what's goin' on than the rest of us."

"Why doesn't he get some help?" Phil protested. "He said there's a total blackout here. No phone, no radio. And only diesels can run. Is that true, Cap'n?"

He nodded his head, pausing momentarily to rub his forehead. A light film covered his eyes. The captain seemed to be preoccupied with something, Phil gathered. He just wasn't his normal self. It was when the captain turned a pair of sad, pitiful eyes in his direction that Phil realized something was wrong. Very wrong!

"It just hasn't been the same around here since you last visited us, lad. Aye, not the same t'all." As the captain spoke, his Highland brogue became more pronounced.

"I've seen for myself those creatures you described, and those flying discs. More than once I've seen them comin' and goin,' They fly around like they own the sky, and the water beneath. I've seen them dive into the water and swim around like schools of herring."

Phil and Linda stared at him, dumbfounded. What the captain was describing was absolutely insane!

"What about the Air Force? Don't they send interceptors after them?" Phil asked incredulously. He knew there was an RCAF Base at North Bay, less than two hundred air miles away. With their fleet of supersonic F-35 Lightning-IIs and F-22 Raptors, they could pounce on an intruder and blast him out of the sky in less time than it would take to talk about it.

The old man shot him back a mirthless smile. "Aye, they have, but they might as well save themselves the trouble. They can't catch 'em!"

"Whaaat! Those planes, I've read, can go faster than a meteor!"

"Aye, maybe so, laddie, but those heathens can also make our planes disappear. There was one I just saw the other day. Bigger than most. A jet chased it into a cloud and neither one of them came out. Vanished, just like that!" He snapped his fingers for emphasis.

Phil suddenly felt his heart beat throbbing in his ears. His memory instantly hardened into thoughts of time warps and fourth dimensions. That vanishing act the captain described could only mean one thing, instant teleportation. How could you beat an enemy with that kind of technology? Enemy! Were these aliens really our enemy or were we just in the way of a higher agenda? Disturbing thoughts began to filter into the firefighter's consciousness. The whole scenario was becoming surreal. World-renowned psychics for decades had been predicting alien visitations to come. They weren't referring to the sporadic kind that had been going on since the days of contactees in the fifties, but vast numbers. It was all in accordance with the end of the millennium, supposedly the end of the world. But the millennium came and went, and nothing happened! Phil remembered the headlines: END OF THE WORLD A BUST! There were millions of people around the world who laughed it off. Now, he wasn't so sure who was doing the laughing. His line of thinking was sinking fast into a War Of The Worlds scenario.

Linda's soft voice thankfully interrupted her husband's weird thoughts of humankind becoming sacrificial lambs to a bunch of bloodthirsty aliens. "What happened to Joe's partner, Cap'n? You said something about him coming up missing."

"Aye, that's true, lassie. Ian Forrester is his name. He went out to investigate a UFO landing on the old Beecher property. Never came back. Joe thought he may have fallen off his horse. Maybe the horse tripped, threw him off and he fell into a gully and cracked his head. Neither one of us are what you call…mmmm…" The captain fluttered his hand to indicate he was trying to come up with the right word.

"Equestrians?" Linda volunteered.

"Not quite in that class, bonnie," said the old man with a tight smile. "More like a pair of tenderfoots on a dude ranch. Ridin' double isn't no fun either. Joe and I went looking for him that same night and all the next day. We found his horse just standin' there in an open field, feedin,' But no sign of Ian. Funny thing, though. There was a round patch of burned grass, maybe twenty meters across, not far from there. About the same size as one of those discs I keep seein." The captain's words echoed ominously in the dead stillness, broken only by the feint background humming of the air conditioner

" I take it there's more than Ian missing," said Phil. He had gotten away from his war briefing with the aliens and was closely listening to what was being said.

Captain Smollet's features took on a downtrodden look as he weighed his answer carefully. "I think half of the village is gone, lad. I don't know exactly since I can't use the tele, but Joe and I think at least that many."

Phil straightened up and took note. That meant over a thousand people abducted! The firefighter in him took over as he bounced out of his chair. "Let's go captain! My car. We can stop and pick up Sergeant Putnam along the way and get help."

Captain Smollet showed a tired smile on his lips. "Don't fret, laddie. We got word to the Mounties weeks ago. They know what's happen' here but they got troubles of their own. The sergeant was just showing you and the lassie here good face. He's probably keeping his options open in case he needs them. But it might be a good idea to turn around and head home yourselves. You never know what might develop here."

Phil took a glance at Linda and then steadied his gaze on the captain. "Well, Cap'n," he said, trying to ignore good advice. The frightening images his imagination was conjuring up were making him second-guess his decision. "As long as the aliens leave us alone from here on out, I'm willing to do likewise, at least until

Steve and Lucienne show up. Steve was all excited about something he wanted us to see. Once that's over, we probably will head home. If the same thing is happenin' in California, I would think the kids would want to come home too."

"Yeah," Linda rejoined, "except I think we missed the deadline. Getting a flight for them now will be a bear."

The captain picked up on her meaning immediately. "Are you sure, lass, that you and Phil left on the day you thought you did? I tend to forget what day it is myself on occasion," he concluded with a forced chuckle.

"Oh yes, I'm positive, all right. And I've still got the turkey to prove it!" Linda exclaimed.

"Steve and Lucienne are flying in this afternoon in their floatplane, Cap'n. He's parking it at Dunk Point and picking up his boat there. In fact, they may already be here by now," said Phil, glancing at his watch. "Why don't you, and Sandy, come over and join us at sundown for that dinner we promised you." Phil bent down and scratched the dog's head. "We can't forget about you, can we, boy?" The dog answered with a short lick of his hand.

The captain's face broke out in a grin. "Now, lad, that doesn't sound like a bad proposal. I could never pass up a woman's touch to a can of beans." He looked at Phil and gave him a sly wink. Linda was used to his strange bantering and paid him no heed. But Phil got the feeling that the captain was just putting on a brave show. From the way he talked, it was obvious the alien's super-technology could outperform anything the military could throw against them. The F-35 Lightning II and the F-22 Raptor were the best we had. Maybe the captain just didn't want to depress them with any more sordid details. Was it worse than he let on? And yet, how much worse could it get? As he and Linda walked out the door, he looked up at the sky, and wondered.

November 29—12:33—Milo's Grocery Mart

On the way back to the cabin, Phil and Linda made a stop at Little Tub's local market. Except for a meager supply of canned goods, five loaves of two-day old bread and a half-empty cooler of canned beer and soda, the shelves pretty much had seen better times. The owner's thirteen-year-old son, Tommy, was sitting behind the front counter reading a trade paperback. Interesting, thought Phil. The cover title read: Voyage to Oblivion. The author was a firefighter from Toledo, Ohio.

"Looks like the delivery truck passed you by, "Linda said kiddingly.

"No, ma'am," Tommy replied emphatically. "It's my ma's doin'. She ain't stockin' no more for the winter. We're lockin' up the store an' goin' to stay with my grandma in Sarnia. She don't want nothing' more to do with this place."

"Oh, why's that?" Linda asked, trying not to sound nosy.

'My Ma says grandma is sick an needs somebody to stay with her awhile." He then lowered his voice in a conspiratorial tone and leaned across the counter. "But I know the real reason. It's because of those things she keeps seein'."

"What things?" Linda prodded.

"Beasts, like. She says they're hairy all over an' got beady, red eyes."

Phil and Linda looked at each other as if they had just been granted a reprieve of their sanity. It seemed they weren't the only ones hallucinating around here.

"Have you seen any of these beasts yourself, Tommy?" Linda asked.

"Nooo, ma'am! An' I sure don't want to, either! Ma says they're as big as gorillas. Some men came from the government and said they were bears."

"What men?" It was starting to become an interrogation, Phil opined, but the information they were eliciting was fascinating.

"Men with red coats. There were two of 'em." Phil realized Tommy was referring to Royal Canadian Mounted Police, who traditionally wore red tunics as their official attire. "And they were on horses," the boy exclaimed, "big black ones! They were really awesome!"

"When were they here, Tommy?"

"Oh,…two, three weeks ago. They were looking' for one of the policemen that disappeared." Paul and Linda gave themselves knowing looks. No question they were looking for Ian Forrester. "So they said your ma kept seeing bears. Is that right, Tommy?"

"Yeah, that's what they wanted her to think. But Ma says she knows a bear when she sees one, and what she saw wasn't no bears. Besides, there ain't no bears around here."

"Where did she say she saw one last?"

Tommy gave them a hesitant look before shifting his eyes to a rear door. "On the road by Mr. Beechers farm. But I'd better not say no more. Ma says not to talk about it to nobody, an' I don't want to get in no trouble." No more was said as Tommy bagged the groceries and handed Linda her change. Tommy was a slow learner. By the boy's nervousness, Phil got the impression he had said too much already and was now in trouble with his ma. To break the ice and make him feel some idle conversation between them would seal their lips forever, Phil espied the book Tommy had laid on the counter. It had an attractive cover, so he centered on that. "Interesting picture on the cover of your book, young man. What is that, a Coast Guard Cutter? Looks like it's headin' for trouble." He established it to be a giant whirlpool with a helicoptor hovering in the background.

Tommy's face started to beam at the mention of the Coast Guard Cutter. "Yes sir, it's awesome, ain't it? It's American but Canada has 'em too. I can't wait till I'm old enough to join up." Tommy said it as proud as any kid could his age. Perhaps even more so than any adult Phil knew. The kid's buttons were almost popping off his chest. "Good for you, young man. Good for you. Go for it, and don't let anybody stand in your way."

Leaving the store, Phil was saddened to think Tommy might never get the chance to fulfill his dream.

CHAPTER 10

November 29—2:45 P.M....Dog Patch

    Phil and Linda heard the rumble of dual exhausts wash over the cabin as two powerful, 500-cubic-inch turbocharged Drohler turbines came thundering down the channel. The sound intensified until the walls of the cabin shook like paper and the normal decibel range of speech was all but nullified under the din.

    They exchanged knowing glances as they rushed out the front door. Steve had arrived. They were immediately assaulted by a flash of bright sunlight reflecting off of metal as it streaked past. A second look told them it was a thirty-eight-foot, twin screwed fiber-glassed Wellcraft with a lavish amount of brass trimming, just completing a 180-degree turn around the buoy. The roar of the boat's 900-horsepower power-plants abruptly diminished to a muted snarl, leaving a cauldron of seething froth in their wake. The sudden transition from cacophony to silence was almost deafening. Neither Phil nor Linda were ever surprised at their friend's loud introductions. It had almost become traditional for Steve to showcase his latest prize by first making everybody sit up and take notice.

    Stepping up to the bow with a painter in hand was a coquettish figure with short dark hair bouncing freely in the air. It was Lucienne. She had on red shorts with a halter to match and the omnipresent dark shades covering her eyes. Phil and Linda were always amazed at the way she got around so well being blind with hardly any help from Steve.

She was about two inches shorter than Linda, and looked somewhat impish next to her six-foot, one-inch tall, athletic husband. But their dissimilarities in height hadn't seemed to affect their sex life any, Phil mused. Even with her handicap, she managed to raise five children practically on her own while Steve was out administering to his shoe factories. Of course, it didn't hurt to have nannies and nursemaids at your beck and call. It didn't hurt to be the wife of a millionaire either.

He heard a muffled "NOW" from inside the boat's cabin the same instant Lucienne cast the line. It sailed within easy reach of Linda's outstretched hands. The engines immediately cut off as she gently maneuvered the Wellcraft alongside the small finger pier Phil had built for the Sea Ray.

Steve's boat was a magnificent-looking specimen of a high-tech racing machine, Phil had to admit, with all the accoutrements of a luxurious yacht. He wouldn't have been surprised if it surpassed the space shuttle for the latest in electronic gadgetry. And in all probability, it was someone else's castoff. Steve had a penchant for rehabilitating old boats, cars, planes, whatever caught his fancy. Last year he had fallen in love with a thirty-year-old Cardita that he had stripped down and rebuilt to the latest engineering standards that claimed him third place in 'America's Cup.'

As soon as Steve appeared on deck, Phil cupped his hands and yelled good-naturedly, "Hey, big guy! How many shoes did you have to peddle for this one?"

"Hey, you like it? I named it the Flying Shoestring." Steve grinned from ear to ear. "Want the quarter tour? For you, I'll throw in the popcorn."

"I'll exchange the quarter for giving you a ride in my new Cadillac. It's one of those Flintstone models." Steve and Lucienne already knew it was what their friends could afford and made no bones about it. That was one of their strongest attributes, Phil discovered early in their relationship, making friends feel comfortable around them regardless of their social status.

"Fair enough," answered Steve with an infectious grin as he greeted Phil with a strong handshake before giving Linda a big hug. Phil reciprocated, thankful of their friend's much needed moral support. It seemed so much had happened since their last phone conversation.

"Glad to see you guys again," Phil piped up, 'glad' being an understatement. 'Thrilled' would have been a better choice of words. "I thought you might have changed your mind about meeting us here." directing his statement toward Steve. "I heard on the grapevine you were breaking ground this weekend for a new factory in Detroit. Good choice. The city could sure use the jobs."

"Not to fear, my friend. My right-hand man, Paul Slater, you met him at my last opening in Montreal, remember? He'll be there for the official ceremony." He slapped Phil on the back in a jovial display of affection. "You think Lulu and I would miss out showing you our big surprise?"

It must be one hell of a virgin shipwreck, Phil mused, still thinking that's what the big secret was all about. But that's who Steve was, like a kid who never grew up. His deep-rooted competitiveness sometimes clashed with his good senses. But when push came to shove, his knack for making the right choices always won out. It was as if the planet Jupiter, the money planet in Astrology, followed him around, like a bee attracted to honey, the moment he inherited his father's fortune. Ironically his father made his fortune in the stock market, not in shoes. Hush puppies were in its infancy when Steve took over the little known shoe manufacturer. It was under Steve's guidance that that little shoe company became Shackter Shoes, the largest shoe conglomerate in Canada. Phil always kidded him about inheriting a fortune to make a fortune. How lucky can you get?

You would think that, with that kind of money, Steve would be a rich playboy. That would be furthest from the truth, Phil would answer. However, he certainly could play the part well, with his Errol Flynn mustache and devil-may-care attitude. Steve took after his father in many respects, with his affable nature and a heart as big as his wallet. Steve would be the first to offer a helping hand to someone truly in need. It was difficult not to like a guy like that.

Steve was also a devoted family man, especially dedicated to the cornerstone of his family, Lucienne. Sometimes Phil got the impression that Steve's entire world revolved around Lucienne. Like a house of cards caught in a sudden draught, Steve's happy disposition would come crashing down in an instant if that cornerstone suddenly collapsed. The fact that she had an inoperable aneurysm lodged at the base of her brain due to a skiing accident didn't help matters either. She had been perpetually walking a tightrope ever since.

"Let's go in and have a beer or two," Phil suggested. "It's too damn hot out here."

"Yes, it has really been hot lately, hasn't it?" Lucienne murmured softly. "The earth is restless." The words had an almost sinister undertone to them. No one would have thought much of it if it hadn't been Lucienne saying it. Her powers of perception since her accident were extraordinary. Everyone stopped.

"What is it Lulu? Why'd you say that?" asked Linda.

"Because I feel change is coming. It's hard to describe. Our planet is reacting to some powerful … force…is the best way I can describe it." For a few long seconds, everyone remained silent, trying to interpret what Lucienne had meant in-between the lines.

"My body is reacting to a severe bout of dehydration right now," kidded Steve to his wife, breaking the awkwardness of the moment. "Let's do what our host suggest, my love, and graciously accept his hospitality, before I die a horrible death of thirst." Spoken like a true Errol Flynn disciple, Phil thought.

"How pathetic," answered Lucienne in a pitiful voice, giving everyone a good laugh. It broke the ice. All of them hustled back to the cabin, boisterously reminiscing of their last get-together.

Unbeknownst to them, two shining discs dropped unnoticed into the waters off Devil's Island. Their gilded surfaces shone like giant lasers in the dying sun.

CHAPTER 11

November 29—3:54 P.M.

The scent of turkey roasting in the oven gave off a pleasant, homey atmosphere. All of them were lolling around the living room in different modes of attire, trying to stay cool. Steve, wearing a glossy pair of black trunks, draped over a worn chaise lounge while Lucienne cuddled next to him on the floor. Phil and Linda were sprawled on the couch with their feet propped on the coffee table, Molson Lites in hand, looking for all the world as if they were going to melt into the fabric. Phil realized that the trickle of cold air spilling through an open bedroom door from their small air conditioner wasn't nearly enough to combat a rising thermal bombardment of one hundred plus degree temperature outside.

"I would suggest we all vegetate on the Flying Shoestring, but I'm afraid my small cabin unit wouldn't do any better than what we've got now," volunteered Steve. Everything seemed to be weighed down by the enervating heat. Even their speech flow seemed to be mired in molasses. It was like watching everyone mouthing their words in slow motion. That's what too much sun can do to your sense of perception, Phil thought. Through the large picture window, he happened to glance out at an unruffled steel mirror, the lowering sun making the seascape shimmer like diamonds. How many times had he and his family gazed through that same window and felt the Bay's magnetism drawing them into its depths? There was no such feelings of that promise today, only one of potential danger the moment you stepped outside. Besides the hellish heat, the ozone layer surrounding the planet was found to have a hole in it over the Artic. Not to worry though, the experts said. It can repair itself in fifty years or so. One little caveat, however. It can recover in fifty years or so only if other new gases aren't released into the atmosphere, like hairsprays, pesticides and refrigerants. And that's only gases we know of. Phil had that feeling of danger looming again, especially after he heard what else was happening in the world.

The news Steve and Lucienne brought with them was not good. Chinese troops massing along the India-Pakistan border had been reported during Phil and Linda's four-day absence. Within 24 hours, they had attacked, using lightweight plutonium warheads delivered by recoilless rifles. Sub-kiloton yields produced the desired effect, leaving a swath of devastation behind as they headed for the new Karachi oil fields in southern Pakistan. It had been rumored for several years that the Chinese oil beds in the central Sinkiang Province had dried up significantly, leaving them with dwindling reserves and insufficient funds to pay for the huge amount of imports their burgeoning population demanded. Phil, being an amateur history buff, was surprised why the Chinese made the same mistake Saddam Hussein made when he invaded Kuwait. Kuwait had the United States, with nuclear weapons, as a back-up; Pakistan already had nuclear weapons as a back-up. Using these small thermonuclear devices against each other, huge amounts of radiation were being spewed up into the stratosphere, to be scattered downwind by the jet stream. Before they decided to use bigger yields delivered by missiles, which would profligate into a major war and annihilate the entire planet, it had to be stopped. Phil didn't have to be a rocket scientist to realize something mysterious was happening to the earth. Volcanoes around the world, many of which had been dormant for centuries, such as Mount Vesuvius in Italy and Mount Pelé on the island of Martinique in the Caribbean, were beginning to erupt. Severe tremors were being felt all along the San Andreas Fault in California. A major quake, registering 8.6 on the Richter Scale, had been reported in the city of Kushiro in northern Japan, killing tens of thousands of people. No further news was being reported from that area. Another seismic disturbance, its epicenter somewhere in the middle of the Indian Ocean, had caused huge tsunamis along the coast of Ceylon. What was strangest about all the disasters, Phil surmised, was that they had all begun to occur during he and Linda's hiatus. Coincidence? Too many variables would have to fall into place to think that, Phil decided.

"You look surprised, pal," said Steve. "Didn't you and Linda catch the news? That's all the CBC's been broadcasting the past forty-eight hours, mostly about the invasion and the atomic war going on. Our prime minister thinks chances are good both our countries will get involved, somehow. The United Nations is in an uproar. What do you think?"

"Believe it or not, Steve, I'm more worried about what Edgar Cayce predicted about future earth changes. I think its starting."

"Wasn't he a healer of some sort?"

"Yeah, he was quite a healer." He was also Phil's benefactor. During a dark period of his career as a firefighter, he had lost all hope of finding a kind and benevolent god. His job as a firefighter/paramedic, especially, had taken him into a world of pain and suffering for so long, he had stopped believing there was a higher being who could stop such terrible suffering to continue, especially to the young and innocent. For what reason, he kept asking himself, did God allow it to happen? He had asked clergy of different denominations, and always got the same response. He soon became disenchanted with their answers. Men of the cloth liked to quote such biblical phrases as, 'It was God's will,' or 'God works in mysterious ways.' "God's will, my ass! Tell that to a young couple who found their six-week-old baby dead in its crib for no apparent reason; to a five-year-old girl he once carried out of a fire, dead in his arms; or to a three-year-old boy who was found face down in a bathtub. Where was God's mercy for those innocent victims? Oh, yes. To those euphemistic posturers who live by quotes, let's not forget about man's free will. What free will does an innocent fetus have after being flushed down a toilet, or a baby being shook to death by a deranged nut case? If God allowed those innocents to be born to begin with, why does he snuff out their lives so cruelly and without purpose before they even know right from wrong?"

His brother, Jeremy, who, among other things, had an uncanny gift of perception, came to Phil's rescue and referred him to a man who devoted his entire life to helping people. Through the Association for Research and Enlightenment in Virginia Beach, Phil and Linda got to know about Edgar Cayce. Cayce died in 1945, but he left behind a legacy of over 14,000 life readings.

From this complex library of stenographic reports emerged many accounts of the evolutionary spirit of man through his many successive lifetimes on earth. Man's ultimate goal, Cayce claimed, was to reach perfection, to "return to the path of reconciliation." (forgiveness) This was man's road back to the Creator. The way it was achieved was through reincarnation and, synonymous with it, karma, the law of cause and effect. By not following God's laws through his commandments in a previous lifetime meant a period of restitution in the next. It's called karmic debt. If he chooses to reincarnate, his free will is the deciding factor as to what direction he must take. Only after death returns him to the spirit world does he learn if his efforts were of any consequence. Time is irrelevant. He may choose to reincarnate for an entirely different reason years later. Perhaps a loved one, still living, needs his/her help. Guardian angels come to mind? The Bible mentions them often. Cayce, in many of his readings, referred to a person having hundreds of lifetimes before he/she chose to stay in spirit form. The whole idea of reincarnation is to help shorten the journey to God. That's what all major religions refer to as being in Heaven. Christianity is the only major religion that doesn't embrace the concept of rebirth or reincarnation. The combined billions of

Muslims, Jews, Hindus and Buddhists can't all be wrong, Phil decided. And when he stopped to think about it, didn't Jesus reincarnate when He came back from the dead? And on more than one occasion He appeared to his mother Mary, Mary Magdalene, and the Apostles. Which brought Phil to the crux of his disillusionment with God. Was there even a God He could identify with? The Trinity boggled his mind ever since he studied it in his catechism book from the first grade.

"Is there really a God, mamma?" From momma, the answer was always the same. "Of course there is, dear."

"Only one?" With the patience of Job, his mother would say, "Yes, dear. Only one. He takes care of everyone." Even at a young age, somewhere in his brain, Phil questioned the logic of such an assertion. In talking to his brother about the One God syndrome…the Supreme Being…the Source…the Creator, Jeremy was of the opinion that a singular God became imbedded in the psyche of all intelligent life the moment they were born. But, as far as Phil was concerned, that was only an assumption. After the firefighter/paramedic witnessed death and tragedy for so many years on the fire department, his psyche was thoroughly saturated with doubt. If there is a God, especially one that can separate himself with love and compassion in one hand, and ignore the cries of the innocents in the other, the Christian faith created an oxymoron in Phil's mind that was irreconcilable. The followers of Eastern religions account for 67% of world religions and yet, somehow, were not able to enter the heaven prepared by Christ. They had their own gods; their own heavens, was the current maxim. If Christ was the true God, how could that be possible? In Phil's perspective, it meant that Christ had deserted more than half of earth's population from his teachings. Even more inexplicable was seeing the pain and suffering, especially of children, continue without pause. Phil had a hard time reconciling the fact that there was even a God at all. Searching for answers, his thoughts carried him down a slippery slope that hopefully, in the end, would provide him the peace of mind he so desperately sought.

Part of the answer lays in reincarnation, Phil was told. Christ reincarnated many times after His resurrection. Christians came rather late on the scene, Jeremy kept reminding him. They've only been around two thousand years. Other religions have been practicing monotheism for thousands of years longer. That's what Phil had the most trouble understanding about the Trinity. As part of the Trinity, Phil was raised believing Christ separated from himself (Father and Holy Spirit) and was made man in order to pay humankind's karmic debt of original sin. (author uses karmic debt not mentioned in the Bible) He died on the cross 'for our sins,' before returning to his Father. On the cross, Christ specifically refers to His Father as a separate entity. "Father, they know not what they do." Who else calls their father 'father,' unless it is a son or daughter? Also, a spirit can return to the earth plane in the same form as when they left. It explains Christ's appearance after the crucifixion with the same wounds in his side, wrists and feet. It explains the appearance of loved ones being seen as apparitions, or ghosts, usually in familiar surroundings, back in the earth plane. Sometimes it was difficult for departed souls to leave the material world; it explains child prodigies and phobias carried over from past experiences; it explains homosexual desires if changing sexes from one lifetime to another.

One God in three different interchangeable houses or dimensions. That's no harder to believe than three Gods incorporated into one. To Phil, it made more sense that Heaven is multi-dimensional. Christ even said, My Father's House has many dwelling places. What Phil couldn't figure out is what part of dwelling places don't people understand? According to Christ, there is a heaven, made up of dimensions (houses) where both physical and spiritual beings coexist. Scientists have claimed up to ten dimensions exist in the universe, so that concept can also be debated on scientific grounds as well.

To support this belief, through a succession of reincarnations, Phil believed Christ returned to start new religions in the likeness of Mohammed, Krishna and Buddha. "Yes dear," his mom used to say. "God can make anything possible, because He's God." It reminded Phil of the movie, Jaws, where Sheriff Brody said in reply to Hooper questioning his authority—"I'm the sheriff. I can do anything I wanna do."

But, for Phil, that was only the beginning of his battle to rationalize his relationship with God. Even Cayce's readings of God's eternal love and compassion couldn't convince Phil there was a just and merciful God. The firefighter/paramedic in him never understood why innocent children, even babies, underwent such cruel punishments, even to the point of being tortured before death. They have no conception of right or wrong so you couldn't blame it on karmic debt. Perhaps having a child suffer or die to punish another soul is God's way of retribution. Like grieving parents, for example. In Phil's reasoning, he kept asking: Why does He allow helpless children to bear the burden of someone else's 'free will?' And in many cases, have to die for it. To any sane person, there was no logic to it.

It was in Cayce's library, sifting through the documents, that Phil happened upon Edgar Cayce's prophecies. In several of his readings he talked about earth changes and the dawning of a New Age. The earth upon which we live, he said, was also subject to universal laws which cannot be changed or altered, and the time for change was at hand. In six of his readings, Cayce predicted a specific cleansing to take place, beginning with the release of energy through earthquakes and volcanic eruptions. The cataclysms would continue and increase in intensity over a three year period until the earth, as he knew it then, would cease to exist. His original prediction closely matched those of other psychic's. History proved them all wrong. As there are bends in a river, so are there bends in the natural flow of future events. Cayce was the greatest clairvoyant who ever lived. His percentage of strikes were head and shoulders above everyone else. Everything that ever happened on earth since time immemorial is stored in what Cayce called The Akashic Records. The records of what a person does or thinks are thus forever preserved. For everyone that ever lived and died on earth, each individual entity patiently wrote upon the skein of Time and Space, as Cayce put it, recording their interests, their talents, their knowledge, their experiences. This is what he tapped into for his readings on reincarnations and predictions of earth changes; countless billions of life experiences. To interpret the twists and turns of every human consciousness that ever lived up to Cayce's time, can be a daunting task. As far as Phil was concerned, Cayce, the master psychic, was occasionally allowed to relax, chill out and regroup.

Cayce's take on the coming earth changes were too horrific to put into words. Phil was leery about bringing up Cayce's predictions to Steve and Lucienne without sounding like Chicken Little. Phil brooded. Even the UFO and the aliens he and Linda encountered sounded insignificant compared to what else was happening around the world. With Linda giving him an understanding look, Phil abruptly changed the subject.

"Let's talk about something dearer to our hearts, big fella. Like, what's the big secret?"

"Not so fast, my friend. I happened to run across an article in the paper the other day. Some filler on the back page about the police checking out reports of a Bigfoot roaming around out here."

"Don't forget a bunch of sightings of UFO's being reported around Tobermory!" interjected Lucienne in an excited voice. "I've never seen one before!"

"Tell me about it," exclaimed Linda. "We got something to tell you that you won't believe."

"So much for insignificant," said Phil under his breath.

Steve and Lucienne sat in stunned silence as Linda, maintaining equanimity throughout the telling, and without any coaxing from Phil, relived her frightful experience one more time.

"You mean, you guys can't account for four whole days?" Steve asked suspiciously. "Okay, what kind of hooch have you two been drinking?"

"We're not kidding, Steve," answered Phil seriously. He finished up the story by repeating what Sergeant Putnam and Captain Smollet had related to them. The wheezing air conditioner suddenly took on the sounds of a threshing machine in the hushed stillness that followed. It seemed everyone was holding their breath.

"Perhaps you better tell them what happened to us on the way up, honey," said Lucienne in her soft, pixie-like voice. "Maybe it's connected some way to what's been happening."

"Yeah, it does look like there might be something to it," Steve replied thoughtfully as he finished his beer with one last pull of the can. "Lulu and I left the Mississauga Airport at precisely 10:40 this morning," he began. "As you know, it's only a two-hour flight to get here."

They knew Steve flew an old war surplus Stinson Sentinel L-13, a spotter plane that used to be named the "Grasshopper." As with everything else he liked to restore and tinker with, he had beefed up the frame and added a few more rpm to the Franklin air cooled 250 hp engine.

"I decided at the beginning to fly my Cessna amphibious today. Lucky I did. It has a bit more power with the new turbo I had installed. I started out my flight plan with a clear ceiling and unlimited visibility. No crosswinds. A milk run. About an hour and half into the flight, all hell broke loose." Steve's face hardened into a look of disbelief. "We were over the bay by then, just about ready to turn onto my final approach, when I started bucking head winds you wouldn't believe. Then, out of nowhere, came these…yellowish looking clouds the size of mountains. I mean these suckers came up fast. And lightning then started hittin' all around us! I mean, this wasn't just ordinary lightening. And then came the buffeting! I felt we were inside a pinball machine. In all my years of flyin', I never experienced anything like that before." With a dead man's stare, Steve stopped to take a deep breath, took another long pull of his Molson, and continued his narration as though he never stopped. "And the horizon just disappeared on me! Where water and sky should have met, all I could make out was a milky-white haze. I even lost track of what heading I was on. My RDF was out, so was my GPS, and my mag compass was spinnin' so fast it looked like a pinwheel."

Steve was usually a pretty levelheaded guy and one hell of a pilot, Phil opined. He could make a plane stand on its tail and do pirouettes. He did dead-man stalls at a thousand feet just for practice. But Phil could tell this latest venture had really scared his friend. After finishing his story, Steve had the haunted look of someone who'd had a brush with death.

Phil went to relieve himself before stopping at the kitchen to get another beer. By the time he returned, Steve had reverted to his former debonair self and was finishing another one of his classic stories.

"…And there was only one way to get out of that mess. It was what any intelligent pilot of my caliber would do." He paused for effect by slowly taking another swig of beer, letting them hang on his every word. He gave Phil and Linda one of his Errol Flynn grins. Phil remembered he had heard the story before as he was walking in from the kitchen. It was another one of Steve's standard climaxes.

"I got out of there tout de suite and I didn't let the door hit me in the arse on the way out either!"

"They all laughed.

"Tell them about the whirlpool, Steve," Lucienne prompted.

"Oui, Oui," her husband replied quickly in French. "I was getting to that," as if he wished he could forget it.

"I spotted this giant vortex in the water. It musta' been ninety…maybe a hundred meters in diameter. Like she said, it looked just like a whirlpool. Stupid me! I decided to make a low pass over it. Wrong! When I did, it was like I hit a pocket of dead air. I had no lift! If it wasn't for my supercharger giving me boost, I would have never been able to pull out of it."

The word 'whirlpool' instantly reminded Phil of the picture on the cover of Tommy's book. What a coincidence, he thought.

"Yes, it was frightening," Lucienne added. "I felt as if my stomach was being turned inside out."

"Yes, I imagine so," consoled Linda. "If it were me, I probably would have upchucked all over the place. You know how I don't like to fly anyway."

"Do you think it might have been caused by some seismic disturbance?" queried Steve. "First time I've run across something like that."

"If I had to guess, I'd say it was a portal for our visitors from Mars," said Phil with tongue in cheek.

"Mars!" coming from Linda and Lucienne in one voice.

"Just kidding, girls. Just kidding. But I do believe there are more than one around and they're entry and exit points for all those flying discs people keep reporting."

"You may be right, my friend, and it might be connected with what Lulu and I have discovered." The big Canadian swung his leg off the armrest and, leaning forward on his elbows, gave Phil a fixed stare, his eyes glittering from the window glare. "About six weeks ago, Lucienne and I went diving off Flower Pot Island. As you know, we like to camp there. So, early one morning, we decided to do a little underwater exploring off the lighthouse area. You know where I mean?" Phil and Linda both nodded.

"Have you ever known the island to have any underwater caves?" He was fishing for anyone to grab the bait. Linda obliged.

"Phil and I dove on the Cedarville wreck once off Lookout Point, but I don't remember seeing any caves, do you dear?"

"No, except for some shallow indentations, it's pretty much shelf rock all the way to the bottom," said Phil.

"And how deep do you think the bottom is?"

"Oh, I don't know. I think the charts say about forty fathoms. Why?" Phil was starting to get impatient with Steve's teasing questions.

"Would you believe 190 meters?"

"Impossible!" Phil was never the quickest on the draw when it came to the metric system, but he knew 190 meters was well over 500 feet.

"I thought so too, until Lulu and I ran across this enormous trench. We followed it, and it just kept leading us deeper and deeper. Lucky we were wearing doubles with our tri-mix. And guess where it led us? Right smack dab into the biggest cave you'd ever want to lay your eyes on. I mean, this sucker must take up half the island!"

"Where exactly were you and Lucienne in relation to the surface?" Linda asked.

"I'd say right below the large flowerpot," Steve replied. "I'll bet you'll never guess what was inside." No one spoke,

"SHIPS! Not wrecks! SHIPS! There musta been dozens of them! And they were all lined up like they were on display or something. There were all kinds, but mostly lake freighters and 19th century wooden schooners, from what I could tell. I even saw some airliners too. I recognized one in particular, that TransCanada 777 that disappeared over Lake Ontario a couple of years ago."

"Yeah, I remember that," said Linda. "Over two hundred people aboard."

"Wasn't it kinda dark down there? No surface light can penetrate that far down, you know," Phil challenged.

"Didn't need any. As soon as we entered the cave, some weird illumination was keeping everything well-lit."

"Where was the light coming from?"

"All over! It wasn't a harsh light. It was like stepping outside on a cloudy day. I had no trouble seein' inside the entire cave."

"You tryin' to tell us what you saw was a cave full of intact shipwrecks and even modern day aircraft lying about. None were broken up?"

"Exactly!"

Phil and Linda looked at each other, not knowing what to make of it. They knew Steve had a tendency to embellish the truth sometimes, but he was never one to tell tall tales, especially ones as fanciful as this one.

"There was something else, too," said Lucienne.

"What's that, Lulu?" asked Linda.

"I could feel a presence. There was someone or something else besides Steve and me down there. And the feeling got stronger the longer we stayed." She reached out and clasped Steve's hand for reassurance.

If Lucienne said that something bordering on the paranormal was happening, you could believe it. Her powers of ESP transcended simple clairvoyance. She could receive impressions simply from touching an object. Parapsychologists called it psychometry. It was amazing, after diving on a shipwreck, for example, to listen to her description of what she 'saw' with her fingers, Phil reflected. Her sense of touch took in the minutest details. Her description of the Bentley Gale was phenomenal. During some of her best recountings, it was as if she were peeking through a crack in time and witnessing a piece of history unfolding on the other side. "Were you able to determine the cave's exact depth?" Phil asked.

"My depth gauge was pegged at 170 meters and we still dropped a short ways to the bottom. All solid dolomite. We hung around as long as we could, but when our air reserve alarms activated, we took off."

"Wow!" Linda was caught up in Steve's enthusiasm. "I can't wait to see it for myself!"

"I think maybe…just maybeeee," Steve drawled, flashing one of his infectious grins, "we hit the jackpot, eh?" In his excitement he almost jumped out of his chair. "What do you think, Phil?"

Phil hated to burst Steve's bubble. What he had just described to him and Linda was so bizarre, it fringed on the supernatural. His father had told him a long time ago that it wasn't wise to fool with things you didn't understand. The supernatural was one of them.

Yet, what a fantastic discovery! He was as hooked as Steve and Lucienne were when it came to finding what every diver longed for—shipwrecks full of artifacts and treasure chests just begging to be opened. Except these were the genuine articles. Unbelievable! It was the pot at the end of the rainbow. As strange as it sounded to him, it demanded investigation. Steve and his bank of lawyers could figure out the legalities later. Any thoughts of going home now had suddenly been shoved to the back of his mind.

He quickly glanced at Linda for her tacit approval. Her eyes gave him the answer he wanted.

"It's your show, big guy. Let's go for it."

CHAPTER 12

November 29—7:05 P.M…Dog Patch

The crackle of the campfire, the smell of wood smoke, and the sounds of singing and laughter seemed just right for Phil that night. It felt good to have Linda next to him and enjoy the camaraderie of close friends. Captain Smollet had brought his dependable ukulele along with his trusted companion, Sandy, forever wagging his tail, glued to his side as always. Steve and Lucienne were sitting cross-legged next to the fire, letting loose with their own renditions of Canadian Bluegrass.

In Phil's mind, the mysterious revelations of the past few hours had been temporarily put on hold. He subconsciously relaxed his body, letting his thoughts roam free as his eyes hypnotically focused on the fire. The night was filled with the moon so clear, you could almost count the footsteps left by the astronauts on the Sea of Tranquility. The stars shone bright around the giant orb like embroidered jewels. The air had turned charitably cooler. It was a beautiful evening, the kind people store in their memory banks for future recall. Phil sensed that this diversion was vital for their own piece of mind. No one seemed anxious to break the magic spell the night had woven.

On the surface, Phil imagined, he probably looked composed enough. But on the inside, his nerves were about

as much on edge as when he was waiting for the test scores
to be announced for promotion to lieutenant. It seemed like
yesterday. When the scores were announced, it was a day
of celebration. His was one of the highest. Settling
comfortably back against a rock, Phil let his stream of
consciousness reach out a little further back in time. The
time when a good friend of his, a lieutenant in a
neighboring fire department, was blocked for promotion by
what was called by people in the know, the crony system.
His friend had also scored high, placing in the top third of
the thirty-nine candidates that were tested. Eighteen were
eventually promoted. At the time this particular officer was
#1 in grade and #1 in seniority. He even acted in a higher
rank for a whole year prior to the test, passing with flying
colors on all his evaluation reports. It meant absolutely
nothing under the crony system. Filling a position
regardless of qualifications or precedence is all part of the
game. You can be as street smart as Columbo, but if you're
not "in the loop" even union protection is not always
equitable. His friend appealed to the International for help.
They didn't even bother answering. Phil remembered the
lieutenant's frustration. He once said the effect it had on
his family hurt the most. It was if the world had blown up
in their faces. Of course, the whole bottom line in the
crony system is the city saving money. Deals are made
between the city and the union. Police and fire departments
especially, are highly scrutinized by the public. Nothing
gets by them when it comes to budgetary costs. Promotions
are great for publicity and are touted as being most cost
effective. The initial costs of hiring new recruits goes down
because stacked up experience in the higher ranks with just

minimal pay raises and overtime is cheaper, especially if the city doesn't have to honor a minimum manning clause in the contract. To most, being "out of the loop" can wear thin when you have to continue associating with people who got promoted over you through cronyism. For Phil, it would have been a hard pill to swallow. To be sure, it always goes under a different guise but, as far as he was concerned, he called a spade a spade. Segregating the contestants into so-called bands, with such variance as twenty to thirty points in the test scores, was a sure way of eliminating unwanted competition. To Phil, the memory of the injustice done to his friend and his family had awakened a sudden awareness in him. It was what his friend had said, "it was as if the world had blown up in their faces," that had struck a chord. Even under different circumstances, in the literal sense, that's exactly what could happen to him and Linda and their friends as they sat in comparative safety on top of the world. The most vulnerable piece of real estate on the planet, in his opinion. The Arctic Circle was only thirty minutes away by jet. Steve mentioned the fact that in the last four days, waves of UFO's had been reported in the Arctic region. Something was going on.

He feared Cayce's predictions were about to come true, for several reasons. First and foremost, the lack of communication. In this technological world of satellites and macro-laser avionics, it was as if Tobermory were being purposely singled out, for reasons unknown, as part of some devilish plan. A test site perhaps, to see how its residents reacted to certain stimuli. Like those beady-eyed creatures for instance, Phil pondered, who seemed to be as abundant as the UFOs. And those ships and perhaps more airplanes down in the cave. According to Steve, they were all lined up like ducks in a shooting gallery. Phil highly suspected it was some kind of trick or an optical illusion of some sort. Magicians can do wonders with mirrors. Things like that just didn't happen by accident. There had to be a vastly superior intelligence behind it all, he surmised. Maybe the aliens were the best illusionists in the universe. Whoever they were, they were nobody to fool with.

UFOs! Or rather, the pilots that operated them— that was the key. Somehow it was all connected. But, out of all the rocks floating around in space, what did they want with Planet Earth, he wondered? His body involuntarily shuddered at the possibilities.

If they were after humans, the aliens needn't go any further than the nearest bus stop. Ever since the famous abduction of Betty and Barney Hill in 1961, people from all races have been scrutinized, tested, examined and experimented upon in ever increasing numbers. Phil knew this after years of studying the phenomena. His interest was sparked in the navy when a fleet of UFOs cruised at high altitude over the ship in a perfect V formation. They were classified as bogeys which in military parlance means UFOs. Two fighters out of Eglin Air Force Base were sent up to intercept. Only one came back. The other one was found later, laying on the ground riddled with what looked like BB shot. The pilot was listed as MIA.

According to investigators, there were basically two types of victims: the ones who were earmarked, usually by an implantation of some sort, to spend the rest of their lives as living specimens. The second type were usually affected by chance encounters, being in the wrong place at the wrong time. Unexplained disappearances, such as what occurs in the Bermuda Triangle, a hotbed of UFO activity, fell into this category. Once you were taken, you were never seen or heard from again. It was a fair assumption that Tobermory's latest statistic, Ian Forrester, was in that category.

Then there were the ones who were burned or maimed or driven crazy. There were many instances of UFOs attacking people who, ever afterward, feared that the UFOs might return for them...might return...

"Phil...Phil...are you all right? You're shaking like a leaf." Linda's voice sounded as if it was coming from miles away.

"Huh? Oh yeah...yeah, I'm okay now. Just got a chill, I guess." But he wasn't okay. He felt like he just walked into a refrigerator. He was doing everything he could do to keep his body from shaking apart. He wrapped his arms around his chest, hoping nobody would notice the frightened look in his eyes. Linda kept looking at him like a doctor does when they're looking for something wrong; squinty eyes and furrowed brow.

"Don't look at me like that, honey. I'm okay." He took several deep draughts of air, trying to force fresh oxygen into his overwrought brain. He looked around anxiously. Everybody else was still serenading and having a good time, thankfully unaware of his brief mental lapse. He breathed a sigh of relief. There was no sense advertising the fact that he was slowly becoming a borderline schizophrenic. Phil laughed silently at his own joke. He had better settle down, or he would end up in a straitjacket. "Why don't you relax and join the others," he whispered close to his wife's ear. "I'm okay now and once I take a pee, I'll be ready for the next chorus." As he hop-scotched back to the cabin, springing from one limestone slab to the next, using the bright moonlight for guidance, his sensory nerves were suddenly on high alert.

He smelled an odor he was very familiar with. It came and went and in a matter of seconds, it was gone. But it was like taking a whiff of ammonia. It was sharp and stinging. Like in some of the fires he fought, the stench of burnt flesh was almost overpowering until he slipped on his breathing mask. It's a smell a firefighter never forgets. It's a smell that tells you ahead of time, the Grim Reaper was already there. When he reached the cabin, all he smelled was the soggy odor of wet suits drying in the shower stall. The humidity was so high he figured they'd still be damp next day. But he couldn't get past what he had smelled. It suggested either he was going crazy or somehow he had been telepathically conditioned to smell death. By the time he got back to the campfire, Phil subconsciously had given in to whatever inexplicable forces were at play. He had a strong feeling that the smell was a warning from the aliens. Death was near at hand and if the world didn't change, they were all careening down a one-way street to hell.

November 29—9:11 P.M...Aboard the Flying Shoestring

"What is it?" Phil asked. He and Steve were standing on the rear deck of the Shoestring, looking at a contraption that appeared to be a cross between a toboggan and a snowmobile.

"It's a sled, an underwater sea-sled that you pull from behind a boat." Steve explained. He switched on a pair of mercury-vapor floodlights that were mounted on each side of the bridge. Instantly, within a fifty-yard radius of the boat, the area was magically transformed into day. In front of them lay a five-by-eight foot molded piece of fiberglass and plastic that roughly resembled the kind of sled Phil used to play with as a kid. But only roughly. For one thing, it had no runners. It was contoured to hold two people abreast, with dual hand grips and a console that sported a gleaming array of electronic hardware. The overall assembly was half-encased in Plexiglas, with an illuminated compass gauge and a fathometer within easy view of both riders. Two swiveling spotlights, mounted in front, allowed the riders a thousand candle-watt of power in all directions. A series of 12-volt heavy-duty batteries, stored below the Shoestring's deck, supplied the juice for the entire package. A towing harness with telephone and electrical cables, plus air hoses and full face masks with hookah attachments tied into 5,000-cubic-foot air tanks aboard the boat, completed the assortment.

It was a very sophisticated piece of apparatus, Phil acknowledged, but it was hardly a James Bond original. He should have known. It was just another one of Steve's customized toys. It was his hobby, to improve on something he thought could be made better, but not necessarily cheaper. He just had very expensive tastes, that's all. "You really want to try this tonight?" Phil asked dubiously. "Don't you think daylight might be a little safer?"

"Whaaat! You gotta be kidding, my Yankee friend. You take away all the fun if you can see where you're going." Steve gave Phil a playful poke in the ribs for emphasis, a wide grin splitting his face with a mouthful of pearly white teeth. With his eyes cast in shadow from the reflected light, He reminded Phil of the Cheshire Cat from Alice in Wonderland.

"No, really, Phil. I want to try out these spotlights with just the battery hookup, just in case the power cable might snap…or something else unforeseen might happen," he added curiously. "Look, over here." He pointed toward tubular brackets that had been welded on each side of the sled, fitted to accommodate 200-cubic-foot air bottles.

"If I wanted to, I could even use the sled in a detached mode, eh? A lot more maneuverability. I had the bottles reinforced. They can hold three times more air pressure than originally designed. And see here", pointing toward clips that could hold extra bottles. "That could come in handy when you least expect it." He gave Phil an enigmatic smile.

When it came to ingenuity, the man who had revolutionized the shoe industry with innovative designs and materials had all the bases covered, Phil noted. "You don't seem to have missed anything, big guy. Show me how everything works."

Steve had won the coin toss and elected to go first. It was just as well, Phil thought, glancing over the side of the boat. The black water just outside the edge of the floodlight's illuminated circle looked menacing and brought to mind things that go bump in the night. On one particular night dive in the past, he met up with a school of northern pike. At first glance it had scared the b-Jesus out of him. He thought he had run into a school of barracuda. No, he was never too thrilled about diving underwater after dark. You never knew what to expect.

November 29—10:13 P.M...Georgian Bay

The brief pocket of coolness they had enjoyed earlier was gone. The night air had turned sultry, almost tropical.

Even the artificial breeze blowing in their faces felt sticky to the touch.

The trio of onlookers on the flying bridge of the Shoestring sat in comparative comfort on luxurious foam padded, silicone-coated swiveling bucket seats. An empty seat was taken over by Sandy, sitting up as straight as a statue to catch whatever breeze he could. Phil was piloting the boat, though it felt as if he were holding tight rein on a fleet-footed cheetah. The Flying Shoestring was definitely a more powerful machine than what he was used to handling. Even throttled down to quarter-speed—twelve knots—the boat felt alive to the touch, ready to pounce at his slightest command. The loud rumble of the dual exhausts shattered the absolute stillness of the night like a throbbing heartbeat.

A dozen channel islands surrounded them, some small enough not to be seen until you were almost directly on top of them. Phil negotiated each one carefully to keep from running aground. If you did slip, there were no soft sand beaches to greet you. It was the same rocks that gutted many of the shipwrecks in the area. They grew into sizeable minefields around lettuce-topped islets that exponentially became bigger minefields after winter ice peaked some rocks to veritable ambushes lying just below the surface. The omnipresent rocks gave Phil very little room to maneuver. He was using a direct sight approach only on the farthest directional markers, two automated lighthouse beacons. One was on Cove Island, the outermost island of the group. The other was two miles distant, at Lighthouse Point, the entrance to Big Tub Harbor. Every fifteen seconds, a pinprick of light flashed alternately between the two landmarks. Stationed somewhere in between were the shapeless masses of North and South Otter Islands, and to the northwest, the small, darker splotch of Echo Island. It was Steve's decision to stay out of the main channel. Marine charts showed the bottom plunging to a depth of fifty fathoms, too deep for his liking. The best sledding was where you could skim the bottom and still have enough headroom to avoid obstacles without breaking the surface. Upon hearing this, Phil decided staying close to the entrance to Tobermory was their best bet for staying out of trouble. The shallower depth of eight-five to one hundred feet would also avoid decompression in case his friends had to surface in a hurry. It was understandable to just use compressed air for the dive and save the tri-mix for the big prize next day. With only his range lights showing, it was as if they were cruising in the middle of a liquid desert. He thought it strange not to spot the familiar glow of house lights on the mainland or to see other boats circumnavigating the outer approaches to the harbor. Suddenly he started to feel alone and separate from the others. The moon was still performing like a chandelier, the boat still performing like a leashed greyhound, but Phil could sense something was inextricably going to happen. It did. In a matter of minutes, dark cumulus clouds had moved in, covering the moon and stars completely and threatening rain. Phil turned on the floodlights to compensate for the reversal to a stygian darkness that was almost palpable. The light managed to cut into the night only a few more feet. The remaining black void made his sense of isolation complete. Nobody else seemed to notice. Except Sandy. He was standing on the seat, ears perked back, looking toward the back of the boat, still as a statue. Captain Smollet noticed it too, but said nothing.

Over the windscreen, Phil could discern the sharp prow, bearing the name Flying Shoestring painted in colorful red lettering with white pin striping, cleaving the syrupy water with fluid precision. Behind the transom, one-hundred and fifty feet in tow, was the underwater sled, at the moment hurtling toward what turned out to be an unknown shipwreck ninety feet below the surface. By the delighted shrieks of pleasure Steve and Lucienne were making over the intercom, to the rest of them it sounded as if they were having the time of their lives. Linda and Captain Smollet were maintaining a watchful vigilance on the sled's twin spotlights. The gleaming orbs looked like large, luminescent fish eyes trailing the boat. They were bobbing and weaving, sometimes getting brighter as they ascended to avoid an obstacle, then fading like a pair of baited codfish plunging to the bottom trying to escape.

Linda flipped the toggle switch activating the speaker.

"How you birds doing down there?" she shouted over the rumbling of the boat's dual exhausts.

"Fantastic!" came back Lucienne's high-pitched squeal.

"Yeah, it's great," blurted Steve in an excited voice. "We just passed over a wreck we're going to have to check out, gang, and the ride's like riding a roller coaster, except smoother. I can even make out schools of steelheads and bass you don't normally see in daylight. These spotlights freeze them right in their tracks."

"Too bad you didn't bring your fishing po…"

Unexpectedly a tight grip on Linda's arm cut her words short. She turned just in time to see Captain Smollet pointing toward the open channel. There, not more than a mile away, were two blobs of light streaking toward them underwater at an incredible speed! She immediately relayed the warning to Phil.

"Phil! Look…look behind you!"

At first his mind had trouble grasping the scene. It was only when, a few seconds later, he heard Linda's garbled scream that something clicked inside his brain. Her finger had stayed frozen on the open switch of the intercom so that Steve and Lucienne were able to overhear her panic-stricken cry.

"What's happening up there?"

"I think we got company, folks," was all she could think of saying before releasing the switch.

The two glowing objects had been no bigger than distant headlight beams when Captain Smollet first sighted them, but as they rapidly drew nearer, their brightness overshadowed everything else around them. By the time the lights were visibly closer, they had turned into dazzling welders arcs of incandescent brilliance. The objects must have followed the sled's spotlights, Phil guessed, keeping in the deepest part of the channel until they were almost directly on top of them. Within seconds the pursuers had climbed out of the subterranean ravine, having to brake to a comparative crawl in order not to overshoot their quarry. The surrounding bottom, within several hundred feet of their approach, lit up with a ghostly luminescence. The lights kept getting closer and closer, like stalking batfish, until they slowed down enough to keep pace with the sled.

"What the hell are those things?" came Steve's voice, quite agitated. "There're blinding me!"

"What's wrong?" demanded Lucienne. Linda had switched the intercom back to open speakers.

"You got uninvited guests," replied Phil. "Steve! I'm maintaining speed and heading back to Big Tub. Stay cool!" From his vantage point atop the bridge, Phil recognized a delineation of shape and body within the two objects as unmistakably spheroid. He had trouble determining their size because of the intense glare. The sled's spotlights had virtually been swallowed up by their radiance. His experience as a firefighter told him to clear out while you can. This was one of those times. Throwing stones at that kind of technology was suicidal. His first reaction was to open up the throttles and get his friends the hell out of there. He checked the fathometer and the underwater GPS. The bottom map showed ninety feet on an even plain with a slow incline toward the southeast. Good! They were heading in the right direction anyway.

"Are you guys okay?" he shouted.

'Yeah, so far!" Steve shouted back. "What are we dealing with here?" The amplifier distorted his voice, but Phil could tell the big Canadian was extremely nervous.

Who could blame him? This was his first introduction to UFOs.

"What is it, Phil?" Lucienne pleaded. She knew something strange was happening for her husband to be acting so uncharacteristic in manner

"We're dealing with a couple of UFOs who just flew in and attached themselves as your escorts," shouted Phil. "Stay with me. I'm headin' back toward shallower water."

"Tell them to come up!" Linda screamed.

"Don't do that, lad," Captain Smollet cut in. "That would mean stopping the boat. Maybe that's all they're waitin' for. You're doing right. Maintain speed and start headin' back into the Big Tub, like you said."

Phil nodded, at the same time steering the Shoestring in that general direction. Because of the fierce glow emanating from the UFO's, Phil was starting to have a problem with night blindness. His sense of direction was totally reliant on the boat's compass. He acknowledged the captain had a good point. As long as the aliens maintained their distance from the sled, maybe he could lure them into shore. That might not be in their flight plan. But first he needed a little bit of luck finding it.

Suddenly, a piercing yellow beam of light sliced the darkness over their heads. Phil readily identified it as Big Tub Light, the landmark signaling the entrance to Big Tub Harbor. Talk about luck. The water was only forty feet deep there. He and Linda had dove in it many times before. Two favorite shipwrecks for sightseers were the Sweepstakes and the City of Grand Rapids lying close to the shoreline. Phil pointed the nose of the boat toward the familiar inlet and hoped Captain Smollet was right.

"Linda! Keep talking to them. Find out what's happening!"

"I tried! I can't get through. Listen!"

She turned the volume up on the bridge speaker. All they could hear was static. "We lost them!"

Captain Smollet motioned at Phil to look down into the water. There, eighty feet below, the UFOs were beginning to change their color right before their eyes. The eye-piercing white globules of light were breaking up into a vivid color spectrum of blues, reds, greens and yellows. Their amazement turned to dismay when they saw that the dazzling orbs were beginning slowly to merge! They were squeezing Steve and Lucienne into an ever-tightening noose! Phil realized he had to do something quick. "Hold on," he shouted.

As he rammed the throttles as far forward as the gear box allowed, a cascade of wintry foam erupted under the stern amidst a tumultuous roar. Beneath their feet the deck trembled violently. The Flying Shoestring lunged like a freed cat, earning its moniker as she began to plane out and literally fly across the water. The towing line stretched dangerously taut.

"Captain!" Phil yelled over his shoulder. "How much clearance do I have near the entrance?" He was approaching from an angle and he didn't want to sideswipe any rocks on the way in. He thought he heard a reply, but the captain's words were savagely ripped out of his mouth by the wind.

Phil kept peering over his shoulder, watching with bated breath while the discs kept pace with the boat. It was as though they were joined at the hip with the sled, not relinquishing an inch. He saw no sign of the spotlights. They were completely absorbed by the colorful lights on display beneath them. Grudgingly he had to give way, easing back on the throttles; otherwise, if Steve and Lucienne had hit anything, there would have been nothing left of them to find. He only hoped Steve had enough sense to stay clear of the bottom.

Meanwhile, something strange was happening. Phil could see Linda and Captain Smollet standing at the rear of the boat, seemingly transfixed like a pair of statues. Their eyes were glued to the slowly changing patterns of an underwater aurora borealis display, compliments of our visitors. They seemed mesmerized by its captivating colors. Phil had to admit, there was something surreal about it. It was all he could do to tear his eyes away long enough to keep the boat on a steady course.

It seemed an eternity before they were close enough to make out the darker splotches of rock outlining the entrance to Big Tub Harbor. Phil throttled down to half speed as the Shoestring swiftly rumbled past the lighthouse. Almost immediately the boat's fathometer began giving them a visual readout of the approaching bottom in real numbers, the audio portion in increments of five…thirty meters…twenty-five meters…twenty meters. At last they were entering shallow water. Phil breathed a sigh of relief as he was sure Linda and the captain did also. Even Sandy had a happy face, if that were possible with dogs. Phil figured they did. By the time they reached the inner sanctuary, the boat would be resting in no more than twenty-five feet of water. He shot another glance over his shoulder, thinking the discs would be hightailing back to where they came from by now. To his surprise, they were still there although they had separated to their original stations. "Damn," he cursed under his breath. The bastards were hanging on to the very end.

Shoestring's powerful floodlights did quick work of cutting through the inky blackness once they were cocooned inside a naturally forged canyon of dolomite and limestone. The nine hundred horses under their feet roared their disapproval at their confinement by blasting decibels of sound against the rock walls. The trees atop the slopes shook as the echoes reverberated through their foliage. The smooth rock face never looked as good to him as it did now.

Linda's voice suddenly broke the tension. "Look! They're leaving!"

The aliens had finally decided to break their stranglehold on the sled and were retreating back to the channel. As if on cue, the sled's tiny spotlights hove into view behind the boat. Automated floatation devices kept the sled from sinking. The slap of water from Shoestring's wake against the Plexiglas canopy made a welcome sound across the intervening gap of black water. Phil cut the throttles. An ominous silence filled the void. A hollow feeling of uncertainty gripped everyone. The blinding glare of the sled's spotlights prevented Phil and the rest from seeing beyond their station. Was Steve and Lucienne okay? Fearing the worst, Phil swung one of Shoestring's floodlights into the darkness. Caught in the beam, he spied two pairs of hands waving ecstatically as the sled bobbed lazily on the surface. He joined in the celebration as a collective cheer of relief erupted aboard the boat.

Phil turned to Captain Smollet. "Evidently, whoever they were, they were only out joyriding tonight, Cap'n."

"Aye, maybe we were just lucky this time, my boy," he replied solemnly.

Phil slowly jockeyed Shoestring deeper into the anchorage. He wanted to get in as shallow as possible in case their visitors decided to return. But by the time the Shoestring was midway into the gorge, the luminous discs were far distant, nothing more than pinpricks of their former selves. When Phil gave one last check, their trail had become completely swallowed by the darkness.

After Steve and Lucienne clambered aboard the Shoestring, they all took a minute to reflect. It had been a harrowing experience for all of them, but especially for Steve and Lucienne, Phil reasoned, who were comparatively new to the alien game. Everyone seemed afraid to voice out loud what they were really thinking. In Phil's mind, this confrontation had brought home an incontrovertible fact. The psychic predictions he had read about were coming true. Cayce headed the list of earth changes about to happen. To Phil's knowledge, Cayce never mentioned aliens, per se, in any of his readings. If he had, Phil wondered what he would have said about visitors from outer space invading our skies now. Whoever pilots the strange craft had to have traveled countless light years to get to our puny planet. Why? Maybe to conquer or subjugate the human race. Cayce must have thought about intelligent life on other planets, if not truly acknowledging them, Phil imagined. He believed in the Universal Consciousness, which implied life in other worlds, other dimensions. Soon perhaps, humankind was going to learn a valuable lesson in getting along with its neighbors. A planet floating around in space poisoned with pollution was not a good way to start a relationship. It might be a good way to end it, though. Phil gave a long sigh. Only time would tell.

CHAPTER 13

July 8—2:12 P.M…Duchesnay Falls, North Bay, Ontario

Philip sees himself as a little boy, four years old. He is with his Mommy and Daddy next to a gushing stream. Right now, he sees Mommy with Daddy. They're lying on the ground, making funny noises, holding each other tight. He thought at first Daddy was hurting Mommy. He was on top of her playing horsy. But she is laughing and giggling like she is having fun. He wanted to have fun too. They told him not to go near the water. But they won't care if I just sit on this rock and splash my feet, he thought. The water's so pretty. It moves fast and goes around in pretty little circles when it hits the rocks. It makes lots of suds, just like soap does when Mommy gives him a bath.

Ooohh, the water's so cold. Near him is a little pool. The water isn't moving very fast there. Maybe the water will be warmer. He'll be able to just reach it if he scoots over to that rock. He slowly inches his way over. The rock is wet and slippery with moss. He can just touch it with his toes if he stretches a little bit more. Suddenly he feels himself falling! He desperately tries to grab hold of something, but the rock is smooth and there's nothing to hold on to.

He cries out, but Mommy and Daddy don't hear him. He slides into the water. Ooohh, its so cold! His head goes beneath the surface and he can't breathe! He begins to cry. Tears begin to sting his eyes. When he opens his mouth, water comes in. He starts choking.. He's scared. "Mommy!" he cries out frantically, but she still doesn't hear him. He starts to kick and struggle to keep his head above water. But it's hard. The water makes his hands numb and he can't hold on to the slippery rocks any longer.

The current carries him away. It pushes him against other rocks that are sharp. Ouch! They hurt him when his body hits them. His lungs are beginning to burn. He keeps swallowing water. It's choking him again, except this time he is caught on the bottom by some rocks. He can't get his head above water. He's screaming underwater and Mommy and Daddy can't hear him.

He scrambles loose and fights to the top again. He hears a roar where the water drops into a big hole. He keeps kicking and fighting so he can breathe, but he can feel his body grow weak. His head hits another rock. Suddenly he feels dizzy and everything is going around and around. He's starting to get sleepy.

The water and the rocks and the trees are all getting blurry now. A mask over his eyes is shutting out the light. But he doesn't mind because he doesn't seem to hurt anymore. I only wish Mommy was here to hold my hand, he sobs. He feels like he's falling. A black tunnel opens up and swallows him.

He opens his eyes and finds himself lying on the ground. There's a bunch of funny-looking men standing over him. They're wearing costumes just like the way Mommy dresses him on Halloween. They're small like he is and have strange looking eyes. Next to them I see a man all dressed in white with long gold hair. None of them move their lips, yet he hears a voice telling him not to be afraid. I want my Mommy! I start crying. Again I hear a voice saying my Mommy is coming. The voice is gentle, just like his Mommy's. It tells him he is safe and they must go now. He feels sad, but the voice says they will return and visit him again someday. All of a sudden, there's a bright light behind them and they're gone.

November 30—2:48 A.M…Cabin

Phil's eyes blinked open and he felt Linda's warm body next to him. He was bathed in a cold sweat. A few seconds passed before he realized he had just woken from the same dream he had many times since he became interested in UFOs.

It all began when Phil read Whitley Streiber's novel, Communion. The story didn't bother him as much as the book cover did. The picture triggered something in his brain. It was a picture of an alien with unusually large almond-shaped eyes. Seeing those eyes brought it all back. It was like opening up a window into his subconscious. They were the same eyes of the little people he kept seeing in his dreams.

He rolled out of bed, heading for the shower, trying not to disturb Linda in the process. Standing under the hot, stinging needles of water, he tried to rationalize once again what the dream was all about.

He remembered reading what Cayce once said about dreams. "Dreams were given for the benefit of the individual if they were interpreted correctly." If that was the case, then having the same recurring dream must mean something to him, he thought. But what?

He quickly stepped out of the shower and began drying off.

The towel grazed three small two-inch overlapping triangles he bore on his left arm. He always thought of them as odd-looking. He didn't remember getting them. His Mom said he had fallen on a piece of glass on the school playground when he was still in kindergarten. She always made light of their peculiar shape, saying it was God's handiwork. But, curiously enough, Mom carried a pair of identically shaped ones on her right hip just above the tan line.

He got to see them once when they were at the beach. As she drew near him after a swim, he couldn't help but notice the pulpy white gashes when her swimsuit had inadvertently revealed part of her buttocks. She hastily readjusted the material, hoping nobody had seen. At the time, he thought nothing of it. But now, every time he looked at his scars, he remembered his mother's furtive glance and frightened behavior, as if she were hiding something. He often wondered why. She worked as a flight attendant for Global Air, but when her plane slammed into the side of a mountain in the Pyrenees, he had lost all interest in the identical markings. Recalling her scars, and eventual death, left him with a deep sense of misgiving. It was later revealed Mom's plane was hijacked by terrorists who got waylaid by some brave passengers.

If any death can have good consequences, though, Mom's certainly did, he reflected. It had brought him and his brother, Jeremy, closer together, that was for sure. They spent a lot more time talking and sharing confidences after that. Phil got to know what really made his brother tick. Even growing up, Jeremy had this intuitive quality, especially in the field of astronomy. It was as if he were born with some cosmic insight. Not only did they talk about Cayce a lot, they talked about the planet, Earth, in relation to the cosmos. As he progressed through school, his knowledge and retentive capabilities for learning became astounding. Even at an early age, Jeremy knew more about pulsars, quasars, white dwarfs, black holes, exploding galaxies and other heavenly aberrations than most astronomers knew in a lifetime. It was only a matter of time before Emmett Carlysle, the world-famous astronomer, had heard of Jeremy's genius and sponsored a fellowship grant for him at the Laboratory for Planetary Studies at Cornell University. Now, Jeremy was one of NASA's leading astrophysicists.

When they were growing up, Jeremy would often preach to Phil about the importance of the role their planet, Earth, played in the grand scheme of things. He said man is unique in the fact that he holds the highest intelligence in our solar system. He stressed the fact that our solar system consist of only nine planets, only one of which is seeded with intelligent life. There are countless other solar systems in countless other galaxies that hold more planets with intelligent life forms than we humans can even imagine, he said. Their technology far surpasses ours in our feeble attempts to explore and colonize other worlds. It's imperative we do better to broaden our chances of species survival. That's why it was so important for us to protect what we can't afford to lose, Mother Earth. But it was a role we too often ignored, he complained.

Phil most times took his brother's ramblings with a grain of salt, but not always. He was extremely curious about such terms as 'seeding earth,' and 'explore and colonize for our species survival' that he found most intriguing. But it was something to be explained in more detail at a later date, Jeremy explained. He said it with a sad face, as if there never would be enough time to pursue the subject to the fullest. Once, Phil remembered his brother sadly shaking his head and lamenting at the end of one of their conversations: "As a species," he had said, "we are doing badly, very badly. Certain planets in other star systems have not fared well, either, because of harmful vibrations brought on by their inhabitants and we are heading on the same irreversible course." Phil inquired as to where that course would lead them.

"The lower the vibrations, the more it impedes Earth's energy field," his brother replied. "This force is vital to maintain alignment with the solar system. It's like a spinning top. When it starts to slow down, it starts wobbling."

"What happens when it stops wobbling?" Phil pursued.

Jeremy looked at him askance as if Phil should not have had to ask.

"If the tilt is severe enough, it will leave its orbit and the sun's gravity will take over. Our best hope is that earth changes will realign the axis before that occurs.

Phil didn't need any further explanations. "How do you know all these things?" Phil once asked. He recalled vividly Jeremy's flippant but enigmatic quip as if it were yesterday. He just smiled and said it was all in the stars. "Just what a smart-ass would say," Phil retaliated, but he remembered how his brother's words had made him wonder. It wasn't until later that he was shocked at how close Jeremy's accounting reflected Cayce's predictions. One thing was for certain, though, the more his brother preached to him about the stars, the more he became sensitized to his own planet's fragile existence.

As Phil stepped up to the small bathroom mirror above the sink, he began to study himself more closer under the built-in fluorescent light. He saw subtle signs of aging. Although he was middle-aged, he prided himself on looking ten years younger through a tough training regimen. Firefighting demanded it. That, he knew, was what kept him young even though, he had to admit, the older he got, the more temperamental he became. He just didn't have the patience he used to have.

There were certain things in life a man just couldn't avoid, he realized—his receding hairline, for example, and the laugh lines around his eyes. Vanity told him he would be getting contacts soon. He sometimes wondered if Paul Anka had that problem. Ever since high school, people commented on the fact that he was the spitting image of the famous entertainer. He smiled. It had made for some memorable predicaments at times.

It's strange how parental genes can amalgamate in an embryonic sac and the results still come out lopsided, he mused. He looked nothing like his Dad, yet they shared an unusual trait. They were sentimentalists to a fault. Not just sentimentalists, but patriotic sentimentalists. He remembered the times Dad took him to a Tiger game, or some other sporting event where they played the national anthem before the game. Dad would stand stiffly at attention, placing his hat over his heart. He always wore a worn, beat-up fedora. Phil would do likewise, giving his three-fingered Boy Scout salute instead, and tears the size of marbles would roll down their cheeks.

He also recalled the times he used to sit on his Dad's lap as his Dad read him the comic section out of the Sunday newspaper. The proud French-Canadian would laboriously mimic the different cartoon characters, altering the tone and pitch of his voice in an effort to make them come to life. It was these characteristics of his Dad that endeared him to Phil the most.

But there were other times with his Dad that he would like to forget, like the times he and his Mom used to argue like cats and dogs, which ultimately led to their divorce. That was shortly after all of them had moved to Detroit, taking advantage of Dad's short stint in the U.S. Army, which guaranteed U.S. citizenship, after the war. Phil always suspected there was some hidden underlying cause for their breakup, but neither one of them would ever talk about it in front of him. After the divorce, there were occasions when he wouldn't see his Dad for long stretches of time. Dad was working on a lake freighter then. Phil recalled how he used to look forward to his Dad's return and the yarns Dad used to spin of his exploits around the Great Lakes. Phil guessed that was what eventually got him interested in joining the navy. The life of a 'sailor man' sounded so full of adventure and excitement; he just had to see for himself.

Then one day came that fateful telegram from the Maritime Association. Dad was killed in a freak accident when the lake freighter he was on collided with a collier a day's steaming out of Duluth. From what the telegram explained, there was a terrific storm and, in the process of passing one another, capricious winds had flung the two ships together like a couple of matchboxes, entangling them in a fusion of flesh and steel. They went down in one of Lake Superior's trenches, in over 1,100 feet of water. There was one survivor who later died of exposure. Dad's remains stayed with the ship.

Gazing into the mirror, Phil could almost feel his Dad's presence next to him. He sure missed him. Sometimes he cherished that closeness more than he cared to admit. Time hadn't seemed to erase the invisible bond they shared. The occasional times he was in trouble at fires, he could always sense a strong protective force near him, like he could now. Somehow he knew his Dad was there, watching him if he strayed too far from the straight and narrow.

Phil let out a deep sigh, resigning himself to another night of broken sleep. Whenever he had those dreams, he could almost bank on seeing those large eyes of the little people for the rest of the night, peering at him from out of the darkness. As he flicked off the light and went back to bed, he wondered what other surprises were in store for him. Only time would tell.

CHAPTER 14

November 30—8:53 A.M…Georgian Bay

Every time Phil traveled over or under Georgian Bay, it stimulated a deep feeling of awe and respect inside him. Its immensity alone caused others to call it the sixth Great Lake. The first Europeans called it "La Mer douce" (the calm sea). Quite a misnomer, he thought. Since that inglorious statement was made, impenetrable fog and vicious storms have sent over a thousand ships to its bottom. To be fair though, Phil recanted, once the early morning sun broke the horizon, history has showed the coordinates of 45.5 degrees N. at 81.0 degrees W. to be clear with calm seas a vast majority of the time. "La Mer douce" eventually became Georgian Bay, named after King George IV in 1822.

He was continually amazed at the cataclysmic forces of nature that molded this giant waterway. It looked as if the formidable mass of water, 5800 square miles, extended to the very edge of the world. He had to keep reminding himself it was only part of the Great Lakes, the southern edge of the Canadian Shield, gouged into a large basin of granite bedrock by an advancing glacier 11,000 years ago, and filled with melted water when it retreated. But its depth was formidable. Analogous to Lake Huron, Georgian Bay boasts some of the deepest spots of 750 feet.

Phil was sitting in the back of the partially enclosed rear deck of the Genny, his feet propped on top of a pile of scuba tanks. Captain Smollet was pushing the boat along at a respectable six-and-a-half knots. The water sloshing alongside the hull looked as viscous as motor oil. The humidity would soon begin its climb, Phil imagined, making everything it touched heavy and oppressive, However, for the time being, the slight breeze from the boat's momentum was keeping everybody comfortable.

Linda was up in the pilothouse with the captain, rehashing last night's events. It seemed ironic to her husband that they were traversing the very spot where the UFOs made their appearance just twelve short hours ago.

They were on their way to Flower Pot Island, where Steve and Lucienne had camped overnight. Their friends were most definitely the fresh air type. Wherever they traveled, they opted for the great outdoors whenever they could. They didn't mind dispensing with the conveniences of civilization. That wasn't to say he and Linda were solely reliant on soft beds and indoor johns, but mosquitoes, gnats and crawly things were not their idea of congenial bedfellows. Maybe Steve and Lucienne were savoring what city dwellers had unconsciously forfeited long ago, Phil pondered—a true bonding with Mother Nature. Maybe that was why people had treated the wilderness with irreverence for so long. Land had become an expedient commodity. Around the world, the rain forests were being trampled and decimated by bulldozers and chainsaws. Watersheds were being destroyed by man's penchant for glass and concrete. Using eminent domain to advance shopping malls and parking lots was allowing erosion to eat away the land.

National parks were being slowly dissected and parceled out to greedy developers. Housing developments ran the gamut of irresponsible builders who thought nothing of sacred ground or unprotected species. Georgian Bay was probably one of the few places left in the world, Phil imagined, whose resources were still safeguarded by iron-clad laws. He couldn't help remembering one particular afternoon when he and fellow dive-club members actually witnessed modern day pirates cruising into Little Tub like they owned the place. Nobody knew who they were or what they wanted. They slid out of the harbor the next morning like a venomous snake. Their poisonous fangs were sticks of dynamite. You could hear them blowing up the shipwrecks one by one for their miniscule scrap iron. What a sickening sound it made. The pirates were hitting the shallower wrecks first before working their way deeper. They were destroying irreplaceable archeological artifacts. Most important, they were blowing up the local inhabitants source of livelihood. Mostly those people were ex-fishermen who were victimized by the sea lamprey. The shipwrecks that they sailed around purposely to avoid getting their nets snagged, were now being used as tourist attractions. Visitors came from all over the world, appreciating the availability of charters and glass bottomed boats to see the shipwrecks and islands for themselves. There wouldn't be any visitors at all if all that was left were the bones of scattered iron carcasses. Thank God for Captain Smollet. Thankfully he knew people in high places. Within hours an injunction was filed and delivered to the pirates to stop all activity until further notice. The rest is history. Then, there was the story behind the story.

Whether it was true or not was debatable. Phil hoped it was true, if nothing else but to imply a 'don't fuck with us' attitude was clearly understood by the pirates. Two of the biggest Royal Canadian Mounted Police on the force, with that 'dare me' look under their traditional wide flat-brimmed Stetsons, wearing black bandolier belts over immaculately starched red tunics, and each with a 45 Smith and Wesson sidearm conspicuously visible, sat astride two big black horses snorting fire, waiting on the dock for the snakes to return back to their nest. When they did, the sight waiting for them must have made them think twice before they decided to ignore the stop order. That's when the process began whereby Georgian Bays 30,000 islands became federal land and its waters in between protected by marine parks. Certainly it took time to iron out all the legalities but Canadians can be proud their politicians wasted no time keeping scum like that under control.

Phil looked out over the dipping bow of the Genny at the growing green bonnet of Flower Pot Island rising up to greet them. He recalled part of a spiel given by a park ranger once. He said the island represented the culmination of the great Ice Age, when massive sheets of ice sculptured what the visitor saw today. Quite true, Phil reflected. A hiker didn't have to go far off the trail to witness striations on the cliff walls where the passing glaciers had left their mark.

As Captain Smollet guided the Genny into the narrow channel marking the entrance to Beachy Cove, large open-mouthed caves yawned down at them from lofty canyon walls. Seagulls, usually swooping voraciously for food at the first sight of visitors, were conspicuously absent.

Steve and Lucienne were waiting for them at the large wooden dock. Lucienne's suntan and olive complexion, with the added wardrobe of striped baggy culottes, made her look like a gypsy, Phil thought. He could see Steve had a troubled look on his face. "How was your night?" he called across the fast-shrinking distance of water separating them. Just before what looked like an imminent crash, the captain smartly turned the wheel and let the nose of the boat gently brush against the wooden pilings before cutting the engine. "Busy," Steve answered in a clipped voice as he caught the painter and secured the boat.

As they followed a narrow cedar-chipped path back to the campsite, Phil got the distinct impression Steve was upset about something. A lingering after-effect from last night, perhaps? He didn't say much, but let Lucienne do all the talking. "You mean your camp was broken into last night?" Linda gasped.

She and Phil knew that their friends had an electronic security system. Sensor beams strategically placed around the camp's perimeter would sound an alarm whenever the circuit was broken.

"Something broke the circuit," Lucienne explained. "It happened shortly after we sacked in. We checked the equipment but everything seemed to be working okay." She paused for a moment. "I don't think there's anything to worry about. Nothing on the island seems to want to hurt anybody."

Linda and Phil exchanged nonplused looks over her strange remark, but kept their thoughts to themselves.

"Did you hear anything?" Linda asked.

"No, nothing. That's what's so strange about the whole thing. All the birds and animals on the island have gone silent. Even the insects. Steve and I haven't even heard a cricket chirp since we got here."

That was weird! Phil thought. The island was usually teeming with wildlife.

"Maybe it's the heat," ventured Linda. It can get to rabbits and squirrels just like humans."

"I don't think that's it," Steve cut in. "Listen to what I gotta tell you." Lucienne started making coffee as her husband began to tell their friends an astonishing tale. It would sound as if it came right out of an episode of the Twilight Zone. At daybreak Steve and Lucienne were suddenly awakened by a mysterious humming noise. "It sounded like a transformer," Lucienne declared.

That analogy sounded familiar, Phil mused.

With a halting voice, Steve described to them what happened next. "I walked out to the beach to see if I could get a better feel where the sound was coming from, eh? And...and then, this ball-like thing appeared out of nowhere. It was very bright, but...but it wasn't an ordinary bright light. It didn't have a glare, more of a fluorescent glow."

"What color was it?"

"Sort of reddish-orange. It's...it's hard to describe. I've never seen a color like it before!" Steve sounded a little flustered at his lack of explanation.

"How big was it, lad?" Captain Smollet asked. Somehow his steady voice seemed to have a calming effect on Steve.

"It was large enough, Cap'n. Maybe thirty to thirty-five meters across and it was rounded at the top. Looked like some sort of dome. It wasn't more than twenty meters away from where I stood. But...here's the weird part. The bloody thing, it just split in two! I mean, I couldn't believe it at first. It happened so fast. I had to rub my eyes to make sure I wasn't seeing double. But they were still there, hovering over me like vultures. I almost felt like they were studying me. Then, all of sudden, they glowed bright. I mean, incredibly bright! They blinded me! Then, in a clap of thunder, they were gone! They just disappeared! It was like they hadn't even been there."

This was an all-too-familiar characteristic of UFOs, Phil remembered reading. Most people only witnessed this metamorphosis at night: UFO's mysterious lights that merged and split like surrealistic will-o'-the-wisps. To actually witness a daylight demonstration at such close quarters was unique.

"Could have been the same ones we saw last night," commented Linda, lowering her voice to almost a whisper. But her husband knew it was her way of covering up a case of nerves.

Lucienne, with her psychic ability, sensed it.

"Let's all relax and have a cup of coffee," she offered, directing her attention toward Linda. Blindness never deterred her of pinpointing where everybody was by the sound of their voice. Although she could not relate to what her husband had witnessed firsthand, Phil imagined that in her mind's eye, the experience was just as real. It didn't take long before Steve was back to his normal self, making light of the incident as though nothing had happened. But Captain Smollet, with an unaccustomed admonishing look on his face, cut the bantering short. "Only fools josh about Satan's disciples, lad. The forces of evil have descended upon our homeland. Those machines are in the hands of devils."

Frowning, he shifted his gaze to the others. His deeply lined face seemed abnormally burdened with the weight of his years, Phil thought. Smollet reached into his pocket and pulled out a biscuit for Sandy. Satisfied, the dog plopped down contentedly at his feet.

"Yesterday, I didn't tell you everything that's been happenin' around here. Aye, I think it's time we stopped fooling ourselves. Those devils have become much bolder. I don't like what I hear." Coming from the captain, the statement sounded like the prophecy of doom had just been given.

"The Ministry of Transport has hired me, on a temporary basis, to keep up the lighthouse here," he continued.

"Where are the Piche brothers?" Steve asked. Ever since the light and foghorn system had reverted back to manual operation a couple years ago, the two bachelor brothers had become fixtures around Tobermory. During shipping season, they would dutifully maintain the lighthouse while living in the government-built cottages furnished for them on the north side of the island.

"They just vanished."

"What do you mean, they just vanished?" Steve barked.

"It happened during a flash storm," the captain resumed, seemingly unperturbed by the interruption. "Oh, she was a nasty one, all right. The next day, I came over to bring them their mail, and they were gone! Just like poor Ian. Mounties came because it happened on government property, you know. I helped them look for the Piches, but we didn't find a trace. It's as if Satan himself snatched them away!"

"Maybe they decided to go back to the mainland for some reason without telling anyone," Linda suggested.

"How could they do that without a boat, lassie?" the captain countered. The question hung unchallenged.

He then focused his attention toward the line of caves emerging out of the half-shadows overhead. The blistering early morning sun was accentuating the hollowed-out rock in rosy-red detail. "Aye, and when I was searching, I happened to get a good look at one of those beasts you saw. It was at the mouth of one of those caves up there," pointing toward a particularly large gouge in the rock.

"Maybe that's where they took the Piches," Linda piped up.

The captain shook his head. "The Mounties and I climbed up to look for ourselves. The hollow goes in several meters, but we didn't find a thing."

There followed an uneasy silence, each lost in their own thoughts. The mystery surrounding the strange disappearances of Ian Forrester, and now the Piche brothers, was coming to a head.

"I guess we're all thinking the same thing," ventured Lucienne. "The question is why are they doing this to us?"

"Aye, it's almost a certainty; aliens are invading our planet, lassie. Maybe, the devils have been doing it a long time. What bothers me is they're gettin' so flagrant about it. Last month the ferryboat was found adrift off Cabot Head. She was steaming to Owen Sound for her winter layup, you know."

"Yes, I remember catching it on the news," Steve interjected. "Something like the crew abandoned the vessel for no good reason. Never heard anything more about it."

"The news people never finish their stories, lad. They like to string it out so the listeners come back the next day for more." He gave everyone a knowing look before continuing. "Folks in the area said they saw several strange lights dancing about in the sky the same day. When they went aboard her, everyone was gone alright, but the crew must have left in a wee bit of a hurry. Not voluntarily, anyway. Their dinner was still sittin' on the stove!"

They all exhibited a look of amazement. "How many in the crew, Cap'n?"

"There was a skeleton crew of seven. Bill Manson, her second officer...Percy LaVigne, the engineer and two of his stokers. The rest were deckhands. I knew them all. Percy was a good friend of mine," the captain finished lamely.

"Do you think a storm came up and they all abandoned ship?" Lucienne's question sounded like a reasonable option to everyone.

"Nay, lassie. All the lifeboats were in place, and no life preservers were missin,' either. There were no storms reported a'tall." He sighed. "Like I said, the devil is now collectin' his due."

Steve stood up, stretching his tall, muscular frame to the limit. He was Phil's junior by two years, but his physique was like that of a man twenty years younger. His chest and shoulders bulged through a light turtleneck T shirt that had the words Shackter Shoes printed across the front. A baseball cap with a shoe emblazoned on the front hid what was his only blemish, a receding hairline. It would have been a trick to pick him out of a football lineup, Phil mused.

"Devil or not, Cap'n, we're not leaving until we finish what we set out to do," Steve snapped. "Isn't that right, Phil?" Steve looked challenging over in Phil's direction for support. His exuberant friend was back to his old form, Phil thought: arms akimbo like a picture of Errol Flynn on a lobby poster, eyes alight, teeth mimicking a tooth-paste commercial, his stance that of a sixteenth-century swashbuckler. Phil felt trapped. How could he belittle his image of manhood to anything less macho than that?

"Let's go for it, big guy," he replied in as convincing a manner as possible. He was glad no one else could hear the flutter of butterflies inside his stomach.

CHAPTER 15

November 30—10:22 A.M...Flower Pot Island

The fifty-foot-tall Large Flowerpot stood like a lone sentinel under the harsh burning stare of a ruthless sun. Several small shrubs had tenaciously found a foothold in one of its many crannies, lending it a disheveled look. Three hundred feet down the beach was its smaller counterpart, the thirty-foot Small Flowerpot. It too was standing aloofly, as if guarding the entrance to the island, Phil mused. He knew the park wardens kept a close eye on both of them. Parts of their stratified rock had been reinforced with cement patches over the years to prevent any further erosion from the elements.

The small group was suiting up under the shadow of the tall monument, taking advantage of its welcome shade. The sky was hazy, cloudless, and the temperature threatened to climb to another record-setting high. "Damn heat," Phil grumbled to himself. Wrapping himself up in a thick rubber suit under a solar heat lamp was anything but enjoyable.

He looked over at Lucienne. If anyone had guts, it was she. She didn't talk much, but that didn't stop her from accomplishing whatever she set out to do. Ever since he'd known her, she had shown a remarkable resourcefulness most women would envy.

Canadian Woman, a leading feminist magazine, had run a feature on Lucienne about ten years ago, he recalled. They lavished her with praise because she was the only blind female diver living in Canada to be actively engaged in the sport. What the article failed to mention was Lucienne's aneurysm, a subject nobody chose to talk about. It was a "not-to-be-divulged-under-penalty-of-death" secret Steve had disclosed to them several years ago, a secret restricted only to close family and friends. He and Linda should have felt honored for their friend's trust, but instead, they felt as though a curse had been placed over their heads. Both realized every time Lucienne dove, she ran the risk of causing the aneurysm to burst due to some errant pressure surge, resulting in instant death. It was like waiting for a time bomb to go off.

"How the hell can you live with something like that and still have her dive?" Phil fumed in exasperation to Steve in private one day. "One false move and it's all over, pal!"

"Don't you think I realize that?" he blurted in a pain-faced rebuttal. He was almost at the point of tears. "But I love her too much to keep her from diving. She insists we're a team, and team players don't quit just because of a little adversity."

A little adversity was the understatement of the year, Phil lamented to himself. But who was he to argue? It was her life.

"Hey, you people about ready?" Linda hollered. She was cinching up her tank straps and looking eagerly at the water. Steve was attaching a ten-foot nylon line to Lucienne's tank harness. It served as a tether between them. Whenever they weren't holding hands or she holding on to her husband's harness, it kept Steve in constant touch with Lucienne's movements.

"Yeah, let's get wet," Phil hollered back impatiently as he smeared saliva around inside his face-piece to prevent fogging. It was getting damnably hot under his suit. He fancied they must have looked like a bunch of pollywogs as they belly-flopped into the water together. The water, as usual, felt ice cold against their overheated bodies. The water surface temperature hardly varied one degree no matter how high the air temperature was. There was hardly a thermocline to speak of. It was a steady drop of frigid cold all the way to the bottom. He was in constant amazement at this phenomenon.

From his very first contact with Flower Pot Island, Phil had found it excitingly different. The subterranean landscape was an oddity unto itself. He never encountered anywhere else such an unusual crop of underwater rock formations. Stone terraces with the dimensions of small landing strips were stacked atop one another like huge stepping stones. He paused briefly. In a flash of insight, Phil envisaged a staircase used by giants when Georgian Bay was still dry. Didn't the bible say there were giants roaming the earth in those days? He continued to follow the descending steps, bringing up the rear of the pack. Whenever they dove together, they always dove in tandem, with Steve taking the point.

The water was crystal clear. Phil couldn't ever remember the time it wasn't. Brilliant shafts of sunlight flung a dazzling ring of colors in all directions. Warm pinks, yellows and oranges blended into a melting pot of flecked gold; the flat, uniform rocks acting as giant reflectors. As Phil penetrated deeper into the slowly, darkening void, the glittering colors faded quickly. In their stead, the cold end of the spectrum began to take over: the violets, purples and deep indigo blues. He knew full well he had entered the outer fringes of a sepulchral world, the world where an all-pervasive loneliness seeped in and gnawed at your psyche. This is where a novice diver discovered if he had any claustrophobic tendencies... darkness closing in...feeling trapped. It was a threshold Phil had passed a few times before, but never with much enthusiasm. He and Linda never had much reason to go beyond the dictates of the sport divers manual of 130 feet...until now. (some manuals showed 150 feet)

They were using the electronically regulated, Tri-mix, a mixed gas combination of oxygen, nitrogen, and helium. The potency of each gas was greatly strengthened in this updated version of deep diving technology. The regulator was the major piece of hardware that commercial divers lived by. It not only gave the diver the needed amount of gas to breathe but continually adjusted the mixture of whatever percentage of gas, or gases, the diver required the deeper he went. It was based on time at depth, and the exertions of the diver in all phases of the dive. To accomplish this, you had to attach a small electrode to your skin that was connected to the regulator. It was a complicated system, fairly new on the market for sport divers, but too much money and not enough simplification for amateurs, in Phil's opinion. But, knowing Steve, he would be working on improving the system in his own inimitable style, Phil had no doubt. But, in the meantime, his firefighter instinct was getting aroused. He would have felt more comfortable if all the bugs had been worked out. He was sure some were still hanging around. He caught himself holding his breath. He turned to look up at his receding link with the outside world. A beautiful silvery necklace of bubbles billowed upward toward the distant light like an endless string of pearls. At this depth, the surface seemed unbelievably remote.

Suddenly a large dark shadow materialized against the rocks. For an instant Phil's blood froze. He took it to be a cloud of some sort, casting its shadow through the water. But it couldn't have been a cloud, he argued. The sky had been perfectly clear when they left the surface..

The shadow began to move! It made a crazy wobbling motion, as if some huge underwater bat was fluttering its wings. Phil was momentarily fixated by it, like a cat mesmerized by its own shadow. He managed to wrest his eyes away long enough to follow its source. Silhouetted against the sun, hovering just below the surface, was a circular object large enough to create its own eclipse!

Phil wheeled toward the others. Why didn't they see it? He realized too late they were focused on what was in front of them. Meanwhile, the distance between him and his companions had widened alarmingly. Darkness was closing in quickly as the fringes of visibility became shorter by each receding foot. Furiously he began chasing their expanding trail of bubbles, hoping he could reach them in time.

By the time he overtook Linda, large gouts of exhaust bubbles were exploding from his regulator. He had trouble catching his breath. Grabbing her leg, he pulled her to a stop and imploringly began pointing. He was beside himself with excitement. She glanced at his flailing arm, then gazed back at him with inquisitive eyes. He realized she didn't see it! He rubbernecked around, but it was too late. Whatever it was had disappeared.

Meanwhile, Steve and Lucienne were hovering a short distance away, waiting impatiently for Phil and Linda to catch up. Phil could just discern their features highlighted against the gathering darkness rising from below. Phil imagined Steve was probably cussing him out by now. He knew for every second wasted, their bottom time was being compromised. Phil shrugged his shoulders in defeat and motioned for Steve and Lucienne to continue their descent. There was no sense spending any more time chasing a ghost, he reasoned.

At the 240 foot level, the staircase petered out. What was once a shrinking pattern of indistinct images, barely within visible range, came to an abrupt halt. The underwater tableau suddenly blossomed into a dizzying chasm of black infinity all around them. The darkness was almost complete. Steve motioned everyone to stop. They found themselves perched on the edge of a vertiginous drop-off. Phil had the ominous feeling they had reached Georgian Bay's bottomless pit. It was rumored it was an entrance to an old Indian burial ground before it flooded. He knew that if a diver got this far without going bonkers, claustrophobia was the least of his problems. The cardinal rule was always the same, stay calm. Rumors of an old Indian burial ground notwithstanding, Steve finally gave the Go signal to continue the dive. Jackknifing smoothly over the cliff, Steve again claimed the lead and headed down at a fast clip. Without any further hesitation, everyone followed suit. Holding his wife's hand, Phil mentally prepared himself for the next stage of their descent. At this greater depth everything took on new meaning...new sounds. His intake of gas doubled, tripled and quadrupled as the abyss opened up to embrace him. His lungs were forced to compensate for the tons of water pressure crushing against his body. What was once the sweet sound of bubbles purging from his regulator changed to an agonizing, stilted wheeze. Every liter of precious gases being sucked into his lungs was like manna from heaven.

Then came the blackness—total and complete. It was the same as when he and Linda went to Carlsbad Caverns and the tour guide turned off the lights to demonstrate absolute darkness. This was no different. There was no up or down. There was nothing he could identify with, to keep his mind from being sucked down a deep, dark sinkhole. All he was able to grasp was the silence, the abominable silence pressing in on him like a vise. In the background was the deep throb of escaping exhalations. This was the deepest level of claustrophobia he had ever encountered. It was a psychological battle to curb his most primal fears.

Phil switched on his hand-light. Instantaneously, a beam of bright white light stabbed the darkness like a dagger. He sighed gratefully. Sight was his liberation. Unlike a smoke filled room, in the blink of an eye, his world returned to the rule of order he was accustomed to. With smoke a firefighter had contaminants to contend with.

One thing they both had in common, however. Even with poor visibility, light meant you still had a finger-grasp to your world. If your time was up, you wouldn't die alone. Phil slowly played his light around, just before two more LED beams made their presence known. Everyone was grouped together in a tight circle, holding hands for reassurance, letting gravity do the work, conserving precious gas for when they would need it most. He saw Steve and Linda gazing with pop-eyed expressions through their masks, as if hypnotized. Phil managed a smile. Lucienne, with her blackened face-piece, looked like the underwater version of Darth Vader.

The illumination brought into focus the perpendicular rock face as it spiraled past them an arm's length away. Free-falling at four feet a second heightened his feeling of being caught on a run-away elevator plummeting out of control. Phil reached out tentatively, his gloved fingers lightly brushing the speeding precipice. Its rough, porous texture felt unearthly in the artificial light.

Suddenly, like a movie screen bursting into life, the changing scene exploded in their faces without warning. Phil recoiled in amazement. His mind was totally unprepared for the dazzling spectacle confronting him. As far as the eye could see were ships, row after row of them, of all vintages, of all sizes and descriptions, sitting upright with their keels wedged in the bedrock of an enormous cavern. Steve was right. Phil remembered him saying they were not shipwrecks in the normal sense. What he was describing were ships plucked out of the sea when they were still in their prime. Ones that just disappeared and were never found. A green phosphorus glow emanated from some hidden source within the ceiling, creating the illusion of fluorescent lighting. The whole scene reminded him of huge scale models in a museum. All that was missing were the tour guides, Phil quipped to himself. By the time they landed at the floor of the cave mouth, he had estimated the height of the cave to be that of a ten-story building. He glanced at his depth gauge. It was registering an incredible 510 feet.

Steve wasted no time getting started. He had his eye on an interesting-looking freighter while Phil and Linda were still trying to recover from their initial shock. Linda was the first to rally, giving Phil a nudge and pointing toward an old wooden schooner. Steve hurriedly synchronized his watch with theirs, indicating they would all rendezvous back at that spot in twenty-two minutes. They would be on a strict timeline. Then he was gone, with Lucienne in close pursuit.

Phil and Linda's ship turned out to be the legendary Jane Miller. Phil was taken aback. The name beneath her transom signified a hundred-and-forty-year-old mystery. For years, divers had been trying to locate this virgin wreck. She was a small cargo and passenger ship which presumably sank on a storm-ridden night in 1881. No trace of the vessel or her twenty-eight passengers and crew was ever found. What he remembered reading about her, she was a sailing sloop before being converted to steam. Tall, gaunt masts stuck upward like oversized matchsticks while he could clearly detect a stovepipe funnel protruding from her superstructure.

Phil and Linda proceeded to circle the ship, feeling and prodding their way along as they went. She was on an even keel, as if sitting on invisible chocks. As they passed the towering wooden rudder, Phil happened to spot the reflection of a three-bladed propeller gleaming dully in the recessed shadow of the poop deck. It looked brand new, without the customary discoloration associated with long use. As he and Linda continued their inspection, they found the hulk spotless, untainted by age or decay. Phil didn't even detect a broken spar or a loose chunk of planking lying about. That, in itself, was highly suspicious, he thought. Storms had a way of tearing and ripping a ship apart. Phil and Linda stopped to examine the hull more closely. Phil rubbed his hand against the vessel's smooth, wooden strakes. He stretched his frame to include an inspection of the bottom timber. He shook his head. This was no shipwreck in any sense of the word, he determined. There was absolutely no damage he could find that would relegate the Jane Miller to an underwater grave. Instead, it was as if she had been put in cold storage. His mind started to search for answers. Perhaps topside he would be able to find what he was looking for. Phil signaled his intentions to Linda, and, with an impatient thrust of his fins, he vaulted upward.

Catapulting over the bulwark onto the main deck, he stopped to reconnoiter. Breathlessly, he looked around. At first glance nothing seemed disturbed or out of place. There was no silt or mud to speak of. It was amazing! The scene was like having a history book open up in front of you. Looking up and around, Phil scanned the cavern for clues. The collection of relics were all being fed by the strange greenish glow that, as well as providing light, seemed to be some sort of energizing field. He could almost feel its penetrating rays saturate his body. Its invisible force hung over the ship like an umbrella.

After a cursory sweep of the deck, there was little doubt in his mind that the Jane Miller was rigged to haul freight as well as passengers. Scattered all about was a wide assortment of deck machinery, seemingly set aside for future use. An antiquated derrick and a skeletal looking object he didn't recognize was bolted to the deck next to a cargo hatch. Further aft was a cargo boom hanging idly in mute readiness. Next to that, he espied an open area which resembled a small promenade deck where the passengers must have lounged.

Phil began working his way toward the bow, passing large cargo hatches that were still battened down for sea. He wondered where Linda was. It wasn't like her to be hanging back from inspecting the rest of the ship with him. He glanced at his watch. Time was going by faster than he thought. He quickened his pace. A minute later he found himself standing at the bottom of the bridge. The pilothouse, with its gaping window, stared down at him like a giant Cyclops eye. Passageways on either side, leading to what he presumed were the passenger's quarters, receded into dark tunnels. Nearby, a lifeboat hung limply in its davits. A loose edge of its drawn tarpaulin flapped sullenly in the breeze. Red flags in his head began popping open. Phil froze. Impossible! There was no possibility of a breeze or a current down here. This just wasn't happening! The tarp kept flapping harder as if it were taunting him.

It was a scene taken right out of Moby Dick. At any second he expected Captain Ahab to come hobbling out on deck. He knew someone was there because he heard voices, a whole chorus of disembodied voices, all trying to communicate to him at once. But they were just unintelligible sounds he tried to shut out. He frantically blocked his ears, but he could still hear them. The sound was insipid, an undulating sea of tongues, murmuring louder and then softer, louder and then softer, like a surging riptide inside his head. "What's happening to me?" he cried out fearfully. Great gouts of bubbles were exploding out of his regulator. Without realizing it, he was starting to hyperventilate.

    Wild-eyed, he wheeled around, disoriented. Where was his wife? She should be with him. Without consciously realizing it, an overpowering urge gripped him. Some unknown force was pulling his eyes back to the bridge. His heart skipped a beat. Ohhhh my god!, Phil exclaimed. He couldn't believe what he was seeing. It was as if a camera shutter had snapped open for a brief instant, allowing the imprint of a hairy creature with fiery eyes to be etched into his brain. He back-pedaled away in horror.

    Panic-stricken, Phil tried kicking, but his legs were frozen in place. Thinking quickly he started pulling himself hand over hand along the bulwark, groping as best he could in a frenzied attempt to escape. Seconds passed away like minutes. Finally, he doubled over in sheer exhaustion. Every muscle in his arms and shoulders was crying out in protest. His entire body had started to tighten up from overexertion. Paroxysms of paralyzing cramps had reduced his legs to useless appendages. He had to rest, if only for a few seconds, he pleaded. His breathing was coming in short, painful gasps and he had the most uncontrollable urge to vomit. He could taste the bile welling up in his throat. For a few interminable minutes, Phil couldn't remember where he was. His head was spinning in a kaleidoscope of revolving images, everyone a likeness of the creature he had been fleeing from inside the cove.

Sucking in deep draughts of air, Phil resorted to his old yoga trick. Slowing down his breathing to a more normal rhythm, he willed his body to relax. Obviously, he told himself, he had been hallucinating. Flickers of happenstances as to why roiled through his head. Only one made any sense—the automated sensor that determined the proper mixture from his tank to the regulator must be malfunctioning, He stole a glance at his watch. Still, plenty of time before rendezvous. According to his tank gauge, however, he was past reserves. In his scrambling about, he must have tripped the reserve valve. He didn't have enough gas to wait for rendezvous or make it back alone. Phil realized he faced a dilemma. Do nothing and wait for help, or try and find Linda, or luckily one of the others, and put an emergency exit in play and buddy breathe back to the surface. It didn't take a rocket scientist to figure out which one he chose.

Phil kneaded his calves and legs to get his circulation flowing again. He could feel it working. He could kick again with some authority. He kept scanning his suddenly enclosed perimeter of visibility in the desperate hope of spotting someone's bubbles. "Where was Linda when he needed her," he cried in silent frustration. Instead of finding Linda, all he had found was an aberration from a forgotten era, the empty pleas of the Jane Miller's passengers and crew still ringing in his ears. He shook his head in disbelief. Was he really hallucinating?

Phil felt something brush against his leg. It took him a few seconds to identify it. It was the ship's capstan. Coiled around its drum before snaking its way into a hawse pipe at his feet was a huge anchor chain. The silt built around it gave it the bulbous, disjointed configuration of a python shedding its skin. He had landed in the extreme bow of the ship.

Slowly, painfully, Phil started retracing his route back to where he last seen Linda. He estimated he was about a third of the way along when he spotted her! She was directly below him, skimming the bottom, heading back toward the bow.

Phil slipped his knife out and started hammering against the side of his tank. The sound reverberated hollowly through the water like a death knell. She showed no response. Funny she couldn't hear that, he reasoned. Without further thought, he dove over the side to intercept her.

Once Phil was in the ship's shadowy underbelly, visibility decreased dramatically. Nonetheless, even in the half-light, the omnipresent green glow kept Linda in sight. Again, he banged on his tank. Still no response. He had no choice but to chase after her. After three or four kicks, he realized right away his legs were not ready for a speed duel. He was losing ground fast. Another few seconds and his wife would be out of sight. But then she slowed down, allowing Phil to make up the distance in just three or four more kicks. He didn't stop to ponder his good fortune. He reached out to grab her leg when, in the blink of an eye, she was gone! He was staring into nothingness!

Phil's brain immediately began assimilating, rationalizing, computing each incoming facet of information through its 100 billion neurons. His brain was desperately trying to come up with a logical, sane explanation, and quickly. His mind absolutely refused to accept any other possibility.

Temperature inversion came the analytical reply: a freak layer of warm water sandwiched in between two layers of cold. Like a magician who used mirrors to hide a subject, an inversion layer could temporarily make Linda disappear, Phil realized. But when a minute passed, and nothing happened, he began to think that Linda had ducked into some hidden nook or cranny of the ship instead.

Phil lay on his stomach and peeked through the underlying gloom. The ship loomed over him like an empty coffin. There were a lot of places a person could hide under there, he thought. Linda could be concealed in any one of a hundred different shadows.

Suddenly, something made him stop—a faint rustling sound, perhaps, or maybe a subtle pulse of kinetic energy caressing his body. Whatever it was, the hairs at the back of his neck were standing straight up. He looked up and saw something only nightmares were made of. Iron flukes, shining menacingly in the green paleness, began overflowing his field of vision with lightning rapidity. Phil realized too late what had happened. Unwittingly he had positioned himself directly below the ship's pendulous anchor. Somehow the capstan had disengaged. He wildly guessed the force of his bubbles, acting like a jet stream through the hawse pipe, might have done it. Without brakes, the unleashed chain came rattling down with the lethalness of a wrecking ball. And now, the anchor was aimed right at him, threatening instant pulverization. He could feel the water being pushed aside, washing over him like an invisible shock wave. And he was helpless to stop it. His body was paralyzed with fear. Split seconds dragged on like an eternity. He closed his eyes and lunged, praying that whatever strength he had left would be enough to escape the deadly missile. Instantaneously he was consumed in a billowing cloud of silt. He felt the vibration through the water as the massive weight of iron jarred the bottom at impact. The anchor had miraculously missed his outstretched, convulsing body by inches!

Phil lay next to his would-be grave marker, waiting for his racing heart to slow down. It was making funny palpitations, like he was getting ready to have a coronary. He felt as if his chest were being drawn into a vise. It was difficult to get gas into his lungs.

The reason suddenly dawned on him. It wasn't a heart attack. It was anoxia. Lack of oxygen. He knew he was sucking on dry tanks. Without wasting time thinking about it, Phil began his dash toward the entrance, his tired legs pumping in short, sporadic bursts. He could see the blackness beyond the cave mouth and the open water he so desperately sought. It was so near and yet so far. There was still hope. Even if his air gauge showed empty, there was always some residual gas left. He started ascending toward the roof of the cavern. By lessening water pressure against his lungs, he would lessen the amount of gas he had to breathe. It wasn't much but it was all he had left. He had run out of options. He pushed on blindly. From here on out, it was going to be a race against time.

Weird memories kept popping in his head. Like the time he had been trapped under the ice in Weller's Quarry. All he had to do was take a compass reading to the edge of the quarry where the ice was thinnest and break through. Hopelessly he looked up, wishing he was back in the quarry. Instead, tons of solid rock met his gaze.

Flashes of more poignant memories kept going through his mind—memories of his family, of Genny and Brian, a pair of always smiling, lovable kids who were at the threshold of adulthood. He thought of Linda, a wonderful mother as well as a terrific wife and lover. He remembered they had spent a lot of good times together.

Then there was his brother, Jeremy, the man with an astral computer for a brain. But, for all his smarts, he was a lousy chess player. Phil couldn't hold back a smile. It was funny how all those bits and pieces of your life whirl through your brain when it's time to cash out. He could feel his legs begin to tighten up on him again. His fins were acting like drag anchors. A relentless burning sensation was seeping into his lungs. He felt lightheaded. His whole body began to feel listless and tired. A bone-chilling numbness began to penetrate the very marrow of his bones. In the back of his mind, he was starting to see no way out of this. The cave mouth may as well have been a thousand miles away. He kept pumping, no matter what his body was telling him to do.

Phil's apprehension turned into cold fear when icy fingers began wrapping themselves around his spine. The burning sensation in his lungs had ignited into a fiery furnace. It felt as if he were inhaling hot volcanic gases with every breath. His stomach was churning in gut-wrenching spasms. A thin veil of darkness had started sending feelers to his brain.

At this stage, he was finding it impossible to concentrate. It would be so much easier if he could just stop and rest for a minute, his body pleaded, but his brain refused to let it quit. His vision was blurry. Focusing on anything at this point was out of the question. He wasn't even sure if he was going in the right direction anymore.

But some inner drive, some compulsion, kept urging him forward. By now, the fire in his parched lungs was permeating his entire body, pushing away the last of his reserves.

Then, something wonderful began to happen. The red-hot vise gripping his lungs began to mercifully loosen. In its stead, a cool, soothing ointment began to spread all over his body. Ohhh God, it feels so good!, he moaned. His pain was gone. He could breathe again. All of a sudden he felt relaxed and at peace with the world. He wasn't afraid of dying. He knew his mom and dad would be waiting for him. He could see a distant white light reaching through a dark tunnel to greet him. It was bright and glowing with immense beauty. It was getting larger and more compelling by the second. He closed his eyes and let the caressing, protective blanket of darkness carry him toward the expanding whiteness.

CHAPTER 16

Planet Earth

A burst of resplendent white light invaded Phil's senses. As if coming out of a stupor, he had to blink several times to adjust his eyes back into focus. The transition was slow but sensuously pleasing. The first thing he became cognizant of was his attire. He was dressed in a beige-colored, one-piece jumpsuit that completely covered his body from head to toe. He was standing on soft, cushiony soles that also felt very comfortable. He could distinguish no buttons, zippers or fasteners to mar the seamless fabric that felt like silk.

Phil found himself standing on open grass in what looked to be a neatly groomed botanical garden. He was bounded on three sides by a variety of palm trees and vibrant-looking flower beds that resembled an ad in Better Homes and Gardens.

Some of the flowers weren't at all familiar to him, nor were other exotic-looking shrubs and plants interspersed throughout the garden.

In front of him, guarded by a three-foot-high railing, lay a flat expanse of blue-green water. Waves were breaking on an outer reef about two hundred yards distant. It was salt water he determined quickly. Besides the fragrant scent of flowers, he could smell a briny tang in the air. Off to the left, low on the horizon, the sun hung like a golden medallion. He had the feeling it was setting, although he wasn't sure. It had a strange crimson halo around it. Small, puffy cumulus clouds floated lazily overhead. The scene had all the earmarks of a late afternoon summer day at a seaside park, he mused.

In the distance, Phil could see a high-level bridge under construction. Its incomplete erector-set framework stood glaringly naked against the reddish-tinged sky. Hovering above and below the steel network of girders and beams were swarms of odd-looking aircraft that resembled overgrown beetles. All were aglow in different colors. They executed erratic aerial maneuvers that defied the law of physics, flitting about like mischievous fairies. Phil stood fascinated by their peculiar behavior for several minutes before he realized that what he was gazing upon was actually happening; it wasn't a figment of his imagination.

Phil stepped up to the railing and discovered it wasn't really a railing in the normal sense, but a beam of green light. It extended for several hundred yards in either direction before eventually disappearing behind headlands of palms and tree ferns. Amazingly, the beam felt as solid to the touch as metal or wood.

Phil was overlooking a wide vista of beautiful white sand beach. The tide was out, he determined, because he could discern tiny seashells and dead seaweed lining the high water mark. It looked like a tropical beach of some kind, except he didn't think he was anywhere near the tropics. Beyond the beach lay a spur of land that was perhaps five or six miles across the water, obviously the terminus of the rapidly expanding bridge. The beetles were still dancing up and down, to and fro, in what looked like self-directed play. Upon closer observation, Phil could tell some kind of intelligent control was manipulating them. Beams of light radiated from their noses, striking the girders like lasers cutting and reshaping the metal to fit specific measurements. Some lifted huge stanchions with invisible tongs, using the same beams of high-intensity light for levitation.

"Hello, Philip."

The voice was smooth and mellow, like the resonance of a harp string. Startled, Phil whirled about. He was staring into the face of a tall, handsome man in his middle to late twenties with hair the color of ripened wheat hanging to his shoulders. He was dressed as Phil was, except the color of his suit was eloquently white. The outfit had a shimmering texture to it, similar to the luster of satin, except much glossier. Around his waist he wore a white belt on which was attached a small, flat-looking device the size of a matchbox. On the right side of his chest was an emblem of three interlocking triangles. It immediately caught Phil's attention. It was a perfect likeness of the secret marking he and his mother shared. It was a moot point anyway. He was all of a sudden captivated by the man's compelling presence. The angelic feeling he was receiving was something he couldn't put his finger on. It was like being in the company of a higher being, but he immediately scoffed at the thought. He impressed Phil as having Nordic features—fair skin, aquiline nose, elongated head. His piercing blue eyes seemed to look straight through him. If it were anyone else I would feel intimidated, Phil mused, but for some incomprehensible reason, he felt no qualms about the man standing there, only a deep sense of kinship.

A thin, benevolent smile played on the stranger's lips as he continued to gaze upon Phil. The expression in his eyes was of pure love and compassion. Phil had the strongest urge to embrace him as a long-lost brother.

"I am called Malik."

As soon as he said his name, Phil felt as though a gossamer-like thread, which had at one time intertwined their lives together, had just been rejoined.

"Haven't we met before?" Phil asked hesitantly.

"Yes, on many occasions, but you may have only a distant memory of them. You were not in your present incarnation then. His words seemed to strike a distant chord in Phil's memory. Malik's soft-spoken tone of voice was like that of a mother talking gently to a child.

"Where am I?" Phil swept his gaze in all directions. He felt like he was on a different planet. The last thing he remembered was the feeling of euphoria sweeping over him before losing consciousness. Was he dead?

"You are in a different space-time continuum, Philip. Your body is still in the earth plane but not as you remember it. Because of that, your vibrational frequency only allows you to remain here for a short while." He began to step away, gesturing with his hand. "But come. Let us walk along the seashore and enjoy the rest of the day together. We have much to talk about." His patrician face beamed with a radiant smile, revealing teeth that perfectly matched the color of his uniform.

Malik slowly began to walk along the railing while Phil just stood for a moment, unable to fathom the strange rapture he was feeling. Malik stopped and turned, waiting patiently for Phil to join him, an understanding look playing on his face. Phil decided not to try to fight the overpowering vibes he was receiving from this man staring at him with such deep conviction. Just being near this individual brought an indefinable lift to his spirits. It was the same feeling he got as a little boy when his mother used to console him after he had a bad dream. Phil pinched the bridge of his nose. It was even more intense than that, he lamented. It was as if he were talking to a…a…

"Are…are you a saint or an angel or something like that?" he finally blurted. For some reason, he didn't feel at all embarrassed at his lack of prudence.

Malik laughed.

"No, my brother. I am not an angel or a saint. I am considered a teacher."

Phil was probably looking at a man far removed from his own insignificance in the scheme of things, and yet for Malik to call him "my brother" didn't seem to Phil the least bit strange. As a matter of fact, it seemed perfectly natural.

They stopped to gaze at the placid waters streaked with gold as the sun continued its plunge toward the horizon. Malik suddenly turned and laid his hands on Phil's shoulders in a tender show of compassion.

"I must tell you this now, Philip, and you must heed my words. The earth will become shrouded in a generation of darkness soon. It is because mankind has disavowed his rightful place in the universe. He has succumbed to disruptive influences and self-seeking forces that have altered his environment considerably. As a result, human consciousness is out of synchronization with the life energies of Earth. This discord has imbalanced the polarization of your planet. In order for Earth to survive, it must realign itself into proper vibrational harmony with other planets. To do so will entail a major shifting of its axis and in the process, many of earth's inhabitants will perish. I am sorry. Mankind did not follow the Divine Plan which the Creator assigned to all his souls."

Phil just stood and listened, trying to mentally absorb what he was hearing. The words rang dully in his brain. Their impact had not fully reached his consciousness. He was confused.

"I don't understand. You mean it's the earth changes Edgar Cayce spoke of?" Phil thought his voice sounded as if it were coming from someone else.

"Yes, he was one of the few in your time who prophesized the coming of the New Age."

So it was true! Phil gaped at Malik with disbelieving eyes. He was shocked at the enormity of what was about to happen. Somehow, hearing it from this man put a finality to it. Malik's words continued to pound into his brain.

"It is a cleansing process, Philip. It has been necessary for the earth to undergo many such changes in its history. Be not afraid. You have been chosen to teach. You will survive, as well as your family and friends to comfort you. There will be places on earth that will offer temporary refuge."

"Yes, I know. Cayce called them safety lands. Ohio, Indiana, Illinois and parts of southern Ontario in Canada would be spared." Once he said it, something clicked inside his brain. "The cave I was in was filled with artifacts," Phil went on. "Would it being there have something to do with the coming earth changes?"

Malik nodded. "Yes, there are many hidden places on earth that will sustain earth's history by its discoverers as the rebirth begins. The cave you speak of is one of them."

Phil's passion for history couldn't resist the thought that it answered what had always puzzled anthropologists for centuries—the sudden rise of advanced civilizations like Atlantis and Lemuria. It was like getting a jump-start by finding one of these time capsules. But the end result was always the same, he painfully discovered. The sudden decimation of countless billions of people in an earth change. And now, mankind was heading for another such cataclysm he couldn't even begin to imagine. Phil began to shake and his knees started to feel rubbery. He knew his emotional stability was not capable of sustaining much more of this kind of talk.

Malik squeezed Phil's shoulders in a gentle embrace. Immediately, Phil could feel a healing energy in his touch.

"There will be others that will join you in your task. You will not be alone."

"Wh…what is the reason for all this?" Phil stammered in a pleading voice. "Why does God have to do such a terrible thing?" It was hard to believe they were discussing humankind as if they were nothing more than expendable coins in a slot machine.

As if continuing to counsel an obstinate child, Malik's tone took on the tolerance of a sympathetic mentor.

"For those people who do not believe, it will be as if a dark cloud is lifted from their minds, Philip. They will come to understand who they are and what their purpose in life is. Those who survive will evolve with a higher level of consciousness, a true awareness of the human spirit. They will be the teachers, like you, who will be able to help those who will come after, through the birthing process, to follow their own chosen destiny. Once that is begun, it will bring to pass the meaning of life as it was ordained to the race of Adam."

"I…I don't understand. Why will I be allowed to live while others die?"

"Death is but a continuation of life in a different dimension, Philip. The Son of God, when He was in the earth plane, often referred to life after death as having many rooms in His Father's house. It is not the end of consciousness as you know it; it is only the beginning. The purpose of reincarnating is to gain the immortality God promised. To do so, karma must be absolved in order for one's soul to return back to the Source. This may require many lifetimes. Mankind must continually strive for perfection in each incarnation he has chosen."

Malik was reinforcing what Cayce had preached all along, Phil thought. Reincarnation was synonymous with rebirth. As a sidelight, it answered why people had certain phobias—abnormal fear of things from birth, like a deathly fear of water, perhaps from drowning in a previous life. Or acrophobia, by falling to their death from a great height. Always curious, Phil sometimes wondered how geniuses came to be, like a Mozart or a Michelangelo, who could create works of art at such early ages—all learned and accumulated from previous lives.

Malik placed Phil's hands in his and squeezed gently. They were warm and supple to the touch, but yet Phil sensed a great deal of strength emanating from them. Malik's eyes radiated a strange, magnetic force. Whatever apprehension was building inside Phil instantly vanished.

"Do not feel troubled. The Creator, in His wisdom, has given you the opportunity to learn and evolve one step higher on the earth plane. You have shown in your advancement a deep concern for your fellow humans. It was a choice you made early in your soul's development."

"How will I be able to help?"

"You have faced death many times in your past incarnations. Once, when you were a Roman gladiator under Augustus Caesar, you learned to conquer fear. Another time, as a soldier in your country's Civil War. Even in this life experience, you chose fortitude as an ideal in order to help others. In so doing, you again prepared your soul for immortality. Fear of death retards soul progression. You can teach others to overcome fear, as you learned to overcome it. That will be a beginning."

Just then Phil noticed a small speck had materialized at the edge of the horizon. From that distance its dimensions were immeasurable, but whatever it is, it was enormous, Phil thought. It streaked over the water and approached them at the speed of a jet. Once it reached a few miles beyond the bridge, the object decelerated rapidly, and Phil was finally able to get a good look at it. A long plume of crimson flame was shooting out the back, and the front gave off a white beam as brilliant as a strobe light.

By the time it reached their position, the red plume had fizzled out like a spent rocket and the beam of light had dulled to an incandescent glow. It was shaped like a bulbous cigar. Phil judged it to be about a city block long and as high as a three-story building. Its surface area gleamed as if it were metal, reflecting the sun's dying embers in a blaze of reddish orange. The craft didn't make a sound or show any means of staying aloft. If it wasn't made of feathers, Phil was accustomed to seeing airplanes with wings and stabilizers that denoted aerodynamic stability. In no way could he call this thing aerodynamic. It was like a giant, polished smokestack floating in the air without any visible means of propulsion. It just slowly glided along as if guided by some invisible force. Phil could see a triple row of square windows lining one side as it passed silently overhead. By this time Phil was having a hard time forcing any sound out of his vocal chords. Beings that looked like humans were looking down at him!

But that wasn't all. Just about the time he thought he'd seen everything, Phil saw the humanlike creatures in the strange machine start waving! And just as amazingly, Malik waved back!

"Who…who are these people, Malik?"

"They are from the future, Philip. Their home is in an alliance of planets called the Interplanetary Council. It is similar to your League of Nations. Their members reject violence. There are no wars or conflicts between them. They are dedicated to interplanetary peace and stability." Phil listened numbly to the words, trying to comprehend their meaning. It seemed Malik sensed his confusion.

"They are here in compliance with Universal Law," the celestial continued. "Members of the Council come in many forms, my brother. Over the passage of millennia, they have visited your planet many times. Some have stayed for their own choosing. Those that did had to obey, above all else, the Supreme Decree given to them by the Creator— preservation of their species."

Phil had the feeling Malik was referring to humankind, in particular. His words pounded in synch with Phil's pounding heartbeat as the spacecraft suddenly exploded into instantaneous acceleration and disappeared. In a flash of light it was gone! Or maybe it just dematerialized into thin air. Phil couldn't decide which.

Without any warning, he began to feel weak and disoriented. His legs almost buckled underneath him as he held on to the railing for support.

"What's happening to me?" Phil cried. He felt as if he were about to pass out. Dark shadows were approaching his retinas from every direction. Everything was starting to get fuzzy. Out of the corner of his eye he could see a light blinking on the boxlike device Malik carried.

"The hour has come," Malik said reassuringly. "Do not be frightened. Your journey is about to begin."

"Will I ever see you again?" Phil asked. It saddened him to think he had to leave the company of such a divine presence. It was a feeling he had never experienced before.

"Yes, my brother. When the time is right, we will meet again."

"What is this...place? Wh...where am I?" Phil had to force the words out of his mouth. He was starting to lose consciousness fast, yet he felt it imperative to know the answer. Malik's parting words echoed resoundingly in his brain. "What you see before you is the Pacific Ocean, Philip. You are in the land of Nebraska in the earth year 2356."

Phil wasn't sure whether Malik's reply had registered in his memory or not. A solid black pall had taken possession of his inert form.

CHAPTER 17

November 30—11:37 A.M...Flower Pot Island

Phil felt hot and uncomfortable. As he lay on a hard surface, he could feel the hot sun bearing down on him, roasting him, and it left him little doubt that he was back in his own world again.

Phil shut his eyes tightly to avoid the pain of the sun's searing glare. It's still too bright, he thought. He turned his head. That was better.

Phil could tell he didn't have any of his scuba gear on, but he was still wearing his wet suit, which was why he was swimming in his own sweat. But at least somebody had the decency to unzip his jacket and remove his hood. His legs had also been propped up to keep the blood from rushing to his feet. He could hear voices in the background, human voices. The words kept bouncing back and forth inside his head as though they were being scrambled with an egg beater. Then he heard his name being called. The voice sounded familiar.

"Phil...Phil...can you hear me? Are you okay, sweetheart?"

A series of auditory memory impulses exploding inside his brain were the first to respond. Nobody called him sweetheart, except his wife, and always in a most sexy voice whenever she wanted to persuade him into something he didn't want to do. Except, this time, the voice didn't sound so sexy. It bordered on panic. Phil's eyes fluttered open. The image bent over him was blurry and distorted, but he immediately recognized the long blonde hair hanging down over a satiny shoulder. It was Linda. She was blocking the sun, and her face was hidden in shadow. Steve and Lucienne were standing a few feet away next to his equipment, looking for all the world as if they were gazing down on a corpse.

Phil struggled into a sitting position. Every muscle in his body ached from the exertion.

"I feel like I just got hit by a truck," Phil croaked.

"I thought we lost you there for a minute, ole buddy," Steve chimed in. "What the hell happened to you down there?"

Phil was temporarily at a loss for words.

"Where did you go?" Linda pressed. "I looked everywhere for you."

Phil suddenly realized that everybody was looking at him for an explanation. But what could he say? That he had talked to a deity from another world? Who was going to believe that?

"I ran out of air. The last thing I remember is trying to get out of the cave." He paused in reflection. "I…I don't think I made it." By the disbelieving look in their eyes, his makeshift words seemed to be melting in the hot sun. Phil could still remember that hot iron poker lodged in his chest, his last dying gasps for air.

"You're talking nonsense, pal. Of course you made it. You're here, aren't you?" Steve snapped, sounding slightly perturbed with his friend's answer. "You probably experienced a touch of narcosis, that's all."

"Yeah, I guess you're right. I don't remember too much of what happened, anyway," Phil lied. His feeble reply was left hanging like a hangman's noose as they started back to camp. From the sidelong looks he was getting, he guessed Linda and Steve could read in between the lines. They knew he was holding something back from them. Just as well, Phil brooded. He wasn't ready to divulge his secret…not just yet, anyway. He needed time to think, to sort things out. He looked up at the burning sky. Just how much time did they have left? he wondered.

November 30—4:18 P.M…Back at camp

"You met him, didn't you?" Lucienne spoke so softly and matter-of-factly that she caught Phil off-guard.
"Wh…what did you say?" He was in the process of helping her filet a batch of fresh walleye Captain Smollet had given them. Steve and Linda were out exploring, looking for the captain's elusive Sasquatch. That's what everybody finally decided to name the creature. There was a good chance, Steve figured, of finding a clue to its whereabouts in one of the more inaccessible caves riddling the island.
"I asked you if you met Malik."
"Yes, yes I did. But how did you know?"
She had stopped what she was doing and was directly facing Phil. Even with her sightless eyes hiding behind dark polaroids, she knew exactly where he was sitting. She had the uncanny ability to pinpoint objects strictly by sound. It was as if she had her own built-in

radar, not unlike a bat. She could also read what people were thinking just by the slightest inflection in their voices. It would be difficult to get anything by her, Phil realized.

"Because he told me a long time ago you were chosen too. I could tell from what you didn't say this morning that you must have finally met him."

"Then you know what's going to happen."

"Oh yes. He told me everything. But it was such a long time ago, I kind of put it out of my mind until now. I also knew you were in trouble down there. I could feel your fear coming through. Remember? I have this psychic gift that many people think is so great. But it can be a curse sometimes, you know," giving a thin smile.

"When did you meet him?"

"The day I died. Just as you did."

Phil sat speechless. He didn't know what to make of her answer. She saved him the trouble by quickly explaining. "After my skiing accident. I died on the operating table. It was only later I found out. The doctor said my heart had stopped beating for twelve minutes. It was during that interim I met Malik."

"What did you think of him?"

"Ohhhh, he's such an extraordinary man," she swooned. "I felt so good just being near him. Didn't you get that feeling too?"

"Yes, I certainly did," Phil answered. Then curiosity got the best of him. "Were you able to see him, Lulu? I mean, before you were blinded?"

"Oh, yes. He was a handsome young man with gold hair down to his shoulders and the deepest blue eyes I've ever seen. He told me I was going to be blind the rest of my life. The doctors were amazed I took it so well. I guess the shock had worn off by the time they got around to telling me."

"Who is he? Did he ever tell you where he came from?"

"No, not exactly, but I can tell you what he is."

"A teacher."

"Yes, that too, but I also think he's a spirit guide."

"A spirit guide?"

"Yes, you know, somebody who oversees the different directions you take whenever you come up to certain crossroads in your life."

"What do you mean?"

"Have you ever wondered how your life would have been different if certain opportunities hadn't come along when they did? Like meeting Linda, for example. Or had chosen a different career, instead of joining the fire department. What made you make those important decisions that, down the road, would ultimately influence the outcome of your life? Life is full of those kind of choices. You know that. Spirit guides just help keep you focused and pointed in the right direction, that's all. Some people call them guardian angels. They help you fulfill your chosen destiny. At times, even by saving your life, if they have to. Did you ever think of that? Certainly you don't believe it was all by chance."

"To be frank, I really never thought about it that much before," Phil replied. He admitted there were times on the fire department when he got unexpected help. At the time he attributed it to pure luck. But it was the way she emphasized the word 'chance' that conjured up a dim memory from his past. It was when he and Jeremy were lying on Detroit Beach one hot summer day during one of his brother's infrequent visits from college. Phil recalled how Jeremy thought most people believed the universe was formed strictly by chance. "How sad," he maintained, "that someone could be so arrogant to think earth was simply made by accident for our benefit. Archeologists have proven that other intelligent life forms had inhabited earth long before homo-sapiens came along. Some went exploring to other universes while others came back to start new civilizations here. Which brings us back to the beginning. Every planet that supports intelligent life has a purpose," he said. "Those who defy that truth by squandering their planet's resources and polluting its environment are doomed to extinction." He then took a handful of sand and sifted it through his fingers. "Even this sand wasn't made by chance," his brother declared. "It took millions of years for a certain type of coral to grow, proliferate, die, get pulverized by wind, rain, have a few thousand tons of ice grind it to little bitty particles, and then deposit it in this exact spot, just so you could squish your toes in it. Get my point, brother? Nothing in the universe is by chance. Not even the lowest, inanimate, tiniest forms. Everything was made to serve a purpose."

Lucienne's voice sounded as if were a million miles away.

"Did Malik explain to you why you were chosen, Phil? I mean specifically."

"Huh? Yes, I think so." Lucienne's question snapped Phil back to the present. "He said fear of death retards soul progression, and since I've learned to overcome fear, I should teach it to others. But, you know, Lulu, I get scared like everybody else. Hell, I used to hide under the bed when I was a kid because I thought the bogeyman was after me."

Lucienne laughed. "I don't think Malik meant it that way, Phil. You're a big boy now. I bet all your past life experiences got you conditioned for what's coming. I would certainly think so anyway. It doesn't promise to be an easy task."

"You got that right. I used to be a gladiator, a soldier, and now a firefighter. I guess I just had to show everybody how fearless I am," said Phil with tongue in cheek. "Malik said it had something to do with a choice I made earlier in my soul's development."

"Well see, there you have it," Lucienne said, beaming. "And I bet your spirit guide helped you along the way too."

Now it was Phil's turn to laugh. It was funny how she could manipulate the conversation to defend her hypothesis. But then again, maybe she wasn't so far off base after all, he thought.

"Okay, hotshot. Now it's your turn in the confessional. Why were you chosen to live again to fight another day?" Phil's lighthearted banter helped maintain his sanity. The words, the end of the world, kept haunting him. It wasn't words he could swallow easily. He held one last hope. Something else his brother had said in passing. "The future is not fixed. The thought energy of humanity's new world leaders could alter the forces of nature." Even more hopeful was what Cayce had predicted in one of his readings—"a concentrated influx of Atlanteans reincarnating in the earth plane. It was possible their powerful creative potential of human consciousness could redirect the flow of events in the physical world."

"You firefighters would refer to it as a firewall," his brother added for clarification. "If so, it would mean..." Lucienne's strident voice kept interrupting Phil's reverie.

"My karma. K-A-R-M-A."

"Karma?"

"Yes. Weren't you listening, my dear? Malik said I was to suffer blindness because of some past digression I committed in a previous life. Heaven forbid, whatever it was, it must have been something dreadful." She said it without a trace of bitterness in her voice. "Now, I must work it out in this life," she continued.

Lucienne gave a pathetic little smile. It was like she wanted to let it all out.

"Malik said my working in the Foundation has greatly advanced my soul's progression. But heck, Phil, it always made me feel good to help others cope with the same affliction I have. I certainly don't expect any favors. He said my sight would return someday, once my debt was paid. God only knows when that will be?"

Phil knew Lucienne was being too modest. Her volunteer work to help support the *Foundation for the Blind* in Toronto had become synonymous with Shacker Shoes. Her monetary contributions were probably nothing to sneeze at, either.

"So, what are your plans, Phil? Are you going to tell Linda about Malik?"

Phil shrugged. "Oh, I imagine I will eventually. I haven't really thought about it a whole lot yet. Right now, my main concern is to get the twins on the first plane home. They're visiting their aunt in California, you know. Once I explain the game rules, there's a good possibility she'll join them. After that, I'm not sure what Malik has in store for me. Same with you for that matter. I guess it's wait and see." He gazed up at the relentless, blistering sun as its rays tried to penetrate a thick patch of white pine and Douglas fir guarding the campground. Huddling in their shade didn't seem to be doing much good, Phil realized. The heat was like being slowly barbecued on a rotisserie. Every inch of his body was dripping moisture. He wiped the gathering perspiration off his forehead with an already soaked towel he kept handy. "It seems to be getting hotter, Lulu. Whatever's going to happen, I don't think we have much longer to wait. I know I don't want to stick around here any longer than I have to. If I were you, I'd think of getting out of here too. Who knows when we'll be getting another visit from out...out there?" Phil absently gestured toward the cerulean waterscape beyond the jetty. He had to admit, even though he was still harboring a resentment that he almost drowned in its cold depths, it still looked mighty inviting. He silently asked himself how long it would be before he dove in it again? They had all agreed to see what tomorrow would bring before returning to the cave.

"I think whoever they are were just curious last night, Phil. After all, neither Steve nor I were hurt down there."

"Well, what about this morning? Don't forget somebody tried to break into your camp."

"I never sensed a harmful presence. I believe whoever it was, was trying to tell us something. Maybe a warning of some kind."

"A warning! Lulu! I don't have to be beaten over the head with a club to know something is going on around here. Too many people have turned up missing since those creatures showed up."

"Oh, Phil. You're just overreacting. There's no proof that any of the disappearances are linked with Sasquatch. Personally, I think they're some type of robot programmed to scare people away. After all, didn't you say…"

Just then Steve and Linda came bursting into camp as if they had just crossed the finish line of the Boston Marathon. "Got something to show you. Hurry! Get into the boat!" Steve wheezed, gesticulating like a wild man, excited and out of breath. He grabbed Lucienne by the hand, pulling her along toward the dock while exhorting them all to hurry. Phil looked at Linda for some kind of explanation, but she already had her back to him, following close on Steve's heels.

"You won't believe it until you see it for yourself. C'mon!" Linda yelled over her shoulder. "We'll explain later!" The trio were already scrambling into the boat by the time Phil decided to chase after them. When he finally caught up, Steve had already unhitched the mooring lines, letting the vessel drift away from the pier. Phil just managed to launch himself across the widening gap of water into Linda's outstretched arms. The racket of the turbochargers starting up sounded like rockets exploding in their ears. In a giant cascade of white water and foam, the

Shoestring leapt away from the dock as though shot out of a cannon. Phil's remembrance of the moment was nothing more than a blur of sound and flying spray as the unleashed power beneath the deck whisked them out into the outer reaches of Georgian Bay in a matter of seconds.

CHAPTER 18

November 30—4:45 P.M…Georgian Bay

As Shoestring roared her way across the Bay, Phil managed to piece together Steve and Linda's story. They said they were combing the other side of the island when they saw something totally bizarre. They couldn't explain it. A solid fog bank had materialized out of nowhere, hovering on the water no more than a league offshore from where they were standing. It seemingly extended for miles in either direction, blocking everything in its path. Although there was no wind to speak of, it seemed to be inexorably moving toward them.

Shoestring was just rounding the promontory that hid Beachy Cove from sight of the mainland when, without warning, Steve suddenly jammed the throttles in reverse. Simultaneously, he spun the wheel as far right as the stops allowed, the engines screaming like ruptured banshees. The centrifugal force of doing a one-eighty at forty knots slammed everybody to the deck in a heap of arms and legs. Amidst a flurry of boiling foam, leaving a trough the size of a bomb crater in its wake, the boat heeled like a subservient greyhound to its master.

Phil was ready to give Steve a piece of his mind for his hot-dogging. Somebody could have got hurt. As far as he could tell, nobody had, although he wasn't so sure of himself yet. Putting aside a bruised ego, he struggled his feet to see what made Steve think he was at Indianapolis Speedway. He was immediately taken aback by what he saw. It was absolutely breathtaking. If Steve hadn't slammed on the brakes when he did, Phil realized, they would have collided into the thickest wall of fog he'd ever seen in his life. It completely swept the horizon like an impenetrable curtain

"It got bigger!" Linda cried in an awed voice.

"And closer!" Steve added for effect.

Phil was no stranger when it came to fog. He and Linda had been caught in its deadly grip many times before. These waters were especially known for the sudden, random appearance of fog banks, as many a shipwreck lying on the bottom of Georgian Bay could testify. But the fog facing them was more than just an amalgamation of water vapor and cold air. It was an aberration. It was as if someone had hung a solid barrier directly across their path. With the sun setting at their backs, the leaden substance appeared to be made of living protoplasm, absorbing the heat like a giant amorphous sponge.

"Have you ever seen anything like this before in all your life?" Steve exclaimed.

Phil had to admit he hadn't. Nobody had. But it instantly brought to mind stories he'd read of similar phenomena happening in other parts of the world. The Bermuda Triangle, for example, where fog banks suddenly popped up out of nowhere to completely envelop a ship without warning. When the fog dissipated, whoever had been trapped inside would mysteriously disappear without a trace.

As an afterthought, Phil glanced at the boat's binnacle.

"Look at your compass, Steve!"

"I'll be damned. It's spinning like a top!"

"Yes, and if my hunch is right, it's probably caused by some strong electromagnetic field close by. Possibly inside there," Phil said, nodding his head toward the fog bank. The mass didn't seem to be moving, as was earlier thought. A shiver ran up and down his spine. He feared the surreal amalgamation had been waiting for them to show up. Meanwhile, Steve was keeping Shoestring at bay, measuring a safe distance of at least a boat length away, just in case.

"Why don't we turn around and..." Linda never got to finish as Lucienne held up her hand for silence.

"Listen!"

At first, Phil heard nothing but the soft rumbling of the Shoestring's idling engines.

"Cut the engines, Steve."

Once the engines stopped, Phil heard it too. The soft, almost inaudible sound of an animal in distress.

"It's a dog barking!" someone said.

"The only dog I know around here belongs to Captain Smollet," Steve remarked. "Who else travels with a dog in these parts?"

Phil shot a quick glance at his watch. The timing was about right. The captain would have been returning home from the north side of the island just about now.

"Maybe he's in trouble," Linda suggested.

Steve stood up on the bow and bellowed through cupped hands, "AHOY THERE! CAN ANYBODY HEAR ME?"

Silence.

Steve hailed again. Still a dead calm met his cry.

"Looks like we're going to have to go in after him," he announced.

He switched on the electronic starter and began reaching for the throttle controls. Phil and Linda could see their friend had a determined look in his eyes.

"Don't go in there, Steve!" It was Lucienne. The fear in her voice froze his hand in midair.

"Why not?"

"Because I'm getting bad vibrations. There's something not right in there."

"That's nonsense, Lulu. It's just an unusually thick patch of fog, that's all. Nothing to sweat. We've been through them before."

"I don't think this is just ordinary fog, Steve," Phil intervened. "Something is making that compass go haywire, and once we're in there, we may never find our way back out."

"I agree," Linda added vehemently. Her voice had that "don't argue with me" finality to it which meant she wasn't taking no for an answer. Outvoted, Steve backed down graciously. "How about if I use the runabout then, eh? If I can't get the Genny started, I'll just tie a towline to it and you can pull me out with Shoestring."

Phil wasn't too keen on that idea either. The only towline available was for pulling the sled, a much lighter vessel than the Genny. Besides, if anything went wrong, his only recourse would be to go in after him, blindly. Without a compass, it would be a hit-or-miss proposition. As a firefighter, he had been trained to search for alternatives on short notice. As much as he hated to admit it, this was the first time he found himself stumped. "How about if I go instead?" he offered. "After all, you know how to handle your boat better than I do in case something goes wrong."

Steve threw his head back and gave out one of his robust guffaws that would have done Errol Flynn proud. "No way, pal. You're an old hand at handling boats, so I'm not worried. You did just fine last night. Besides, it's my party, but thanks anyway."

"I'm going too," Lucienne piped up. There was an obstinate set to her chin that discouraged any argument. Steve gave her a reproachful look, but Phil knew Steve would probably have been disappointed if she hadn't volunteered. "Okay, okay, we're wasting time. Let's go!" Steve wheeled around and was halfway to the bow storage compartment before anybody had a chance to take their first step.

"It looks like he means now," Lucienne giggled.

November 30—5:22 P.M...Georgian Bay

The suspense was almost palpable. Once Steve and Lucienne were swallowed up in the fog bank, it was a matter of waiting it out...and not letting your imagination run away with you, Phil mused. It was as if their friends had entered a different world, separated by a wall of silence. He and Linda kept up a running commentary with

them with the use of a pair of walkie-talkies Steve kept
aboard the Shoestring. Hearing their voices helped, if no
other reason than to feel close to them; to make sure they
were okay. Whenever they talked, their voices sounded
muffled and suppressed, as if they were being filtered
through a wad of cotton. The zodiac's ten-horse motor
didn't sound so good either, as its off-key pitch reached
Phil and Linda in sporadic coughs and spurts. Steve was
having a difficult time keeping it running. Something was
wrong. Even Steve's breathing was coming in short gasps
whenever he talked. Whenever questioned about it, the tall
Canadian kept insisting he and Lucienne were okay.

Another worry that was starting to play on Phil's
mind was the polyethylene ski rope they were presently
using as a lifeline. It was a separate entity unto itself.
Once it entered the fog bank, the yellow appendage
disappeared completely, as though it had been severed with
a knife. Linda kept feeding it out slowly, not allowing any
slack, as the small runabout pulled it along. Phil kept the
Shoestring's stern perpendicular to the fog bank with its
powerful diesels idling. He had every intention of yanking
Steve and Lucienne out of there at the first sign of danger.
The only question was, the ski rope only had a test rating of
eight hundred pounds. Could it sustain pulling anything
heavier…like a two-and-a-half-ton fishing boat?

Phil knew that, on the other end of the three-
hundred foot line, Steve and Lucienne were trying to zero
in on Sandy's barking like homing pigeons. If that failed,
they were to attempt a modified version of the sweep
method. It was often employed by underwater salvage
divers in murky water. The plan was simple. Play the line

out to its furthest most point, then, with the Shoestring acting as a fulcrum, the zodiac would begin a one-hundred-and-eighty degree swing, sweeping the tow line across the surface, in ninety degree increments, back and forth, snagging anything within its radius. With a little bit of luck, it just might work if the Genny wasn't beyond reach, Phil thought.

He glanced at his watch. It seemed as if hours had passed, but instead it had only been seventeen minutes since they had broken out the runabout. By now the line was stretched almost to its limit. They could hardly hear Steve's or Lucienne's voices anymore. The fog was playing havoc with the walkie-talkies. Static was jamming the airwaves, producing a sizzling sound, like frying bacon. Not knowing what was happening was making Phil and Linda especially nervous. Neither of them liked what their imaginations were envisioning.

Phil jumped as he heard Steve's faint cry through the fog. It was the moment he and Linda were waiting for. Success! Their friends had found the barking dog. It was Sandy, as Steve presumed, sitting impatiently aboard the Genny, wanting attention. Except for being overly ecstatic at Steve and Lucienne's arrival, the dog was okay. As Phil had suspected, Lucienne's keen hearing had zeroed in on the barking like radar is to a bat. Wait a second! Was he hearing correctly? Yes. Even through the opaqueness, Steve's words were unmistakable. The captain wasn't there! Oh my god! Phil's first thought was that he must have fallen overboard. But, he quickly surmised, that would be a stretch. Unless something happened that made him fall overboard, like a heart attack or a stroke.

Steve immediately wanted to search for the captain, but after a hurried exchange, Phil convinced Steve to stick with their original plan. Trying to find the captain in this fog was like trying to find the proverbial needle in a haystack. He could have fallen overboard anywhere between there and the other side of the island, for all they knew. And the Genny probably drifted for who knows how long before they found it, Phil pointed out. Getting the Genny free and clear of the fog bank was their first priority. But that soon went by the wayside when Steve discovered the Genny's engine wouldn't start. And for good reason once Steve inspected below deck. All the engine's wiring and electrical cables were burnt to a crisp. They figured a tremendous force field had to have been the cause. It was the same phenomena that was affecting the spinning compass, and reason enough to keep the Shoestring out of the mysterious fog. Which meant they had no choice but to revert to Plan B. Back to the questionable ski rope.

"SECURE THE LINE AND HANG ON. I'LL START PULLING YOU IN," Phil hollered across the void. Once he got momentum going, he figured, with a little bit of luck, the ski rope would hold. Something else was starting to bother him, though. His thoughts were starting to gravitate to only one thing; getting Steve and Lucienne out of there, with or without the Genny in tow. And to be quick about it!

Phil revved the Shoestring's powerful turbos, put her in gear, and gradually eased the dual throttles forward. Once the slack was let out, the ski rope hardened like a rail. Now came the real test, Phil thought. He and Linda held their breath as the fog bank, inch by inch, began to recede.

So far, so good. All conversation between them had ceased. Neither had to talk anyway, just pray. The seconds began to drag into minutes as progress became painfully slow. A snail could have kept up with their pace but Phil was afraid to nudge the throttles higher. The towline, as he had feared, was beginning to stretch like a rubber band. If only a few more minutes were granted by the good Lord, he prayed. Seventy-five more feet to go. Once the Genny was free, they could flee this anomalous muck that had consumed their world like an evil shroud. The whole scene was starting to give him the creeps.

Phil and Linda suddenly began to hear a strange droning sound above the deep-throbbing diesels. Curious as to what it could be, Phil slipped the gears in neutral and listened. With the drag off the engines, the mysterious drone suddenly jumped a hundred decibels, torturing their already overtaxed nerves. It was a sound that struck an all too familiar chord of fear in their consciousness. There was no mistaking its meaning.

"Oh, Jesus," Linda shrieked. She was pointing frantically at the fog bank. "It's coming from inside there!"

Phil's blood froze. A greenish glow was beginning to take shape inside the fog.

"STEVE! LUCIENNE! ARE YOU OKAY?" Phil yelled at the top of his lungs, but what now sounded like a whirring dynamo began to overpower every other earthly sound, including his own feeble cries.

Phil and Linda exchanged horrified looks.

"GET THEM OUT OF THERE!" she screamed.

Without thinking, Phil jammed the throttles forward, releasing the full potential of Shoestring's power plant. That was a mistake. The boat lunged with a convulsive shudder, whipping the ski rope taut again like an overdrawn bowstring. The engines clamored in protest, but they obeyed unhesitatingly. All sixteen pistons instantaneously began churning at once, sending out teeth-chattering reverberations throughout the boat. A cauldron of spewed water seethed beneath the stern. The din was deafening. Glancing back, Phil was amazed the ski rope was still holding together. Meanwhile, the Shoestring was gathering steam. He expected at any second to see the Genny's white-and-green-painted prow come popping through. But something was wrong. Shoestring was acting funny. It was slowly, but steadily, decelerating! Phil and Linda could feel the boat fighting to keep from being dragged backward, but it was like fighting a losing tug-of-war. Shoestring was being overridden by an extremely powerful force. Within a minute all forward progress had ceased. It was as though some inexplicable magnet was trying to pull them back into the fog bank! And it was happening! They were starting to creep backwards!

Incredulously Phil stared at Linda, not knowing what to do next.

There was a dazed look on her face. He could read her lips as they mouthed mute pleas in the unearthly cacophony.

"Do something, for god's sake!"

Frantically Phil played his eyes over the console. There had to be something he could do, but what? He was in a quandary. Cutting the towline? Not an option. Make a mad dash into the fog bank and out again, if they could? A good possibility the Shoestring would end up like the

Genny. But it was a chance he had to take. He was within a heartbeat away from turning the boat around when he spied it A red button with a small brass plate underneath. The lettering on it read 'powemer.' It was almost hidden in between the fathometer and the GPS and could easily be missed if you weren't looking for it. It looked like something Steve had added as an afterthought. Another one of his brainchild's, perhaps? Phil glanced back at Linda. Her whole body was trembling with fright. What did he have to lose? Boldly, he pushed the button.

A surge of unleashed power suddenly erupted under their feet. Shoestring reacted as if it had just been kicked in the rear end with a Saturn V rocket. The thrust of the engines rose to an indescribable pitch. Their eardrums were immediately hammered by the blast of nine hundred horses trying to break loose of their mountings. The reverberations rattled every bone in their bodies. The smell of burning hydraulic fluid hung heavily in the air. At any moment, Phil thought, a rod or piston would come flying through the deck. The ski rope began stretching to intolerable limits.

Linda had her hands clasped over her ears. She was yelling at Phil. He couldn't hear her, but he knew what she was saying. It was working! The extra horsepower had somehow broken the deadlock. The Shoestring was moving forward again! Their progress was excruciatingly slow, but their luck was holding. The ski rope was still providing the only connection they had with their friends. Phil made a mental note to contact the manufacturer and thank them profusely for making such a lifesaver.

Ten minutes later it was all over. He realized he had been holding his breath almost the whole time. The Genny, with its toothless green turtle regaling the stack, had suddenly popped into view like a magician's rabbit popping out of a hat. Free of the clinging fog, Shoestring reacted like a racehorse released from the starting gate. Phil quickly eased off on the throttles and let out a long sigh of relief. His pulse was still racing like a trip hammer as he carefully maneuvered the boat closer to Genny. He could faintly hear Linda's plaintive calls for their friends to respond. A long minute passed before the ringing in his ears finally subsided and he could reasonably hear normal again. Meanwhile, a death-like stillness had descended over their little circle. Inside the fog bank, the emerald-like glow had thankfully disappeared. Phil and Linda exchanged questioning looks. With the distance narrowing rapidly, it was strange they weren't spotting any movement aboard the Genny. Where were Steve and Lucienne?

Linda nimbly leaped across once the gap separating both boats had closed. She was back almost instantly.

"They're gone!"

"What do you mean, they're gone?"

"Come and see for yourself," she sobbed. "The bastards took them!"

Phil jumped aboard the Genny's open bow and quickly scanned the tiny pilothouse before making his way aft to the rear compartment.

"Not quite," he replied. Phil nodded his head toward Sandy as the dog came crawling out from beneath an overturned deck chair. He was whining softly and quivering with fright.

Linda bent down, her hands open. "Come here, boy." Phil could sense his wife was trying desperately to overcome her feeling of deep despair as the dog slithered pathetically into her arms.

The feeling was mutual. Phil's mind was completely numb. Like everything else happening to them within the past forty-eight hours, it was like living in the Twilight Zone. He and Linda had just witnessed a most flagrant act of piracy, and they had been helpless to stop it. Phil racked his brain in futility. What could they have done to stop it? What could anyone have done? It brought back the inescapable truth of their missing four days. Complete amnesia as to what happened to them and yet, they seemed not to be any worse for wear. If Malik was responsible for safeguarding Phil and his spouse, it would be reasonable to assume Malik was responsible for safeguarding Lucienne and her spouse as well. The Council would protect its own. The thought brought some measure of hope that his friends would be okay. So, if Malik was one of the good guys, it seemed to Phil there was more than one type of alien life form responsible for all the disappearances around there. According to Captain Smollet, they were confronting an alien technology far more superior to man's. Even more disconcerting, their agenda was still unknown.

"Phil, we need help." Linda's voice was completely devoid of emotion. It seemed to Phil his wife had come to fully accept the hopelessness of their situation. They couldn't fight the aliens alone. Phil had reluctantly come to the same conclusion.

"Yeah, kid. I…I know."

Just then, a tenuous flow of energy rippled through his brain. It was potent enough to make him pause, as if his whole being was waiting for something to happen. He realized his subconscious was receiving some vague signals. Someone, or something, was trying to tap into his most subliminal thoughts. Then, as if turning on a radio, he heard a voice. He wasn't hearing it with his ears, but from inside his head!

"Return to the cave," it said. *"Those you seek are waiting on the other side."* The message repeated itself once; then, as mysteriously as it had come, it was gone.

Phil looked over at Linda to see if she had heard anything, but she seemed oblivious to anything around her except the dog cuddled protectively in her arms.

"Let's head back to camp, kid. We can't do anything more here. Everything's going to be okay." The conviction in his voice must have surprised her. She looked up at him with a teary look in her eyes, but she didn't say anything. She just nodded in reply, a picture of dejection masking her face as she disappeared into Shoestring's lower cabin.

Phil shortened the towing line and started the engines. Somehow he knew they would find their friends alive. Whoever the mysterious voice belonged to, it provided the catalyst he needed to start searching for their friends without delay. The cave was as good a place as any to begin, he figured. But the road leading to the other side, as the voice indicated were where their friends were, was a road shrouded in mystery. On the other hand, it was the only road, and that's the road Phil and Linda had no trouble deciding to cast their fate.

He pointed the Shoestring's bow toward the setting sun. Her sharp prow, acting like a honed chisel, cleaved a wide swath over the mottled surface. The sunlight's reflection on the bow wave radiated a sparkling mosaic of iridescent pinks and mauves, creating a spectacular illusion of rubies fronting the boat. Thus began their long retreat back to camp. By the time they reached Beachy Cove, the fog bank had all but evaporated behind them. Only traces remained, withering tendrils trailing away in the gathering dusk. It was as though the whole terrible nightmare had never happened.

CHAPTER 19

December 1—02:12 A,M…Big Flowerpot

Phil tossed and turned fitfully like a kid on
Christmas Eve, but rather than visions of sugar plums
dancing in his head, they were emaciated dwarfs with
wrap-around eyes staring at him. It was like reliving a bad
dream. In the background he could hear the rush of
waterfalls. It was getting louder and louder. The intensity
scared him and immediately he awoke bathed in sweat. He
lay there quietly for a minute, his heart racing like a trip
hammer. It was hopeless to think he would get anymore
sleep, at least until the turmoil in his head subsided. Phil
slipped out of his sleeping bag and stepped into the night.

Looking back at the last few hours before night fell
had been anything but reassuring for the firefighter and his
wife. They were almost certain that Captain Smollet had
suffered the same fate as Steve and Lucienne. When they
had gone back to the mainland to report the disappearances
to Sergeant Putnam, they found an even more depressing
sight. The place was deserted. The office was locked, and
the dock, where the police launch was normally tied up,
was empty. The black gelding was still roaming free in its
stall. As conscientious as Linda was of animal cruelty, they
couldn't leave without checking to make sure the horse had
plenty of feed and water. Linda somehow felt, as did Phil,
that Sergeant Putnam might not be back for a while. Bea's

Kitchen and Milo's Grocery Mart were also under lock and key. So were several motels, a dive shop, and a souvenir/gift store lining the harbor front. The streets were barren. With the exception of a double pump BP gas station, with a conspicuous hand-written sign saying diesel fuel was available, the remainder of the town looked as if it had been evacuated. But not quite. Phil recalled Captain Smollet saying his closest neighbor, crotchety old Mrs. McGreevy, who was forever faithful to him, would be home. The captain always thought she was waiting for him to pop the question to her after his wife died. Poor woman, he sadly reiterated to Phil one day. His wife died twenty years ago, and she's still waiting.

"Everything's fine, Mrs. McGreevy," Phil had lied. "Captain Smollet asked us to bring Sandy to you because he's staying on the island longer than expected, and he's out of dog food. He said you know where he keeps it and you wouldn't mind babysitting the dog until he gets back." Phil was only guessing that she knew where the captain kept the dog food. He wasn't for sure the dog even ate dog food. He hated to lie to her, but she seemed to guess, by the look in her eyes, that something was amiss without making him dig deeper for further excuses.

"Aye, ever since Cora died, he's been messin' on that island more than he should. That man's going to be the death of me yet," she had blustered.

On the way back to the campsite, Phil and Linda had stopped by the cabin to pick up their sleeping bags. They opted to begin searching for their friends at the break of dawn, spending their last remaining night under the stars on a large flat slab of limestone next to the Big Flowerpot.

It was their way of being close to their friends; the same rock from where their first dive to the cave was launched earlier that morning. Except, for this dive, they were adding a newcomer, the underwater sled they nicknamed Shoehorn. Its self-contained propulsion system, Phil opined, would give them extra mobility and longer bottom time for the search. He was almost tempted to abandon any more thoughts of sleep and start preparing for their return to the cave. He was anxious to shed that lone survivor syndrome; 'why them instead of me,' stigma? They say the sooner you can retrace one's steps back to the scene; the sooner you can rid yourself of its haunting memory. He knew Linda felt the same. They were like two castaways caught up in their own self guilt. But waking Linda now would be foolish, he thought. She had been so distraught, she had cried herself to sleep. Who could predict how long it would be before sleep would provide solace to her again?

He remembered the dead silence the moment they entered the campsite. It was like walking into a mausoleum. There was no screeching of sea gulls or forest sounds of rustling branches and scurrying wildlife. It was as if the island was exuding its own brand of exorcism. Phil recalled what a depressing sight it was to see their friend's empty tent, personal effects lying about, wet suits hung up to dry, the fish filets Lucienne had been preparing laid neatly in the skillet, ready to fry. Neither one of them felt like eating, but to sustain their strength for the coming ordeal ahead, both agreed it would be wise to listen to their growling stomachs. They felt like condemned prisoners eating their last meal. It was a do or die mission. It was a personal vendetta silently shared between them. With steely eyed resolve, neither he nor Linda were planning to return without their friends. There was vengeance in their hearts. It was in this atmosphere that Phil related verbatim the telepathic message that told him to return to the cave. When Phil started to think what he had heard might have been delusional, Linda caught him short by emphatically shaking her head. Her take was that the summons implied a doorway had opened to finding their friends. It might only stay open for a short while. It was their only hope, she sobbed. Phil suspected his wife was dangerously close to slipping back into catatonic shock. Phil's paramedic mode kicked in. He decided he would delay her introduction to Malik and the coming earth changes. It would be hard for her to conceive the earth changes as justified after the shock of losing their friends was still so painfully fresh in her mind.

Phil shuffled his way over to the water's edge, reaching his toe into the dark liquid, causing a tiny circle to form. Freckles of dancing lights played on the ripple like tiny jack-o'-lanterns. He gazed vacantly at the mantle of diamonds blanketing the heavens, a night of glittering cold starlight. He focused his attention on a small cluster of stars. Somewhere up there could be a planet those creatures called home, he reflected. Was that planet in Earth's solar system, or a solar system a million light years away (six trillion miles). He pondered the thought. It was hard for Phil to conceive of such distances until his brother had enlightened him in one of his monologs. "The universe is infinite," he had said. "What we see with our telescopes and space probes is only what we call the observable universe—about 46 billion light years in radius and still expanding as we speak. (a light year travels 186,000 miles per second) Beyond that is a new frontier never before seen by man. Hopefully, someday, we'll have the technology to explore it to its most distant horizons."

"There you go again," Phil recalled rebuking his brother one more time. "How do you know these things. And don't keep telling me it's all in the stars."

Jeremy gave him one of those fatuous smiles that smacked of a cat that just swallowed the canary.

"Let me explain, brother. Space and Time is synonymous with the heavens. There is no beginning and there is no end. The Big Bang Theory stems from observations of supernovae that indicates outer space is beyond dimensional..." Jeremy cut short. By the expression on Phil's face, Jeremy saw his words were flying right over his brother's head. "Okay, okay, I'll keep it simple." Jeremy said obligingly. "Let me use an analogy instead. Take a railroad car full of sand and pretend you had ten-thousand billion of them."

"That's a hell of a lot of sand," Phil had said half-jokingly.

"Yes, it is," Jeremy answered without hesitation. "And pretend every granule of sand in those box-cars represents a galaxy. One of those granules would be the Milky Way, our galaxy. Are you with me so far?" Phil nodded numbly, knowing what was coming next. Like talking to a computer, he thought.

"Take for example our infinitesimal planet, which is hidden in one of billions of galaxies just like ours. Just think of it, Phil. There's four hundred billion stars in our galaxy alone! What are the odds, let's say, of at least one planet having the right DNA to support intelligent life out of four hundred billion solar systems? The existence of Mother Earth has proved that the odds are well within the law of probabilities. And how many galaxies did I say there were out there? Every granule of sand in ten-thousand billion box cars represents a galaxy. We're talking 'infinity,' brother. Each one of those galaxies has at least one planet that contain the same properties as our earth had to propagate intelligent life forms ten-and-a-half million years ago. (Cayce's time scale) And that's not all! There are parallel universes next to ours which we are only beginning to understand; collapsed stars could be our gateway to those universes."

"You mean black holes?" Phil had asked.

"Yes. They could be conduits in time, for all we know. There are forms of energy out there we know nothing about yet; like dark matter and dark energy and wormholes that we could apply for our own use. With all the UFO sightings being continually reported worldwide, it seems most aliens have already bridged the gap. So you see, brother," Jeremy had finished with one of his disarming smiles, "it would take a very arrogant person to think we humans were the only intelligent life forms in this vast cosmos of ours."

Yes, Phil acknowledged, his thoughts flashing back to the present. But some aliens are playing games with us. Why are they picking on some backwater species like us from a planet buried inside some faraway galaxy? How did these aliens find us in the first place, considering the immensity of space, he wondered? And why are they abducting humans on such a massive scale as witnessed in such legendary regions as the Bermuda Triangle and the Devil's Sea? Now, among others, Georgian Bay had been added to their nefarious feeding grounds. He had read that even cattle were not immune to their antics—their reproductive organs surgically removed as if cut out with a scalpel. And nary a trace of blood to show for it. 'Who cared,' he silently cried out as he kicked the water in frustration. He didn't care about earth changes, or aliens, or dissected cattle. All he wanted was his friends back, safe and sound.

The firefighter/paramedic from the Detroit Fire Department gave a long sigh, shrugging his shoulders in resignation. He tried to keep his thoughts in check, but it was like trying to overcome a raging fire storm in his brain. The turn of events in his and Linda's lives the past forty-eight hours was almost too much to absorb in one sitting. The aliens had inextricably wound their hidden agenda around them with such insidiousness, it was hard to believe even Malik could be involved. Phil shook his head. He was starting to get paranoid. From he and Linda's abduction to that of their friend's sudden disappearances, the firewall he so meticulously maintained to ward off defeatism had finally toppled, like Humpty Dumpty, into a thousand pieces. And, like Humpty Dumpty, he knew it would take more than all the king's horses and all the king's men to put the pieces back together again. It was a foregone conclusion that, barring a miracle, their lives would never be the same.

Phil's thoughts kept returning to his conversation with his brother. It was Jeremy's wakeup call that got Phil interested in studying about his infinitesimal planet; a

hackneyed description of earth his brother had used often.
He discovered it was a lump of rock that's been floating
around the galaxy for four-and-a-half billion years. The
more he studied its history, the more he became fascinated
with its pre-dawn civilizations—antediluvian civilizations,
to be exact. It was through their abstruse writings and
lavish artwork painted on cave walls that archaeologists
first learned of mankind's great civilizations, civilizations
that survived great floods and catastrophic polar shifts.
Each succeeding generation, thanks to artifacts found in
repositories, such as the underwater cave under Flower Pot
Island, began on a higher plane of learning than the one
before. It explained how some inventions came so
opportunistically, and in other cases, simultaneously, from
different parts of the world. By leaps and bounds some
cultures, Phil learned, had achieved scientific wonders that
rivaled and even surpassed modern technology: megalithic
structures such as gigantic pyramids, mammoth temples,
stone fortresses and puzzling statues with undecipherable
markings that reminded the casual observer of flying discs
and extraterrestrial beings. Even by today's standards,
these ancient constructions would be impossible to
duplicate, Phil acknowledged. Some of those cut stones
that were used as foundations in vast complexes weigh over
2,000 tons, and were transported from sources hundreds of
miles away. And the Nazca lines in Peru—a weird
collection of lines, squares and triangles that form
geometric designs of monkeys, spiders, fish, crabs, and
other creatures that are only distinguishable from the air.
The Crop Circles—another bona fide mystery reminiscent
of looking through a kaleidoscope. Its colorful patterns

have been magnified to I-Max proportions onto farmer's fields throughout Europe and North America for the past half a century. Nobody as yet has come up with a legitimate reason as to how the Nazca lines or the Crop Circles were made with such precision and for what purpose. Yet, somehow all these oddities had a common thread running through them. Nevertheless, they represented only the tip of the iceberg. A thousand other clues lying dormant around the globe showed that mankind had outside help. The mass of literature written by paleontologists and ufologists alike led Phil to believe mankind was visited by extraterrestrials in some bygone era, and has continued to the present day. Legends and myths are filled with stories of a race of super beings helping mankind achieve greatness. Could this be what was happening now? Were they here to help mankind, now that the earth changes were coming...or enslave them?

Phil absently let his gaze fall on the humpbacked shadow of Bear's Rump Island across the way. Its off-shore waters were also home for the Forest City, a deep-water schooner that crashed into the island in 1904 while enshrouded in fog and sunk. It was one of the more intact wrecks to dive on and fun to explore. At the moment however, his concentration wasn't able to dwell on pleasantries. Thankfully the fire in his skull had died down to that of smoldering embers, but his worries still persisted. If what Malik said was true, he needn't have to worry about Steve and Lucienne's fate. They were under the same umbrella of protection as he and Linda were, but by nature, he trusted his instincts. If his instincts triggered a sense of danger, as they did now, it told him to tread softly and carry a big stick. He found what he was looking for aboard the Shoestring. The C4Urukay 120 spear gun he had lashed to the Shoehorn was his big stick.

Facing east, a sultry breeze had kicked up in his face. It seemed a change in the weather was brewing, or maybe it was a portent of an ill wind blowing. Phil tried to dispel the thought from his mind as he slowly made his way back to the slumbering figure huddled beneath the shadows. He snuggled as close as he could to his wife without waking her. He was hoping the added sleep would overtake the gremlins starting to do battle inside his head.

December 1—6:45 A.M...Flowerpot Island

Phil woke with a start to the acrid stench of burning sulfur. A buzzing, crackling noise filled the air.

"Phil, wh...what is it?" Linda stammered sleepily. Her body automatically tensed as she slid over next to him, matching her husband's gawking face at the strange sight before them. She started to scream. Phil quickly clamped his hand over her mouth. "Shhhhh," he whispered hoarsely in her ear. "Don't move and don't make a sound!"

He and Linda were lying within twenty feet of the Large Flowerpot, its darkened profile back-lighted in stark detail against a pale yellow sky. Dawn was about to break. At the Flowerpot's summit, bobbing and weaving, were a dozen or so small oval objects the size of basketballs. As they sizzled and crackled intensely, they shone brilliantly in the air. It was almost like gazing at a swarm of welder's arcs, Phil opined. They must have heard Linda's stifled scream, because they all stopped at once and began advancing in her and Phil's direction. Phil guessed they were electronic probes of some sort, remotely guided. He held his breath, clutching Linda, who was as still as a statue. They didn't dare move, he reasoned, for fear that whoever was directing the "basketballs" might think he and Linda were being too aggressive.

The strange-looking devices danced around their heads for several minutes as if they wanted Phil and Linda to join them in their frolicking. Then one of the fiery balls got tired of that game, separated from its companions, and hovered within inches of their faces. It was like staring into the mouth of a miniature nuclear reactor, Phil thought, gasping. Its interior blazed with the incandescence of pure energy. He couldn't feel any heat, just the sound of electrified air, like bacon frying. Once the probe satisfied its curiosity, it seemed to lose interest in them and swiftly darted back up to rejoin its companions. Then, in the same playful fashion in which they began, the entire flock went bouncing and skipping down the beach. A few would occasionally jostle each other for position like overzealous school kids, eventually disappearing from view behind a promontory that concealed the far end of the island. Phil was too shocked to be frightened. Were these the same devilish lights Captain Smollet claimed he saw hanging around the Devil's Pulpits before an approaching storm? Phil left the question unanswered. Instead he just gave Linda a blank look. "Well, what next?" he whispered.

CHAPTER 20

December 1—7:15 A.M...Large Flowerpot

The waxing sun had just ducked behind a wave of fast-scudding clouds. It looked like the harbinger of an approaching storm, Phil thought uneasily; its serried ranks being pushed by an evil wind. They were dark and disfigured with jagged streaks of heat lightning flashing menacingly. The heat index was building fast, making sweat rivulets find new courses beneath his wet suit. The repetition of the early dawn did nothing to assuage Phil's feeling of surrealism. The unchanging rocks and trees seemed to press in all around him. It was as if the atmosphere itself was holding its breath, waiting for the final curtain call.

Phil and Linda had decided the night before that there was no time left to get outside help. They didn't know how long the communication blackout would last, and as far as Phil was concerned, he didn't care. It was time to act before it was too late, although "too late" was strictly an arbitrary term in their case. Their friends could already be beyond reach. Nevertheless, they had conceded early on that they were probably the best qualified to effect a rescue, unless there was a SWAT team being airlifted in that they didn't know about. There was only one other option, run away and hide, and that was too unconscionable to even consider.

According to Steve's first assessment, the cave was packed mostly with an assortment of ships and aircraft of by-gone era's, both military and commercial. Phil assumed that if their friends were in the cave as the message indicated, they would be in there somewhere among the artifacts. That, in itself, would be like looking for a needle in a haystack. The more he thought about it, the more it didn't make any sense. Without the proper diving gear, there was no chance of survival at that depth; at that pressure. He and Linda would be on a mission of retrieving dead bodies. No, he said to himself, there had to be more to it than that. "Those you seek are on the other side." All he could think of was that there had to be a continuation of the cave somewhere. Using Shoehorn was then the right choice to assist their efforts. It would, without question, save them time and energy. The cave could extend for miles under the bedrock beyond the island's perimeter for all he knew. He rigged Shoehorn so that it would operate on the independent compressed air tanks Steve had ingeniously incorporated into its design. There were four of them—size 200's in cubic volume—connected to the sides like booster rockets. Steve had said he preferred air tanks instead of batteries because of their lighter weight. Regardless, Phil wasn't worried about weight this trip. It was storability he wanted, not speed. He strapped extra Trimix tanks to the sled wherever he could find room. He figured if he and Linda were down for any length of time, they would need them. He had plenty to spare. Phil even found two oxygen bottles that could be used for decompression back to the surface. Thanks to Steve's generosity, the Shoestring was a floating dive shop. It seemed like Shoehorn was starting to look like one too, Phil thought cynically, as he perused his handiwork. It reminded him of a crammed underwater version of the Beverly Hillbilly's jalopy stacked to overflowing with their family heirlooms.

When the time came to enter the water, Phil found it difficult to summon the same exuberance he had exhibited with Steve and Lucienne the day before. Nevertheless, he knew he had to prepare himself mentally for the same bracing coldness, the same eternal night, the same abysmal loneliness he had learned to endure on previous deep dives.

This time Phil was able to focus his mind on the sled, which helped some. He had attached several air lifts around its periphery to keep it from plunging to the bottom. By bleeding the air out slowly as they descended, he and Linda were able to keep the sled in check.

Once they reached the cave entrance, Phil immediately began to prepare the sled for boarding. First, he hooked up the coaxial feed lines to the pneumatic controls which would operate the steering vanes and rudder. The sled could turn on a dime, thanks to its dual water-jets. He then checked the electrical system to make sure none of the wiring, which was sealed in plastic tubing, had worked loose. He double-checked the gauges. These were supplied with small photon cells which, even when separated from the surface, kept the instruments from losing power. Again, he checked all the connections holding the various tanks and made sure the spare equipment and tool compartments were sealed tightly. Full facemasks with a state-of-the-art wireless PTT system allowed subsurface communication between driver and passenger. Including the hookah assembly for surface communication, Phil had to admire the entire setup. The unit was completely self-reliant. He was glad Steve was insistent on showing him how everything worked that first night. It was strange. Sitting around the campfire, Phil had overheard Lucienne's cogent reminder to her husband that it was imperative Phil be shown the whole nine yards of the sled's operation. It was as if she was passing on some warning her psychic powers had picked up on.

Underwater sea-sleds had been around for a long time. They were mostly used in times past for survey work before modern appliances, like scooters and submersibles, took over. Apparently Steve didn't like what he saw on the open market, Phil reasoned, so the big Canuck had modified this particular sled into his own prototype. Phil was amazed at his ingenuity. Unlike most sleds, two could ride abreast in comparative comfort onto contoured padded bench seats with a thirty degree incline that could be adjusted to accommodate a person's prone body. Situated within easy reach were grooved handgrips, independently operated. One lever controlled the steering vanes; the other was for impulse power. Phil lovingly stroked the smooth Plexiglas canopy. It curved so it covered half the sled. Even without the overload of equipment, Shoehorn looked ungainly on the surface, but down below, the sled took on a different perspective. Phil fancied it was modified, for reasons unknown, by Steve, to see what it could do independently. Whatever its purpose, Phil was forced to admit that he and Linda were relying on it heavily for their search. "Now's the time to find out what this baby can do, Steve," Phil said under his breath. "It's all yours."

Linda, and then Phil, slid effortlessly onto the soft padding. Once the intricate network of cross-feeds and interconnects that fed air into the system was activated, Shoehorn was ready to get underway. After the communication testing was complete, Phil glanced over at Linda and gave her the OK sign. She responded in turn. Her eyes burned with a ferocity Phil hadn't seen since their friends were abducted. She was on a mission. They both were.

They heard a faint gurgling sound as Phil gently kicked in the thrusters. The sled began to move ahead slowly. He took it easy at first, trying to get used to its crazy yawing and fishtailing when he would accidentally jerk too hard on the controls. Right away he was impressed with its deceptive quickness. It's probably a little like manipulating a hang-glider, he thought. After several minutes of practice, he was able to keep the nose of the sled on a fairly straight course, all the while keeping his sights leveled on an intriguing pocket of darkness at the far end of the cave.

Phil and Linda could only gaze in wonder as the rows of ships filed by them like a parade of specters— square riggers, frigates, cabin cruisers, sailing sloops, freighters, destroyers, yachts; then came a row of private and military planes—prop fighters, jet fighters, transports, bombers, passenger jets, private and commercial— hundreds of museum pieces caught in a grisly time warp. From a distance Phil happened to spot the Jane Miller laying at rest among her peers. A flashback of the deadly scenario of the day before immediately sent a cold chill down his backside.

"What does all this mean, Phil?" came Linda's inquiry, her voice sounding high-pitched through the mask. "How can all these ships and planes help mankind after the earth changes?"

"Through reverse engineering, my dear. You notice how they all run from the low to the high end of human technology. For survivors to advance to a higher scale, higher technology has to wait for human initiative to catch up. When that happens, mankind will have the tools to invent whatever they can discover from these artifacts." Phil paused. In his studying of earth's history, there was only one civilization that closed the gap quicker than all the others—Atlantis. "It's the same as when miniaturized circuit boards and stealth bomber invisibility to radar jumped on the scene in our era. The knowledge came from crashed UFO's. We weren't able to apply that knowledge until our technology was up to speed. What else do you think they do at Area 51?" he asked chidingly.

It was a rhetorical question in which no answer was required to satisfy Phil's playful taunting. Linda knew it was his way of breaking the tension. She filled the void with a tap on his shoulder instead, pointing toward something at two o'clock. Phil understood and banked Shoehorn in a gentle dogleg to the right. As soon as he leveled off he could see for himself what she was pointing at.

An open-decked cabin cruiser had been ignominiously squeezed in between a 17th century baroque and a modern-day sloop. Phil immediately recognized it.

It was Sergeant Putnam's patrol boat. The unit designation OPP HARBOR PATROL 76283 stenciled in black lettering on its raked prow stood out from the white hull like an epitaph.

Phil could guess with one-hundred per-cent certainty what had transpired. The good sergeant had seen the same fog bank that had swallowed up Steve and Lucienne and had gone out to investigate. Once he entered its clutches, he more than likely suffered the same fate as Captain Smollet. Phil suspected he and Linda would have seen the Genny down there too if it wasn't for their intervention.

Phil had seen enough. He steered Shoehorn back on course and opened up the thrusters one more click. The machine tremored ever so slightly under the increased power. The deeper their push into the cave, the more exposed he began to feel. It was as if they were sticking their heads into an ever-tightening noose. Even the hairs at the back of his neck were starting to stiffen with their customary warning. He noticed the greenish glow never diminished one kilowatt since they arrived. The eerie lighting seemed to saturate every nook and cranny of the cave. He wondered why? The only living souls that ever traveled in those wooden and metal coffins were all dead now. Or were they? What he heard, or thought he heard, on board the Jane Miller was either brought on by hallucinations or those poor bastards crying out were stuck in some time warp, some other dimensional world. Phil's trained mind only accepted conclusions that could be verified. Which meant that all those passengers and crews could still be alive. The thought gave him a sudden lift in his spirits; some measure of hope that all was not lost. He reached over and gave Linda a tight squeeze of encouragement.

Off to their left was an Air Canada Boeing 747 with a large red maple leaf emblazoned on its tailfin. Reaching deep into his memory bank, Phil faintly recalled the mysterious disappearance of a large jumbo jet over Lake Superior just about the same time the Edmond Fitzgerald vanished in a killer storm. They eventually found the giant ore carrier but they never found the 747. Witnesses testified that they saw several UFOs in the area at the time. Phil shook his head in amazement. It seemed the devilish machines were always around whenever an unexplained disappearance occurred.

Once Phil and Linda were past the gauntlet of abandoned relics, the cave began to narrow perceptibly. By that time the sled's odometer showed that they had penetrated a distance of three kilometers into the island's infrastructure. Phil did some quick mental calculations. The figures he was grappling with meant that they had to have gone two miles. That was impossible. Flower Pot Island wasn't that big! Which meant his hunch was right. The cave was larger than it had first appeared. It extended beyond the island into the very heart of Georgian Bay.

Suddenly, ahead of them was the dark splotch that had intrigued Phil from the start. It was a large tunnel, its yawning black maw hungrily inviting them in. Phil cautiously nosed Shoehorn inside the entrance. The light dimmed, as if they had just entered a church vestibule. As a firefighter, his mind detested open spaces in confined areas. Openness meant vulnerability and danger. Safety came from hugging support walls or parking yourself under interior arches. He hugged the left sidewall of the tunnel, thinking that if he was going to get blindsided from some unknown source, it would be from his open flank. He activated the sled's two powerful halogens positioned within easy reach of his fingertips. Switching to wide-angle beams instantly irradiated the tunnel with a yellow-white brilliance. Stopping the sled, Phil and Linda gazed transfixed at the scene confronting them. What they were seeing was truly amazing. The dolomite bedrock was as smooth and round as if it had been bored by a gigantic drill bit. Phil immediately thought of the Detroit-Windsor Tunnel. Whoever had engineered what they were gawking at made it so a locomotive could pass through it with comparative ease, he thought.

He and Linda exchanged questioning glances. "Well kid, wadda you think?" Phil asked, his voice sounding hollow through the liquid ether. "Shall we blindly forge ahead or go back and keep looking?" He knew what her answer would be but he had to ask to keep it fair. Both their lives were at stake on making the right decisions. Both had only one desperation shot left at finding their friends. Phil always liked to follow the law of probabilities on any important decision making, and Linda knew that. In the end, her mind usually sided with her husbands.

"Let's do it your way, Sherlock. We'd run out of gas wandering around trying to find them back there. If we go forward, the worst we can run into is a blind alley, and then run out of gas. Your law of probabilities suggests we have a better chance if we continue forward."

"The shortest route between two points is a straight line. Just elementary, my dear Watson. Just elementary." Phil answered with a crooked smile."

Once they were past the spilled light from the cave, they found themselves in total darkness. The only light keeping the walls from closing in on them was from Shoehorn. The thought of surrounding yourself with tons of rock was like cave diving in the springs of northern Florida. He and Linda tried it once, Phil recalled. He especially didn't like it any more than if he was going for search and rescue in a heavily smoke-filled building without a safety line. Your chances of survival are greatly reduced. The obvious choice of survival would be to not go in a heavily smoke-filled building without a safety line. Unfortunately, firefighting sometimes doesn't leave you any choices. You play the cards you're dealt. Not left with any choices in this situation, Phil preferred to play the law of probabilities. His and Linda's safety lines were the twin spotlights of Shoehorn and the clear visibility of Georgian Bay leading them out of there. Except for stopping briefly to change breathing tanks, discarding the empty ones in the process, he and Linda conducted a lonely vigil. They expected the tunnel at any moment to taper down to nothing. But, surprisingly, it kept going without showing any signs of ending. Another surprise. It was hard to tell without a inclinometer, but they both agreed, the tunnel was slowly inching its way downward. The sled's fathometer was showing a definite increase in depth. That meant using up more tri-mix the deeper they went. That was not good, Phil said to himself. They had already gone over three kilometers. By now, he guessed, they were well beyond the boundaries of Flower Pot Island.

Then came the moment of truth. Phil signaled to Linda, pointing to their air supply gauge. He didn't have to explain. They had reached the point of no return. Going any further meant they wouldn't have enough tri-mix to return the way they had come. From here on out both of them were holding a one-way ticket.

Five minutes later Phil's nerves relaxed sufficiently enough to slow down his racing heartbeat as a welcomed green-shaded circle of light began to form. They were approaching the end of the tunnel. Shoehorn continued to race toward the swelling orb like a moth attracted to flame. Upon nearing the exit, Phil powered down and switched off the spotlights. In the semi-darkness of ghostly green hues, he felt more conspicuous than ever before. This cave was much smaller and quite empty; which made the sled stand out like a sore thumb. The sides fell away sharply to expose a barren floor of bedrock and hard-packed clay. Phil judged the water clear enough for him to easily assess the distance to the far wall at no more than three hundred feet. Instinctively he steered the sled to the nearest wall. Whoever or whatever was waiting for them on the other side certainly had to know they were coming. He and Linda would have never gotten this far without some compulsive force driving them on. It was a powerful enough force, Phil realized, for them to be assured of drowning like rats in this underwater tomb if they didn't find another way out soon.

Linda's exclamation broke the silence. "Check our depth, Phil!"

Phil pulled his eyes toward the fathometer. It was pegged at 240 meters! (over 700 feet). This was crazy, he thought. It meant their trimix, what precious little they had left, would be used up in the next five minutes. Phil shrugged futilely. They knew it could come to this; a suicide mission. Even if they could get back to their entry point, they could not decompress properly with only two oxygen bottles. They had stayed too long, too deep. It was out of their hands now. Whatever was going to happen, it had better be quick, Phil cried out in a silent plea. It didn't matter now trying to hide from someone who had to know we were there anyway, he finally conceded. Boldly, he nosed Shoehorn toward the middle of the cave.

They hadn't gone more than twenty yards when something out of the corner of Phil's eye caught his attention. A movement of some sort! Linda saw it too and clutched her husband's arm in a reflexive lock.

Off to the far edge of the cave appeared a large luminous object. Phil was certain a moment ago the cave was empty. The object seemed to have materialized out of nowhere. It was surrounded by an unearthly white light that shimmered with the intensity of a signal flare. It momentarily blinded him and he raised his hand over his eyes to block out the glare. Linda had turned her head away, fearing the worst. Phil peeked through his fingers, just barely discerning a round, dark shape within its nebulous borders. A gut feeling of recognition invaded his senses. As he continued to study the strange image, he knew what it had to be. The white light had metamorphosed into a rainbow of colors. Phil became fixated by its dazzling beauty. It was that same gripping spectacle that had consumed his companions aboard the Shoestring the other night, Phil realized. As he continued to watch, a saucer-shaped UFO emerged, rotating on its axis, with red, green and yellow lights blinking in an oscillating fashion around its perimeter. It was about twenty feet high, fifty feet across, and looked like a thick spinning top. A red light pulsed from a cupola on top of the domelike structure. There seemed to be a continuous band of openings at the base of the cupola, but the blinding light was keeping Phil from seeing inside. He took his hands off the controls and let Shoehorn coast to a gentle stop. He and Linda slowly disembarked, all the while Linda holding on to Phil's arm in a deathlike grip. The whirling lights were seducing them to keep their eyes concentrated on the UFO as though they were being drawn toward it by some invisible force. A gut-tightening lump was beginning to form in the pit of Phil's stomach. It was the same feeling he used to get just before entering a burning building. For the next few interminable moments, his fate would be in the hands of a higher authority. When Linda started pulling him backward in a frenzied dance to escape, he looked at her in disbelief. Her face was contorted in horror. She was screaming out sounds that were muffled and indistinct. Their wireless was down. They had no way to communicate. He took hold of her wrist and reassuringly led her toward the waiting spacecraft. She broke free, pointing ogle-eyed with frenzied movements over his shoulder. Phil turned just in time to see another UFO, identical in size and shape to the first one, materialize in a mirror image of blazing lights.

Off to the right, two more glowing spheres were just making an appearance. They had entered a nest of them!

Their only option was to play it out, and see what happens, Phil thought, his mind swirling with indecision. Logic was telling him that to turn back now would be suicidal. They were literally on their last breaths of air. He urged Linda to follow him, holding her tightly with one hand while making beckoning gestures with the other. But she wanted no part of it. She was in panic mode, Phil realized. She kept resisting, her body jerking fitfully in vain attempts to escape. It was taking all of Phil's strength to keep her from bolting.

Almost stealthily, the conclave of spinning lights began to move in their direction. Their coalescing colors was mesmerizing, filling Phil and Linda with wonderment. The leading UFO hovered over their frozen bodies like a hawk getting ready to pounce. Then, a piercing beam of light reached out from below the spacecraft, bathing them both in a rapturous green glow.

Instantaneously Phil felt his arms and legs grow numb. He tried maneuvering his body, but it was like swimming in a sea of molasses. His mind cried out in frustration as he could feel Linda slipping out of his grasp. He tried desperately to hold on to her, but it was hopeless. His mind was rapidly becoming ensconced in the beautiful, irrepressible light.

Phil had just enough mental acuity remaining to recognize Linda's limp form drifting away from him, her outstretched fingers gesturing silently for help. Then, in a heartbeat, she was gone, whisked away like a leaf caught up in a gust of wind. But by now he was beyond caring.

Phil was consumed in a world of his own, an all-encompassing world of contentment and sublime bliss. He gazed steadily into the light as long, tentacle-like wafers of brilliant colors swirled themselves around his upright body. He felt joined with its life-giving force. He closed his eyes and let the dazzling rays embrace him in their loving, tender grasp. It felt wonderful.

CHAPTER 21

Earth Day Plus One

 Phil was abruptly interrupted by a feeling of bewilderment. His body had left its watery grave behind, only to be trapped inside a pocket of pressure pushing in on him from all sides. His diving gear was absent. In fact, he discovered, his whole body was completely naked. 'What was happening to me?' he cried out in silent bewilderment. He tried opening his eyes, but he couldn't seem to concentrate his thoughts. Hot, slashing knives were tearing at his stomach. He felt nauseated. He got on his hands and knees and started to retch uncontrollably. Some kind of device somehow evaporated the vomit by an overhead beam after Phil leaned back, exhausted.

 Phil realized he must be in some kind of air lock. In its cold vacuum, the sound of his heavy breathing resounded loudly against the walls of what felt to be a hard rubber surface. The walls were rounded and emitted a luminescent white glow. The air smelled dank and fetid. It had a metallic taste to it. Mixed with the taste of his vomit, the combination made Phil feel even more nauseated. His throat hurt with every heave. He felt cold, yet his insides were burning up. It was becoming unbearable! Phil began to squirm with discomfort. If only he could open his eyes!

 A wave of fresh air suddenly washed over him. Now he was being lifted, although he didn't feel anything touching his body. It was the same sensation as weightlessness. He was floating in the air, being guided by some unearthly force. The next thing he knew, he was being placed on some sort of hard surface. It felt rough and unyielding against his skin. He was freezing. Goose bumps layered his entire body. He was overwhelmed with an almost violent urge to relieve himself. He tried moving his arms and legs, but they were paralyzed. All he could move was his head. He tried opening his eyes again. He hated not being able to see what was happening to him. Perhaps if he concentrated harder, he thought, he could crack them open a little. Yes, it was working! He could see a dim light with blurry images moving about. He shut his eyes tightly, waited a few seconds, and tried again. This time he was able to bring his legs and feet into focus. He found himself spread-eagled on a low-lying table in the middle of a strange-looking room. It was similar to the one he came from, but larger. The interior was immaculately white with several orange blinking lights scattered randomly about the glowing walls. Staring down at him from the ceiling was a curious contraption that looked like a huge eyeball. Its one large pupil shone reddish-purple and was attached to some kind of metallic arm.

Phil couldn't help but shiver. His nakedness didn't help. The air was cool and had a sweet, sickly smell to it. Not unlike death. That, plus the white harsh glare of the room itself, made Phil feel nauseated again. He found it better to squint than to keep his eyes fully open. His shoulder and back muscles ached. The table he was lying on was like lying on a slab of concrete. The only sound he heard besides his own labored breathing was what sounded like a ventilator fan humming in the background. For all intents and purposes, he should have been scared to death. This was totally foreign to anything he had ever encountered. It was like living out in virtual reality the weirdest sci-fi horror movie ever made, yet, for some inexplicable reason, he felt very calm and relaxed. Other than being physically uncomfortable, a dim realization slowly began to take root inside his brain. He was actually inside a UFO!

A movement next to Phil brought him to full alert. Three strange-looking humanoids were standing beside him. They were about three-and-a-half feet tall, dressed in skin-tight gray-colored uniforms with just their heads and hands exposed. There was no apparent sign of what sex they were. All were hairless with four long, skinny fingers. Their heads were bigger than Phil would have expected for the size of their bodies. They had slits in their faces for mouths, tiny orifices for noses, and narrow apertures in the sides of their heads which Phil mistook for ears. He later learned they were breathing vents. But it was their lidless, unblinking eyes that were their most striking feature. The eyes kept staring at him. They were the same eyes he had seen in his dreams. They were spellbinding. He couldn't seem to tear his gaze away from them.

Phil heard a voice. It took him a few seconds to realize it was his own voice trying to utter words through a set of parched lips and a raspy throat. After several minutes of inhaling the atmosphere of the spacecraft, his mouth felt as if it had a wad of cotton in it. The air was as dry as the Nevada desert. The aliens seemed to understand Phil's difficulty and it wasn't long before his breathing became easier. Finally, he was able to make something intelligible come out.

"Wh…what are you doing? Let me go!"

One of the humanoids stepped closer. Phil could see a pair of almond-shaped pupils floating in pools of black liquid scrutinizing him. He felt intimidated and grossly embarrassed by his nakedness. He began perceiving words, alien thoughts imploding inside his brain.

"You are a chosen one. No harm will come to you."

Even though Phil didn't hear any distinctive sound emanating from the alien, he knew the words, through mental telepathy, were coming from him. And Phil didn't believe any of what he said was true for a minute.

"What are you going to do to me? Why am I naked?" Phil asked in a shaky voice. The eyeball was hanging over him like the Sword of Damocles. He suspected he had been placed beneath it for a reason. Some sort of scanning device, he thought.

"You must be prepared. Human waste is not desirable."

Phil was having trouble deciphering the alien's message. "Prepare me for what?"

"Do not be afraid," were the last words he understood the humanoid saying as it stepped back from the table. It signaled the others to back off as well. Phil heard clicking sounds starting to emerge from the eyeball as it slowly began to descend. Even in his somnambulistic state, a trickle of fear began to force its way into Phil's consciousness. 'This wasn't happening,' he mumbled as he gritted his teeth for what could be the worst to come.

The mechanical arm lowered the eye to within inches of Phil's quivering stomach. But instead of a scanning device as he originally thought, the pupil popped open, revealing a thin, six-inch needle fastened to the end of a long cable. Phil stared at it in morbid fascination as the cable extended the needle over his navel. His body began to cringe in anticipation.

"Don't touch meeeee!"

The needle plunged into Phil's skin. A thin flow of blood oozed out and began to trickle down his sides. Phil couldn't believe this was happening to him! His body was completely desensitized. He didn't feel any pain whatsoever. It was as though he was a party to some grisly ceremony being performed on a corpse. The needle just kept penetrating deeper and deeper into his body, and all he could do was lie there and watch.

Phil tried talking, pleading with his captors, but it was no use. The humanoids were bent on accomplishing whatever procedure they had started to do on him. He watched as another long cable with a glass ampule attached slid out of the eye. It resembled a thin neon tube tapering down to the size of a piano wire. One of the humanoids came over and held Phil's penis up for inspection. To Phil's amazement, the creature began stroking the member while the catheter hovered patiently.

"Please...Nooooo! Don't!"

Once Phil's libido became aroused and his penis stiffened, the probe entered unhesitatingly.

"Ow!" That hurt. Phil could feel the unnatural thickness of the catheter sliding a painstaking path into his scrotum.

"Ahhhhhh!" Phil laid his head back and watched curiously as the attached neon tube became filled with his liquid sperm. When the catheter started retracing its path, he thought the ordeal was over. But it wasn't. The ubiquitous catheter began a circuitous climb into his urethra canal instead. He could feel the pressure of it sliding directly into his bladder. Phil was suddenly overcome with a powerful desire to urinate. He began relieving himself, the instrument somehow acting as a siphon. After completing its task, the catheter and its payload withdrew back into the eye in a silent, businesslike manner.

But, as Phil soon found out, there was no end to the inquisitiveness of the needle still impaled in his stomach. A multitude of titillating sensations started to torment him. It felt as if they were burning a hole right through his intestines. He later learned the needle was injecting an agent into his colon to counteract the germs and bacteria of what the humanoid described as 'human waste.'

Finally, Phil couldn't take it any longer and he began to scream. Gratefully, one of the humanoids placed its hand on Phil's head and the fire in his stomach stopped almost immediately. He closed his eyes and envisaged a middle-age man, wearing a worn fedora, standing on the bottom of a grassy knoll. Somehow the man looked awfully familiar to him. That was the last Phil remembered before sliding into a deep, dark chasm.

CHAPTER 22

Earth Day Plus Two

Red-yellowish lights of intense brilliance kept infiltrating through his closed eyelids. They were revolving around him so fast, Phil thought he was in the middle of a giant centrifuge. What was happening, he wondered. He hadn't forgotten where he was. He was sure he was still in the spacecraft, and yet he felt much warmer and comfortable than he last remembered. Maybe it was because, instead of being naked, he was wearing something more suited to his piece of mind, a form-fitting one-piece jumpsuit similar to the inner garment of a dry suit. He could feel it was made of a stretchy material, covering everything but his extremities. Sooner or later, though, he knew he would have to wake up to find out what else the aliens had done to him. Reluctantly, he opened his eyes.

He saw he was lying on a chaise lounge that seemed to conform to every peak and valley of his body. Inset in the left armrest was a panel of miniature twinkling lights. He could see stars, tens of thousands of them, hanging suspended for a split second in the deep backdrop of space. He could see them through the ceiling and walls whizzing all around him.

"We are traveling beyond the dimension of time and distance as you know them. If you are upset by what you see, I can shut out the image for you."

Phil sat up abruptly at the sound of a soft voice. It surprised him. The sound had come through his ears. He swung his legs around and sat upright at the edge of the seat. Although the room was dimly lit, he could distinguish sharply angled walls, octagonal in shape. The room was about twenty feet in diameter, with its ceiling rising to a convex dome. The only light came from the multitudinous stars, but it was more than enough to help him make out the profile of a small humanoid standing next to him. It was obviously a female. She had straight, raven-black hair down to her shoulders, slanted dark eyes, a small pug nose with well-proportioned lips, and a somewhat pointed chin. She looked Oriental, Phil thought, although her skin was unnaturally pale in earthly standards. The rest of her body, encased in the ubiquitous gray uniform he was getting accustomed to seeing, showed small breasts to match her diminutive figure. She was no more than five feet tall and in a more earthly setting, Phil probably would have considered her beautiful. He fancied that, with a halfway decent suntan, she could have passed for any bathing beauty on a beach.

"Who are you?" he asked.

"I am called Ninlil."

"Where am I?"

"You are on a vimana, an observation ship. Do not be frightened. We will be leaving Gaia orbit soon. Meanwhile, I am to stay with you. Do you wish nourishment?"

For a long moment, Phil had to stop and think. Nourishment? It seemed ages since he had even thought of food. But that was the least of his concerns. Right now, he wanted to find Linda and get out of there. The warning flags in his head were urging haste. Once past a certain stage, it would be too late.

"NO! And you have no right to keep me here. I don't like being used as a guinea pig." Phil hadn't forgotten the mistreatment his body had been subjected to, nor the degradation. He felt violated. He now understood what a rape victim felt like.

The directness and forcefulness of his voice must have startled her, for she hesitated. She continued to gaze at him with those limpid, dark pupils, as if she was studying a bug under a microscope.

"The Vrishnis meant you no harm. The procedure was necessary in order to remove your body wastes. Your body wastes would poison your system if you retained any of it in our atmosphere. Your body is now going through a quarantine process. Once that is completed, it will be time for us to leave. It would not be safe for us to return to the earth plane now."

Phil stared at her with disbelieving eyes. The monotone of her voice made him think of a mechanical voice programmed inside a computer. She didn't say anything about taking a sample of his sperm, he noted. But that could wait. Right now he wanted to get Linda and find a way to rescue his friends too.

"I don't believe you. You're lying to keep me here."

"I cannot lie. Come with me. I will show you." She turned and walked a few steps, then waited for him to follow her. She moved with the agility of a cat, he thought.

As Phil got off the couch, the dazzling luminary display around him became less and less visible until it finally winked out completely. The room correspondingly lit up with a warm glow. The walls themselves, he discovered, performed as incandescent lamps. Somehow, the release of his weight on the couch had triggered the transformation. Ninlil was standing in front of one of the eight-sided walls. It didn't appear to have a doorway.

"Hold my hand," she directed, "and do not leave go until we pass."

As Phil did as he was told, Ninlil began leading him THROUGH THE SOLID WALL! He felt a slight tingling sensation, nothing more. It was like walking through a dense vapor, Phil thought. The wall immediately resealed itself once they were on the other side.

"Do not be alarmed. We have learned to channel the energy force within our bodies to that of our surroundings. When we touch, you are in equilibrium with the ship. Do not attempt it yourself until your procedure is complete. In time you will have the same capability. Come."

She was halfway down a seven-foot-high, narrow circular corridor by the time Phil started after her. He could tell it had a downward pitch. It was constructed of the same material as the room they had just left—a hard Styrofoam rubber that reminded him of insulation material—with the same indirect lighting through the walls. He hurried to catch up, reveling in the fact that he was being given such freedom of movement. That will help my chances of escape, he plotted silently to himself.

At the bottom of the corridor, Phil and Ninlil seemed to have reached a dead end. He got the impression they were at the lowest level of the ship. After going through the same procedure of holding hands and stepping through the wall, Phil found himself in a cavernous chamber that resembled an airplane hangar filled with bright latticework. Sprouting from every direction were glowing neon tubes of light flashing in a variety of colors and intensities. He took them to be structural supports of some kind. At first he was confused as to where he was, until he looked up. He was awestruck. It was like gazing into the maw of a Titan missile!

Ninlil guided Phil onto a narrow catwalk that circumvented three transparent globes he likened to wrecking balls, only much bigger. They were arranged symmetrically overhead in an equilateral triangle. Floating inside each one was an arrangement of glowing rods wrapped around a circuitry of coils, crossed bars and T's. To Phil it suggested negative and positive fields working together somehow, each ball surrounded by an ionization haze of blue. The end result, he was told, was a miniaturized, contained, self-sustaining process of fusion reaction; the future of space travel he had read about in science magazines. It was powering the vehicle, tapping into an inexhaustible fuel supply, the dark matter of space itself. It was technology earth scientists would have given their eye-teeth to have, Phil imagined. From the containment field came a stream of energized light traveling through conduits that gave the ship all the power it needed. His sense of comparison was having trouble grasping the dimensions of the craft. It was at least as tall as a seven-story building, yet he was sure the UFO he and Linda originally approached wasn't anywhere near those proportions. It was as though Ninlil could read his mind.

"Your three-dimensional world is but part of an illusion. Do not always believe what you see," she said noncommittally, "but see what you believe." It wasn't until later that Phil understood what she meant.

The catwalk they were standing on led them deeper into the bowels of the ship until it ended at a small viewing platform adjacent to two of the three wrecking balls. Their internal glow highlighted Ninlil's features as she stepped to the walkway's edge and waited for Phil to join her. He hesitated.

"You will not fall. See?" She tried to step off the edge but an invisible barrier held her back. Phil tentatively inched his way closer. It was a good twenty-foot drop to the bottom of the chamber.

"Look down." Something in the intensity of her diminutive voice made Phil comply without argument. What he was about to see would make him have nightmares for the rest of his life.

Four vertical panels spread apart like the petals of a flower. It was as if he were suddenly looking through a magnifying glass. Through the opening, countless specks of light leaped into focus. Stars! But, in the center of it all was a planet slowly spinning on its axis that held his attention. It was Earth, a blue marble being skewered on an invisible spit. Parts of it were cloaked in vast sheaths of clouds. It was an exact replica of a picture he and Linda had hanging in their family room, a photo taken by the

Apollo 7 astronauts. It looked beautiful, yet extremely fragile.

But something was wrong! The earth was acting strangely. Every few seconds it would convulse and shudder, as if a dog had it in its mouth, shaking meat off a bone.

Phil recognized the continent of Africa, its eastern shoulder just starting to roll past him as the Gulf of Aden slid into view under white cirrus clouds. Crisscrossing the ochre-red continent were miniscule lines, like a cardboard cutout. What he saw next, a hammer blow into his solar plexus couldn't have given him more pain. Huge rifts and fissures were tearing the landscape apart. Mountains were being thrust upward as others were crumbling like papier-mâché. And deserts that had been cleansed of water thousands of years before were reemerging under newly swollen seas. Long-extinct volcanoes belched fire and smoke while new ones were breaking through weakened crust. What emerged were huge gouts of lava disgorging voluminous amounts of ash and poisonous gases thousands of feet into the stratosphere. Phil was watching the earth rendering its soul to the heavens.

On the Dark Continent's extreme western edge, the Atlantic Ocean was just starting to make its appearance. Dark green and brown patches, which Phil construed to be the Azores and, further south, the Canary Islands, lazily swam into view. And as he watched the last remnants of those islands being gouged and dissected apart, new land masses were taking form and shape further west. All along the mid-Atlantic Ridge, the exploding vestigial crusts rising out of the depths were forming new massifs, expanded plains and deep valleys. Could this be the legendary Atlantis Edgar Cayce had predicted would rise again?

As the spinning earth kept advancing toward the night-side meridian, so too were successive walls of white ripples moving irresolutely westward. Tidal waves! Ohhhh God! Phil grimaced. Tsunamis as tall as skyscrapers were literally sweeping across the eastern seaboard of North America, stripping away everything in their path.

The lowlands from Labrador to Florida had become completely inundated. Avalanches of water had already engulfed New York, Virginia, Georgia and parts of the Carolinas were already swept away. Florida had all but disappeared under the onslaught. The crinkled, maroon strip that delineated the Adirondacks and the Smoky Mountains were the last bulwarks of defense against the onrush of crushing waves.

South of the 30th parallel, the Bermuda Banks, Virgin Islands, Cuba and the Lower & Upper Antilles, lands that had been flooded by 300 feet of melting ice at the end of the last Ice Age, were being driven upward to form new bottomland. As the seafloors heaved and tilted, other submerged lands of the Caribbean were discarding their secrets, revealing former traces of lost civilizations. In the Gulf of Mexico, fast-escaping waters exposed gargantuan pyramids, temples, and roads and walls leading downward to constructions buried even deeper.

Rotating counterclockwise, the land kept continually changing its features while the ocean encroached wherever it found new depressions. The earth had no time to settle before it was reeling under another vicious spasm. Again, more lines began etching their way westward, across vast stretches of Canada and the northern plains of the United States.

Phil stood transfixed at the earth's torment. A heavy weight of guilt was increasingly pressing down on him. He felt ashamed he was there, still alive and comparatively safe, while millions of his fellow human beings were being annihilated by a world gone mad. His suit of impenetrable armor of staying cool under pressure had suddenly disintegrated. He slumped to his knees, bowed his head and began to cry. Ninlil stood and watched in stolid silence as her charge's cries of pain and anguish fell disconsolately on alien indifference. Through blurred vision Phil began looking for the long, familiar coastline of California. The twins were down there somewhere in that maelstrom. He gasped. The state wasn't there! It was gone, as well as a dozen other western states, just as if a giant scythe had come along and sliced the country in half. A crescent-shaped gulf remained, its newly formed shores cutting a jagged edge through the Dakotas, Nebraska, Kansas, Oklahoma and Texas. West of the Rockies was nothing but water and broken up isles poking up through the haze. Millions of people were gone. The kids. What about the kids? Malik said they would be safe. Phil turned away in disgust. The memory of standing with Malik on the Nebraska coastline was like a raw sore in his psyche.

"Please, I don't want to see anymore," Phil pleaded.

By some unspoken command, the petals closed.

"You should not regret what is happening. You are safe here." Ninlil's words echoed hollowly in the giant chamber.

"I don't belong here, Ninlil. I belong on earth with my own people."

She perked her head up for a second as if she were pondering what Phil had just said. Perhaps, Phil thought, his words had sparked a touch of compassion in her. But, he was being overly generous. "Come, you will talk with the Controller," she said. "He has requested to see you."

CHAPTER 23

Earth Day Plus Three

Facing him stood a humanoid that Phil took to be quite old. There was nothing Phil could compare him to in earthly standards of aging, but Phil just knew the alien was old. Perhaps the minute wrinkles on his forehead was an aging indicator or perhaps even being slightly taller than the other humanoids he saw earlier could be a clue, but he didn't think so. The alien's demeanor was that of someone who held some degree of authority and intellect in whatever hierarchy was observed aboard the spacecraft. Ninlil had obediently melted into the background after their arrival, without so much as announcing their presence. It seemed introductions weren't necessary when someone such as the Controller wished to speak with you.

But he didn't seem to be in any hurry about talking to his newly arrived guest, Phil discovered. Bent over what appeared to be a child's writing table, he raised his head and peered at Phil inquisitively for a moment before resuming his task. Phil took the opportunity to examine his surroundings more closely now that he was getting more time to look around. He couldn't shake a firefighter's inbred instinct to look for an escape route whenever entering uncharted territory.

There wasn't any doubt in Phil's mind that he was standing in the control room of the spacecraft. It was about sixty feet in diameter, diametrically opposite to what he thought he saw in the cave. Do not always believe what you see. The entire room was surrounded by a low-slung console that reminded Phil of a child's playroom. Dissecting the floor and ceiling in the exact center of the room was a flagpole-sized shaft of sharply edged high-intensity light. It was encased in a translucent tube of some kind. Phil guessed it had to be the same continuation of light stemming from the propulsion chamber. He couldn't imagine the amount of energy it pumped, like a maze of illuminated arteries, coursing through the spacecraft. It probably could have powered an aircraft carrier with ease. The way Ninlil described the vimana, it was like a living, breathing entity. Where the wall and ceiling molded together was a built-in 360-degree view-screen, a three-foot-wide band of darkened transparency that separated the cupola from the main body of the ship.

Inserted in the console, in front of three plastic molded chairs rising up out of the floor, were what looked like spheres the size of soccer balls. Each was half-filled with some kind of gelatinous red liquid. Every few seconds, the jellylike substance would lean off the horizontal like a pilot's attitude indicator. Then, as if programmed by some automated sensor, the level would adjust back to its original setting. Phil could feel no tilting or movement under his feet whatsoever. A slight humming in the background was all he heard since he was taken aboard. Inscribed under each level were weird-looking symbols that resembled Egyptian hieroglyphics. Except for a single row of flashing red and green lights over a bank of monitors that typified TV screens, the circular chamber looked rather plain. Noticeably absent were arrays of gauges, switches and dials, as well as even the barest trace of computers and telemetry equipment Phil would have expected to find in this high-tech machine.

A familiar symbol suddenly flashed before his eyes. Phil had to stop and concentrate for a brief second before he recognized what it was. He turned his head toward one of the monitors across the room without trying to be too obvious. There it was, he told himself, three tangled triangles locked together. There was no mistaking their similarity between the marking on his arm, his mother's thigh, and the insignia on Malik's uniform. Phil was not a gambling man, but if he was, he would have bet a month's pay it was the alien's symbol for earth.

The Controller was still hunched over the table with an odd-looking device in his long fingers. It appeared as if he was doodling on a clear plastic overlay. What was underneath the overlay was what caught Phil's attention. The alien was marking coordinates on what looked like some kind of star chart. They were being superimposed over a network of variegated lights which flit across the chart like Fred Astaire skipping across a stage. It suggested to Phil a celestial field of some kind. At its hub was a concentric pattern of luminous rings. Each time the Controller would place a mark, a halo of light would expand and flair outward into beautiful shades of red and lavenders, like a ripple on a pond. He found it fascinating.

"I see you are adapting well."

The words boomed into Phil's consciousness like a loud thunder clap. It came so unexpectedly, he was momentarily stunned. He had been so engrossed in the star chart, he hadn't noticed that the Controller had laid his marker aside and was staring fixedly at him. Contrary to public opinion, trying to converse telepathically with an alien was not the easiest way to communicate. There were too many nuances and inflections in the tone of a human voice when someone talks normally. Your body's visual expressions, such as the look in your eyes or your body language adjust instinctively to everything you say. In cyberspace, there was no such symbiotic relationship. There was nothing to visually and audibly condition the tone and meaning of your words to the receiver. The message could be interpreted entirely different then what was originally intended. So, he didn't try. It seemed Ninlil was the only exception on board. Except for the lack of emotion, she talked with the use of vocal cords. Phil was starting to catch on. Maybe that was the idea why she was there—to be used as back-up.

"Uhh...yes. I feel fine now." Phil tried to match his gaze, but it was like trying to outstare a viper. At least a viper had eyelids.

"I wanna know what you did with my wife? Where is she?"

"She is safe aboard another vimana. She is in a state of calm and relaxation." The Controller's thought patterns came across concise and distinct. Phil had no trouble understanding him.

"What did you do to her?" Phil's voice started to rise in pitch. He kept a fear at the back of his mind that the aliens would perform some kind of pregnancy exam, or worst still, impregnate her with some alien life form. The Controller seemed to pick up on Phil's concern.

"We are not allowed to continue any experiments until Gaia resolves her difficulties and regains stability. In the meantime, the woman called 'Linda' will not be harmed."

Phil was reminded that aliens, or at least certain ones, could read minds. "What do you mean by 'experiments'? I don't understand."

"Long before great ice sheets covered your planet, a race of divine beings migrated there from a star system humankind later called Sirius. It was their duty to seed earth, through copulation with lower life forms, with beings in their own image. The race of Adam was their progeny."

Shades of the missing-link controversy, Phil opined. Since the famous Scopes Monkey Trial in 1925 brought it to a head, paleoanthropologists have tried to find empirical proof of Darwin's theory of evolution. So far, the Neanderthal was found to be the closest cousin to homo-sapiens. As for the bibliophiles, the only empirical proof they had is the faith they have placed in the written word of their sacred manuscripts and bibles. In the same breath, the Controller confirmed Malik's assertion that Man Came From The Stars. Paintings and sketches of UFOs and extraterrestrials were a mainstay in dozens of caves that were inhabited by the first hominids that walked the earth. Artifacts of materials not of this earth have been found in such strange places as mummy's tombs and the Peruvian Alps. A flash memory of how many times Jeremy preached to him about the diversity of the universe came to mind. The sage's words continued to lance into his consciousness.

"Through genetic breeding, the deities succeeded in propagating a higher intelligence, but they failed to compensate for the frailty of the human mind. With only a few survivors your species started new civilizations, even great civilizations, but did not learn from them," the Controller finished. Phil filled in the gaps. Man's abuse of free will over the millennia, and in defiance of Universal Law, sealed his karmic fate. The planet Gaia (Earth) would soon have a new facelift.

Phil was flabbergasted. It was absolutely incredible! The Controller was talking about retributive justice; karma reaching out to other civilizations, other planets. He stayed silent for a moment, beginning to wonder where all this was leading.

"Why would that have to do with experimentation?" Phil finally asked.

"We have done many experiments with human DNA specimens, the Controller answered. To correct the cause of free will abuse is by enhancing human consciousness. We are slowly succeeding in that direction, but humankind has indicated it is not yet ready to comply. They seem to be ignorant of their plight and continue to defy Universal Law. You must understand, man's free will is not on trial here, but what he has done with it is not acceptable. It is the Creator, in tune with the energies and life forces of all the planets, who decrees when absolution is necessary. It is the Council's responsibility to evacuate survivors, such as you, when that decree is given. The Council has proclaimed all our resources be directed toward that cause. As caretakers of Gaia, it is our obligation according to Universal Law. Nevertheless, it has caused conflicts between us. We have other issues to contend with that must be addressed soon. However, as far as your species is concerned, Gaia's axial shift is now approaching its zenith."

Strange he should confess something Phil figured would be their dirty laundry. He remembered Ninlil saying they cannot lie. Might mean something later, he thought.

"You say you're caretakers of earth?"

"All members of the Interplanetary Council have assigned duties as caretakers to rogue planets. We are in contact with all their governments who are engaging in the wasteful blight of a planet's resources. We have dealt with their military on many occasions to stop the excesses they are committing. Gaia has been no exception. All must follow Universal Law.

"What is the purpose for all this?" said Phil, raising his voice. Why can't each planet choose its own destiny without interference? "

The words of the Controller did not waver. "All living organisms throughout the universe are joined with the Creator. Even the planets, and the lower life forms that exist on their surfaces, are under the Creator's guidance and operate under His principles. Failure to follow these natural laws affects the entire ecological system of the planetary alignment. The human species has violated that responsibility. Without that energy force, your galaxy would be a galaxy of wandering planets, crashing into each other, destroying each other. Your asteroid belt was the result of one such calamity. The Council cannot allow that to happen again."

"But...but you're taking away man's freedom to..."

"FREEDOM!" The intensity of his exclamation shot into Phil's head like a lance.

"Freedom to pillage Gaia, to defile its waters and atmosphere with human wastes? The planet has become incapable of stemming the tide of pollution because of man's wantonness. He has dug out its vital organs and poisoned the air it needs to breathe, stripping away its forests so that the soil cannot refortify the energy it needs to replenish itself. The added plight of wars with atomic weaponry, with resultant clouds of deadly radiation, and droughts caused by deterioration of the ozone layer, has shifted Gaia's magnetic polarity. Erratic weather patterns have emerged. Rivers and streams that hold bountiful supplies of fish are decimated by runoffs caused by overuse of fertilizers. Nuclear waste has infected large tracts of land and sea—not good for habitation. Human evolvement did not stay in harmony with Universal Law. The displacement of Gaia's axis is imminent. The warning signs were ignored. Your earth, in its present form, is doomed."

"But..."

Phil stopped. He felt like a child that had just been castigated by his teacher. The Controller's words were almost the same utterances spoken by Malik. The expression on the wizened old alien's face was immutable. He turned his back on Phil, picked up the strange-looking device he had in his hand earlier, and resumed his doodling. Phil heard no other thoughts being projected his way. It seemed their little meeting was over. Ninlil sidled over to him and discreetly led him out of the room. Phil felt beaten, defeated, crushed. Not for a second could he dispute the logic of the Controller's words.

CHAPTER 24

Earth Day Plus Four

Phil had no concept of time. His watch was missing and there were no clocks aboard the spacecraft. During the course of his stay, he was neither tired nor hungry, nor did he have to relieve himself, thanks to the alien's 'procedure.' He grew no beard and felt continually clean and refreshed, as if he had just stepped out of the shower. Ninlil explained, "Here, we are not bound by your time. There is no past, present or future as measured by earthly standards. Time is."

"I don't understand," Phil said bluntly.

"The vibrations of all living matter is controlled by electromagnetic forces. We are able to control those forces within the ship so that all energy particles, including those in our bodies, are joined together in suspension. Once you leave the ship, you are no longer imprisoned in a three dimensional form.

"Does that mean we can travel in time; that we can reach other dimensions?" Phil asked disbelievingly. It sounded like the space/time continuum was in play when it came to dimensional release. The Philadelphia Experiment immediately came to mind when the U.S. Government, using powerful generators, in an experimental attempt to avoid enemy radar for its ships, accidentally found the secret to teleportation…and time travel.

"Yes. Your government learned the ability to explore. Otherwise, the universe would be very small."

Phil looked at her with a new appreciation. She also had the ability to read his mind.

How can your spacecraft travel across a universe that only can be measured in light years?" Phil was not afraid to ask as many questions as he wanted. He got the impression Ninlil wanted him to learn all he could of the vimana. "By earth's antiquated standards, it would take one of our moon shuttles, 25,000 light years just to travel to the middle of our own galaxy."

"By energy tubes." Ninlil answered. This ship does not have the capabilities to travel long distances on its own."

That was a laugh, Phil mused. A long distance to Ninlil was probably not less than a million light years away. Ninlil told him that the Vrishnis kept powerful solar batteries in the form of power crystals beneath the earth's oceans. It was the same energy form that the Atlanteans had developed, mostly to power their machines and weapons. These crystals were stored inside huge domed structures, strategically placed, to be tapped only when their observation ships entered and left Gaia's gravitational field. Once in outer space, they used the fuel available for them there, " she pointed out.

"How do the Vrishnis use these energy tubes?" Phil grilled the alien beauty. He was starting to think she may question his motives on why he was so interested in their means of travel. He feared, sooner or later, she would start getting suspicious of his plans to escape. But Ninlil didn't seem to mind. As a matter of fact, it was as if she was enjoying playacting the role of an informant giving out company secrets.

The arrival and departure points of the UFOs were in the shape of wormholes, or space/time warps, she went on, which looped through Gaia at various locations. These energy fields extended into the far reaches of intergalactic space. But the biggest threat, to humans anyway, was that the energy fields were unstable. They were continually moving in concentric patterns, in conjunction with earth's rotation, sometimes attaining diameters of two miles or better. Earth had ten such regions in all where time warps waited like invisible booby traps. One of them was off Florida's east coast: the infamous Bermuda Triangle. Another was off the southeast coast of Japan, commonly referred to as the Devil's Sea. Closer to home, Phil discovered one was located off Bruce Peninsula, smack dab in the middle of Georgian Bay. He also learned that since these three places were most frequented by travelers, they took the biggest toll of ships and aircraft who mysteriously disappeared in those areas.

"What happens to the people who sail or fly into these vortexes?" Phil asked.

"They simply cease to exist on the earth plane," Ninlil offered matter-of-factly. "But those who have only skirted the edges have lived to warn others to stay away. That is good. We do not wish to harm anyone." It sounds like Steve and Lucienne were two of the lucky few who managed to barely escape one of those energy cores, Phil thought. It was apparent from Steve's description of the whirlpool he encountered was that the lack of molecules in its air space made his plane lose power. According to statistics, there weren't many who skirted one and lived to tell about it. A celebrated case suddenly jogged his memory. The Lost Patrol. In December 1945, five TBM Avengers and a Martin Mariner PBM rescue plane, with a combined crew of 27 men, all vanished without a trace inside the Bermuda Triangle. Such last-minute radio transmissions as "we can't be sure of our direction" and "the ocean doesn't look like it should," sounded like what Steve had described. The Patrol's last transmission of "entering white water," seemed to be the coup de grace for them. What ever happened to the PBM was anybody's guess. Phil continued to persist in his line of questioning. It was starting to get interesting.

"There are times when ground observers or radar operators see a military plane disappear when chasing a spacecraft. And there are times people are never seen again after spotting a spacecraft on some lonely country road. What about those people?"

"There are those who have chosen to defy Universal Law. Theirs is a mission of allurement and corruption of souls. They will not stop until all who believe in the Law of One are dead or made workers to serve their own primitive needs. Others are of a combative nature and do not understand human paranoia. They perceive your aircraft as enemy projectiles. Those species are easily provoked by violence. There are others so different in physical form, they would make you tremble in fear. The Vrishnis, and races like them, are gentle in nature. Most are gatherers and inhabit planets for exploratory and biological reasons only. The most esteemed are the celestials, a highly evolved race of beings that oversee the Interplanetary

Council." It was obviously the world Malik came from, Phil deduced.

"What race are you, Ninlil?"

"I am of no race. I am a hybrid. I am a beginning generation of the New Age of Gaia. Eventually we will begin exploration to other planets to spread our seed. One's species must survive. It is Universal Law."

The speed of UFOs streaking across the heavens gave rise to questions scientists have been asking ever since Kenneth Arnold precipitated the phrase, 'flying saucers.' Arnold was flying in the Cascade Mountain Range of Washington State in 1947, looking for a crashed plane, when he spotted a flotilla of UFOs. He said their aerial acrobatics seemed to follow the topography of the mountain chain, occasionally rising and falling to match their profile. They were traveling over 1700 miles per hour.

"When not traveling in the wormholes," Phil inquired, "how are your machines able to attain such tremendous velocities in our atmosphere?"

The hybrid beauty replied without hesitating. "All planets born of the explosive beginning of the universe share the same qualities—a magnetic core and gravity. When we use on-board positive to negative force fields, the spacecraft is instantaneously pulled toward the planet. When the process is reversed, the spacecraft is instantaneously pushed away."

It was the most logical answer, Phil conceded. The earth was nothing more than a giant magnet inside a big rock floating in space. As the UFOs skimmed the earth's surface, puzzling onlookers with their bobbing and weaving, not realizing the aliens could parallel or reverse polarities at will.

That being the case, Phil reflected, how can the crew inside the spacecraft withstand G-forces beyond human tolerance and survive? Witnesses have reported UFOs making 90-degree turns and then just blink out of sight as if they were never there. Is alien physiology so much superior than ours?" When Phil broached that question to Ninlil, her answer surprised him.

"No. Our extremities are different, but inside our bodies, we are all carbon based. We all bleed when one of us is wounded; and we all die if the wound is too great. Our technology keeps us from getting hurt when power maneuvering one of our spacecraft. By increasing the resonant frequency of the ship, we can create our own force field. And at higher frequencies, we can bend light waves, allowing us to disappear from the visible spectrum. That proves necessary sometimes when one or more of your aircraft chases us."

One last question remained unanswered. It pertained to a term Ninlil used once or twice in their conversations, Phil recalled. She kept referring to the 'Source' as if it were a Supreme Being.

"No, not a Supreme Being, but all," Ninlil retorted.

Phil decided to play devil's advocate. "Wasn't Earth the center of all creation," he asked? "Didn't Christ die for our sins, the Lord and Creator of all things? Didn't He create humankind in his own image?"

"Yes, He is all what you say He is because your bible says so, so you believe. Buddhist, Muslim, and Hindu sacred literatures have preached the same to their followers, and so they believe. All of them represent truth and knowledge, do they not? That is also the basis of Universal Law. They are the same judgments the Creator handed down to Moses in the Ten Commandments. If we constantly seek the enlightenment of their teachings, then we are on the right path. It does not matter from which direction you travel that path. Your God and mine all lead to the same Source. He is One. Others just have different names for Him, that's all."

If this alien beauty were capable of a smile, he could have sworn she was giving him one now.

CHAPTER 25

Earth Day Plus Five

Although Phil was in constant amazement of the technical marvels surrounding him, he was quickly growing despondent. He desperately missed Linda and his friends. His mental stability needed to be reassured that they were okay. Phil didn't like the feeling that he was the only one left alive. If he thought that for sure, he would have no desire to continue living. And when it came to listening to his mounting concerns, Ninlil was about as receptive as a rock. But he didn't believe trying to escape was the answer anymore. He was made to feel safe and secure in the vimana. Ninlil kept assuring him his wife and friends were also safe and secure where they were at. Besides, Phil pondered, where would he go? Where could he go? As far as what was happening outside the vessel, it was beyond his control. But inside, he sensed a game-changer was in the mix. Whenever a positive feeling overtook his moods of despair, Phil always knew some intervening force was at play. He felt it most strongly when he miraculously escaped death in a smoke-filled upper duplex one time. There are never any atheists working a fire nozzle inside a burning building, was a firefighter's mantra. Phil believed in Lady Luck too. Some days, you just flipped a coin.

However, this time, more than luck was involved. Something else was gnawing at Phil's insides. Something more devious. From all outward appearances, Ninlil seemed to be the perfect hostess. She provided him with everything he required, even feeding him with some kind of tasteless liquid that seemed to quell his appetite. She was also his own personal tour guide of the ship. Phil was allowed to go anywhere he chose, as long as Ninlil was with him. In his wanderings, he saw marvels no human being had ever laid eyes on before. She answered all his questions as though she was programmed to do so. She even showed him how to operate the controls. It wasn't that difficult to learn, as long as he remembered where the heat sensors were located. Those devices activated the automated systems, all hidden behind smooth, eggshell white walls that revealed no trace of the maze of technology behind them. Tiny computers, fiber optics and circuit boards filled the enclosed spaces. The control room wasn't as plain as he had first imagined. He had guessed correctly when he first espied the soccer balls filled with gelatinous liquid. The vimana was currently on automatic pilot circling the earth at orbital velocity. Once decided it was time, the ship's inertial guidance system would lock on to an energy core, either to enter a portal into outer space or enter the fiery hell of reentry back to earth. Ninlil had no answer as to when that time would come.

Meanwhile, Phil learned all about a vimana. They were airships once used by ancient India, as described in their Mahabharata, a Hindu collection of over 200,000 verses dealing with India's customs, history, the cosmos, etc. When earth was invaded by a hostile race of beings, horrific super weapons were introduced that defined atomic warfare for years to come. On the desert floor were found traces of fused glass dated to when the battles took place 16,000 years ago. It was the time when vimanas changed from harmless terrestrial craft fueled by mercury cells to high-tech warlike machines fueled by the energy of deep space. The knowledge left him with an unsettling feeling. The invaders were eventually defeated, but it seemed to Phil the victors did no better than set the stage for their own eventual self-destruction.

Subconsciously, the firefighter kept hearing the red flags fluttering again. There was no way Ninlil could fool those built-in sensors, acquired from years of outwitting the Grim Reaper, when it was warning him he was treading on thin ice. And at the moment, Phil had a strong suspicion that that ice was beginning to crack.

The moment of truth came when Phil followed Ninlil into a room he had not been in before. Its dimensions were bigger than most and the air had a rich musk smell to it, so strong it was almost nauseating. But it was what was in the center of the room that dominated his attention—a glowing pillar of white light, spreading its radiance in all directions. It extended from the ceiling to the floor like a stage spotlight. Phil hesitated momentarily, but he felt irresistibly drawn to it. He felt no fear, only a weird sense of anticipation. Surprisingly, he found he had no will to resist the sudden urge to copulate. Even his warning signs had fallen inexplicably silent. He stepped inside the circle of light, feeling like an unwilling guest who had just overstayed his welcome.

CHAPTER 26

Earth Day Plus Six

Phil stepped out of the pool of light feeling like a new man. He was standing naked in a room filled with whiteness. Any anxiety or apprehension he may have harbored earlier was gone. He felt rejuvenated. He could feel the growing hardness in his groin. He craved companionship—female companionship. He needed someone, ravenously, to share his most intimate desires with.

As though someone had tuned in to his basest thoughts, Ninlil was there waiting for him. Her naked body was wreathed in a glow of opalescent beauty. The sight of her small protruding breasts and hairless crotch, stimulated Phil with an overpowering lust. He wanted her more than he had wanted any other woman in his life. His penis stood erect with desire.

Ninlil began to float, ever so gently, swaying back and forth, to and fro, erotically maneuvering her body in a rhythmic dance of passion. Her legs slightly apart, body tilted backward, she held her arms outstretched, beckoning to him. All Phil had to do was project his thoughts and he began floating in her direction. He automatically positioned his body in preparation for the release of pressure building between his thighs. It was as though they were performing an underwater ballet in a waterless vacuum, pirouetting around each other in an ever tightening circle. Finally they touched, their bodies interlocking in a firm embrace.

The intoxicating sweet fragrance of Ninlil's body acted as an aphrodisiac. She caressed Phil's body, brushing her bloodless lips along his cheek. Her mouth parted slightly, revealing a tiny pink tongue that began to squirm delicately around his neck. Her legs spread wider. In one smooth motion Phil slid his rigid penis into her vagina. She made a small groaning sound from deep inside her throat. As he pushed deeper and began to rock his hips back and forth, her orgasm steadily building with every thrust, a lubricating spray from her urethra was gradually released. Phil felt the warm discharge soothing around his penis. Their bodies became as one as she intertwined her legs sinuously around his. They began to see-saw together, slowly at first, and then in a teeter-totter motion, gradually increasing the pumping of their hips to a climatic frenzy.

Ninlil had reached her point of release. A steady stream of fluid gushed past Phil's penis, her hips thrusting in maddening fury. But her orgasm followed in weak fashion. It was as if she was able to shut off her emotions completely. To Phil, in an alternate state of mind, Ninlil was just as desirous. Her sudden lack to reciprocate his lovemaking only heightened his hunger for more. Mimicking a ravenous infant, Phil began to suck one of her upturned nipples savagely. But this was obviously not what Ninlil had in mind. Before Phil realized what was happening, he felt a pressure behind his right ear. As if suddenly opening up Pandora's box, it triggered a demon within him he couldn't contain any longer. Phil climaxed in one gigantic spasm, crying out loudly with bestial pleasure as he penetrated deep into Ninlil's womb. Continuous spurts of semen were ejaculated and for several minutes Phil's contractions continued in spasmodic jerks. Ninlil stayed silent, her legs spread apart, looking at him with curiously unwavering eyes, unemotional, impassive, anticipating his every movement. As one orgasm would subside, another would begin until finally, like a spent whore, Phil lay prostrate against her motionless body. He instantly collapsed into a dreamless sleep of exhaustion.

CHAPTER 27

Earth Day Plus Seven

That's funny, Phil thought. His mind had suddenly gone blank for a second. The last thing he remembered was being compelled to step into the spotlight. Strange. It felt as if he had just been awakened from a deep and refreshing sleep. A small seed of doubt began to form inside his head. There had been no feeling of a time lapse, yet his brain centers reported a period of activity had occurred. It had been a period of intense pleasure as well, but he couldn't seem to bypass the mental trapdoor that was preventing any details from surfacing. He was still immersed in the light, somewhat groggy and disoriented, but he could tell it was acting as some kind of energy boost. He squinted his eyes, trying to pierce the wall of brightness, but it was like looking through a curtain of stage lights. Phil could sense a presence close to him, coming from outside his illuminated prison.

An inhuman pair of obsidian eyes met his gaze as Phil tentatively stepped out of the light. It was the Controller. As Phil's eyes were slowly adjusting, he looked past the alien leader and espied the three humanoids who had examined him earlier. Ninlil had told him they were a race of beings of a lower order who were made as look-alikes—basically clones—to serve as workers for higher intelligences. They were huddled against the far wall, making clicking noises that sounded like a muffled chorus of sea crabs. From their excited twittering, Phil guessed they were either playing a game or sharing some prankish secret among themselves. As for Ninlil, she was nowhere around. He held the strangest feeling that he would never see her again. She had somehow served her purpose.

"In zero four soltecs, you will rejoin your companions," the wizened alien stated flatly. "Jovii is near."

Phil let out a silent sigh of relief. (a soltec was a unit of time vs. distance, equal to about fifteen earthly minutes) He was glad to hear he was finally getting off the ship. He was starting to get a case of cabin fever. But there was something else too. Something that bothered him ever since he was allowed to witness the earth tearing itself apart. Ninlil had told Phil 'his three-dimensional world is only but part of an illusion. Do not always believe what you see,' said during times when he was trying to grasp the incongruity of what he was being shown. He felt he had been deceived by Malik when he saw the earth tearing itself apart, while his family and the people he loved, were nowhere to be heard from. Was it all a trick, or an optical illusion, to isolate the survivors on some other planet while the earth could be taken over by another race? It would take eons to accomplish in linear time, but linear time was a joke to the aliens. Phil would be laughing at his own words if he didn't seriously consider the possibility. With all the smoke and mirrors of a technology that defied the laws of physics, who could blame him?

"Humanoids will return to Gaia when it is safe to do so," answered the Controller telepathically. "That will not happen until Gaia completes its orbit around the sun. That will begin within your time scale of three hundred years."

"Three hundred years! As you must know, Controller, humans don't live that long," Phil answered directly.

"It is true your three dimensional world is not complete. It is simply an illusion. Your scientist, named Einstein, was correct when he said a mass, such as a space vehicle, cannot exceed the speed of light. But he was restricted to only the law of physics he knew in his own time. We operate within rifts in the matrix of time and distance. To travel millions of light-years in the universe is not possible unless the resources of black holes and energy tubes are used."

"Using that scenario as a basis," Phil replied excitedly, "can't we go back in time?"

"Yes, we could, but not the planet. Your Gaia is locked in a time frame that cannot be changed."

Phil was starting to reach the point of panic. He wasn't talking about just one house fire as a simile, but a conflagration of them. And in Phil's continuum, time was not an option he had at his disposal.

"You said the earth was doomed because of man's ineptitude. Can anything be done to break the cycle? Anything!" Phil was almost pleading with the alien.

"Yes, a symbiotic relationship can be restored if natural laws are followed. To accomplish this, a higher level of consciousness among humankind must be attained. Beware of entities who have chosen the path of Bellial.

They have chosen false gods. Their followers come in many forms. Many are among you now. They continue to kindle strife and bloodshed on your planet. They will not rest until the prophecy of the Battle of Armageddon has been fulfilled."

"A little late to be warning us about monsters from the Id now, isn't it?" Phil blurted out in indignation. Humankind's inability to control his own destiny did not seem to be relevant here. Earth had been up against just as great an odds in the past, such as devastating meteor impacts, ice sheets miles thick, world-wide floods, and the planet still survived, Phil asserted. And now, because the clock had run out for them, it was a matter of pleading for God's mercy once again. There were no more options. Just like when he pleaded for His mercy in a burned-out ghetto two days before he left home. Was it too much to ask God to give back a little girl's disfigured body he found under the bed with seventy-per-cent of her body with second and third degree burns. To Phil's disgust, there never was an answer. He didn't expect one now.

Phil's temper flared. "And when the Battle is over, you'll be here to pick up the pieces," is that right?"

For some reason, Phil was not afraid to challenge the Controller, although he realized belatedly, that he might have been pushing his luck. It was simply frustration, and he knew it. The twittering in the background had suddenly ceased, as if the aliens were all collectively holding their breath. But the Controller seemed to be in a better mood than he had been during his first meeting with Phil. His thought projections had a pleasant tone to them that Phil had not picked up on before. In the same breath Phil forgot the old alien had a lot more practice reading someone's thoughts than he had.

The Controller hinted to himself that a touch of compassion was not out of the ordinary, even for an old alien. He reached out and laid his hand on the firefighter's arm. Without giving it a second thought, Phil clasped his hand over the alien's in a mutual exchange.

"Humankind have always fascinated me with their displays of emotion," the Controller finally said.

"Was that a part of Adam's legacy to us?"

"Yes. My ancestors visited Gaia long after the progeny of Adam began to decline. They observed many generations ascend to power, only to decline by their own inbred weaknesses. After each axil shift, my ancestors helped restore order out of chaos. They built shelters in the form of pyramids and monuments. For untold centuries these shelters have withstood earthquakes and floods to help future generations safeguard their past."

"You know, there was a man in my Dad's day called Edgar Cayce, a famous psychic who predicted the coming earth changes," Phil said. "Among other things, he talked about the Great Pyramid of Giza. He called it the Hall of Records. Is that what you're talking about?"

"Yes. Many secrets of the universe are recorded there. But in order to gain knowledge from those secrets, mankind's consciousness must be nearest the Creator."

There was a short pause as Phil followed the Controller to one of the chairs in front of the console. Sitting down in it sideways so he could face Phil, he motioned to the firefighter to do the same with the adjacent chair. When both were settled, he could hear the

Controller's message starting to come through again. It felt odd hearing words coming from him without seeing his lips move.

"My race came from a planet not much different than your own, the Controller began. But unlike your planet, it was destroyed when we fought a race of beings whose superior technology was greater than ours. Their use of poisonous gasses became ingrained in our DNA's ability to propagate. We were doomed to extinction. We committed the ultimate transgression against Universal Law. There is no difference whose fault it was. For our punishment we were banished from our system and relegated as guardians to a faraway galaxy. Your galaxy, the astronomers of your planet call Canis Major. It is part of the Milky Way in which Gaia belongs. So, as you see, we are neighbors."

"And that's why Ninlil is here, your first hybrid," Phil exclaimed. "But she doesn't look anywhere like your species."

"We cannot duplicate our DNA. Only the Creator has that power. I tell you this because humankind, in the next Age, should not make the same mistake we did."

Phil sat quiet for a moment, astounded as to what the Controller had revealed. However, in man's quest for universal knowledge, many questions still remained. Like pieces of a gigantic jig-saw puzzle, Phil knew his part in the grand scheme of things was insignificant at best. It was time someone else took the reins. His job was survival. His family's survival. And for the moment, even that was in question. Something strange was happening. The walls were starting to pulsate in some queer fashion.

At first he thought he was experiencing a delayed reaction to the pool of light. He shook his head and squeezed his eyes shut. When he reopened them, the walls were still moving, coming alive, like some giant heartbeat.

"Wh...what's happening?"

"Do not be afraid. Jovii, our mother ship, has synchronized your energy field with theirs," he heard the Controller announce inside his head. "You will not be harmed."

Easy for him to say, Phil thought anxiously. It was hard getting used to the pulsations. Everything in the room was being bathed in a blood-red glow. Even the humanoids in the background were beginning to get visibly excited.

But what disturbed Phil the most was the temperature. It was getting uncomfortably hot. He could feel fiery blasts of heat washing over him like a raging fire. Oh no...not again, he groaned. He had no desire to experience the insufferable heat he had undergone when he first came aboard.

The area behind his temples began to throb to the beat of the pulsations. He began to grow dizzy. He felt as if he were falling, but he was floating instead. The fading image of the Controller's elongated eyes was the last thing Phil saw before his dematerialized body turned into molecular particles of pure energy.

He was ejected outside the spacecraft in a flash, hurtling through space at an incalculable speed. An array of intense, exotic colors suddenly embraced him: vivid, absorbing. Just as quickly he broke free, finding himself soaring into a vacuum of blackness dotted with light. Manifestations of ephemeral beauty swam before his eyes:

vast constellations, their stars twinkling at him with eye-piercing clarity; planets girded with diaphanous rings of colored gas; streaking comets with gelatinous trails of cosmic ice, and strings of dust whizzing by on their circuitous galactic journeys; blue-hot plasmic explosions signifying the death throes of some supernova far on the other side of Creation. He gazed, fascinated at clumps of dead asteroids floating like scattered piles of discarded rock. Light years away, he could still recognize the effects of a collapsing star, the abscess of space surrounding a black hole. With hypnotic fixation, Phil witnessed massive yellow-white nebulae of swirling clouds and gasses spinning and twisting in a convoluted dance, heralding the birth of a new star. For one immeasurable moment of time, he was one with the universe.

CHAPTER 28

Earth Day Plus Eight

Phil's trip ended as suddenly as it began. He realized he wasn't aboard the vimana any longer. A whole new dimension had opened up before him. Everywhere around lay a surrealistic world of vivid colors and intense contrasts that merged with sounds and impressions he couldn't identify.

The light was so bright he had trouble keeping his eyes open. Dazzling rays of purplish-white light emanated from somewhere overhead. They seemed to radiate downward in concentrated waves, flowing with some kind of self-induced energy. It was like being bombarded with mega doses of ultra-violet light in a tanning salon. But, instead of a relaxing interlude, Phil could feel his whole body being charged by the light's dynamic force.

Towering all around him were tier upon tier of cubicles honeycombed like a giant beehive. The colors, like those in some beautiful patchwork quilt, fascinated him with their exquisite variety. No two were alike, and there had to be thousands of them.

He was standing on a balcony protruding from an aisle wide enough to accommodate a Mack truck. On every level were the same uniform aisles separating individual balconies from the maze of interconnected cells. He wasn't alone. Busy-looking creatures, about three feet tall, kept scurrying up and down the aisles, seemingly heading nowhere. Their arms dangled awkwardly at their sides and their spindly legs beat a staccato step as they marched heedlessly along, totally ignoring his presence. They kept their upper torsos rigid; their heads sat on unswerving, skinny necks. Some had hair, if you could call it that. It was more like a thatch of yellow straw stuck atop their asymmetrical dome-shaped heads, but most of the creatures were bald. Their skin color matched their skin tight uniforms; a bland, pasty look of dough. Their eyes and mouths looked as if small black buttons had been sewed into their faces. As far as Phil could tell, they had no ears and their nostrils were two black dots. Apparently they have a purpose in life, he thought. They looked like an army of automatons.

Phil reached out his hand in an attempt to grab one of them. That was a foolish mistake. He was suddenly on the floor writhing in pain. It was as if a jackhammer was splitting his head wide open. Thankfully, the pain only lasted a few seconds. Once it was over, he managed to crawl into a sitting position and wait for his senses to clear.

What was even more unnerving was the fact that when he fell to the floor, his landing was as soft as a feather. He was moving in slow motion! The gravity was only a fraction of what he was accustomed to.

But there was something else. Phil could feel, rather than hear, a deep throbbing, about two decibels lower than an idling diesel engine. It had been there all along, he suspected, but only now was his brain cognizant of the subtlety. It was coming from straight ahead, where the balcony seemed to come to a sudden stop. He half-walked, half-crawled to its edge, almost afraid to look down for fear he would face some unimaginable horror. Since he could feel no safety barrier as there was in the vimana, he made doubly certain not to get too inquisitive. The drop-off was comparable to looking down from a fifty-story high-rise. What he saw was enough to convince the most hardened skeptic that UFOs were alive and thriving. Row upon row of alien spacecraft were neatly assembled in a vast amphitheater of light. They ranged anywhere from mini-saucers only a few feet in diameter to the garden-variety type, thirty to fifty feet across. And then there were the asymmetrical, distorted ones, the type people have trouble describing: a potpourri of crescents, cubes, triangles and trapezoids, arrayed with either lights, portholes or antenna-like devices sticking out their tops. Phil spotted one with a Saturn-style ring circuiting its middle. Some appeared as spindles resembling king-sized toy tops or oblong eggs the size of Volkswagens. Others mimicked fat, rounded pencils with red-tipped beacons in place of erasers. Asking his mind to grasp the bizarreness of the scene, Phil realized, was asking it to strain his sense of credulity to the bursting point.

As strange as everything was, he wasn't surprised when he saw even stranger-looking spacecraft pushing the envelope to technology gone berserk: upside-down ice cream cones hanging suspended in midair, or house-sized chandeliers ablaze with lights. But there was one thing they all had in common: an air of expectancy, as if they were waiting...and feeding. Phil had trouble conceiving of this notion, yet he clearly sensed it.

Overhead is where he saw his suspicion confirmed. Through a spectacular luminary display, Phil was able to discern two glowing red orbs burning in the ebony of space. A binary star system! The twin suns were shooting out their rays through a gigantic round dome, bombarding the spacecraft on the floor below with voluminous concentrations of dark energy. This place was nothing more than some kind of nursery, a space station perhaps, Phil surmised. But the Controller called it a mother ship. Maybe not. His first impression was likened to the time he was aboard an aircraft carrier. Its flight deck was only an outer shell. The real inner city was hidden below decks.

"Phil! Phil darling!"

I'm starting to hallucinate, Phil thought. He could have sworn he heard Linda's voice calling him.

"PHIL!"

Phil whirled around just in time to catch Linda running into his arms. Launching into his arms because of the lessened gravity would have been a better description, he thought. But it was her alright, letting her body press tightly with his in a joyful reunion. It was wonderful to hold his wife close again; to smell the fragrance of her hair and feel the smoothness of her cheek against his. They ended their embrace with a long kiss. Phil could taste the salt from the tears streaming down her cheeks.

Phil noticed Linda had a disheveled, strained look about her that bespoke lack of sleep. At first he couldn't understand what she was saying. She kept mumbling unintelligible words that didn't make any sense. His brain was subconsciously rejecting certain words he didn't want to hear. Finally, Phil held Linda at arm's length and looked directly into her blood-shot eyes. After watching her lips mouthing the words, the message she was articulating suddenly struck home like a dagger.

"Lucienne's dead, Phil. Lucienne's dead!"

CHAPTER 29

Earth Day Plus Nine

The cell Linda led him to was invisibly interwoven amid the thousands he had gawked at from the balcony. The round module was spacious by alien standards. It had no furniture except what looked like a stone sarcophagus standing in the middle of the room. Draped over it was a covering of purplish light coming from a small aperture in the ceiling. Phil cringed as he peeked inside. Although all he could see was her upper torso, it was Lucienne alright. The rest of her inert form was shrouded under a luminous blanket of thick vapor, constantly in motion, swirling and eddying as if being whipped by an indiscernible hand. Her eyes were closed and she wore a relaxed expression on her face, as if she had just dropped off to sleep. Her coloring was good, he thought, unlike the cadavers he had labored over as a paramedic.

He turned to Linda. "Are you sure she's dead? She doesn't look dead."

"Yes, she's gone," Linda sighed. "Steve said that right after they were taken aboard the spacecraft, Lucienne became unconscious. When her breathing stopped, he immediately performed CPR on her but…but it was too late. Rigor mortis had already begun to set in. She…she must've died instantly…" Linda's voice trailed off into a whimper.

"But…" Phil motioned back toward the coffin. "What about…?" Linda anticipated his query.

"It's the vapor or…or whatever they're using to keep her that way. Steve said Lucienne began looking normal again only after the aliens placed her in this thing." Linda gave Lucienne a loving glance. "Oh, Phil, I feel so terrible." Phil could see fresh tears spilling down his wife's cheeks. Before he could question her further, Linda continued in a faltering voice.

"Steve's very upset. He thinks it would never have happened if the aliens wouldn't have abducted them. He…he refuses to cooperate and…and he's gotten obstinate. They finally had to restrain him. I've never seen him this way before."

Phil couldn't blame Steve for being bitter. It was evident what had happened. When Steve and Lucienne were levitated aboard the spacecraft, the difference in pressure must have been enough to expand the aneurysm in Lucienne's brain to the bursting point. Oh God, I can't imagine how his friend must feel, Phil thought. He could envisage his own despair if Linda were lying there instead of Lucienne.

"Where is he?"

"C'mon, I'll show you."

Linda led Phil by the hand to the back of the cell. It was shaped like an igloo, tapering down to a circular tunnel which served as a short passageway. They had to crawl on all fours to get through. Phil figured it was about the same height as one of the little robots he encountered. On the other side was a room identical to the one they had just left. The light inside the room was dimmed, as if in shadow. On the far wall Phil saw his lanky friend laying supine on a low table with his feet hanging over the edge. His eyes were closed and his arms resting at his sides. He looked haggard, as if he had just been in a bar-room brawl. According to Linda, it had almost come to that between Steve and the aliens.

An odd-looking machine was bracketed to the top of the table. It was shaped like a U and held Steve's head centered between its two prongs. Red laser beams on either side were boring an intersecting course right through the temporal lobes of his brain. "Oh, God!" Phil wailed. Seeing his friend like this was more than he could stand.

"Turn it off! Turn it off, goddamn it!" The sound of Phil's outcry cracked like a whip in the dead stillness of the cell. Instantly the lasers shut off and the prongs snapped open with a hissing sound. Obviously, somebody was monitoring their every move.

That 'somebody' just came walking through the wall behind them. He had the same similarities in appearance as the Controller, but less wrinkles, Phil opined. The sound of his voice in his head was as authoritative as the Controller's, but less masculine. It also told him right away he was facing the second-in-command of this little foray. His words spoke for themselves.

"I am Orlock, in command of Jovi. We are members of the Interplanetary Council. We did not know of the female's condition prior to her being brought aboard. According to your friend, it was because of our negligence that she is now at minimal existence. That is not true. To us, only an unfortunate delay. We must leave before the forces of evil infiltrate our consciousness. As directed, we will continue to monitor her life force." And with that brief declaration, he spun on his heel and lightly stepped back through the wall. Phil would never forget the feeling of betrayal the alien's words stimulated in his brain. It almost seemed a certainty he was referring to the 'Council' as the forces of evil, causing some unresolved issue between them and the Vrishnis. Phil assumed the Council did not approve of their abductions of human life. He remembered what the Controller had said. The abductions were necessary in order to feed their gluttonous demand for DNA samples. The Council did not seem interested in the fact that it was the Vrishnis last desperate hope for survival of their species. Universal Law was sacrosanct. It kept in play rigid compliance to karmic debt. It was also the Vrishnis death warrant. It was now payback time, and since he and Linda and their friends happened to be at the wrong place at the wrong time, it was time to get the hell out of there. It seemed certain, in Phil's mind, a higher order of Vrishnis were getting ready to revolt. From all the information he learned aboard the vimana, he felt certain the Controller was not one of them. It brought him little comfort. Phil's red flags of warning were coming back to haunt him.

With Linda's help, Phil managed to prop Steve up to a sitting position. Steve's eyes slowly opened, and he gazed at Phil and Linda with a blank look on his face. "It's me, pal," Phil soothed. "Everything's going to be okay. Just hang in there." Steve's befuddled brain finally recognized Phil, clutching his arm like a drowning man in panic.

"She's…she's gone, Phil! My Lulu is gone…" He buried his head in Phil's arms and began convulsing in huge sobs. Steve's spirit was completely broken, Phil, the paramedic, realized. His friend was nothing but an empty shell. He had seen it many times in highly emotional cases when death had been so sudden or unexpected. Sometimes he felt like crying right along with them. It was as if someone very close to him had died too. It was strange. After his senses were dulled from watching the Earth's population being eradicated, he still possessed enough feeling to share a grief-stricken moment with a dear friend. It was a humbling experience for a firefighter who always thought himself as wearing impenetrable armor plating.

CHAPTER 30

Earth Day Plus Ten

    Phil came to realize that he and Linda had lost their former concepts of time and space the first moment they became entangled with extraterrestrial beings. The aliens had the ability to manipulate molecular structure at will, changing it into whatever form suited their purposes. Flying through space and walking through walls were just ordinary feats for them. He remembered in one of Edgar Cayce's readings, he stated that Atlanteans were able to control the energy forces in their bodies through mind control. Somehow they boosted the electrical impulses of the brain by way of using the energy in crystals. Cayce claimed that by tapping into unused power cells of the brain, ones that mankind, over the millennia, had let atrophy through their evolutionary cycles, the latent force still remaining could convert the atomic particles of carbon-based matter into pure energy for brief spurts. These mental powers were passed on through reincarnation.

    He and Linda were also dealing with a multi-dimensional entity that could twist time around as easily as he could position the hands of a clock. The three dimensions Phil grew up with—height, width and breadth—were irrelevant terms in light of time displacement. By Linda's perception, he had only been gone a few minutes, whereas in his reality, it had been hours, perhaps even days. Phil didn't argue the point. There would be time later to enlighten Linda of his sojourn aboard the vimana. Right now, they had to deal with a more important issue.

Because of Steve's refusal to leave Lucienne's side, Phil and Linda were having a difficult time convincing him that they needed his help. They agreed that, in Steve's distraught condition, there was no telling what he might do. It was not wise to leave him alone with Lucienne. But, as much as they argued with him, it was to no avail. Steve had entrenched himself next to the sarcophagus and was adamant in his refusal to leave Lucienne's side. It was like watching a leaf wither at the end of a dead branch.

As a means of coping with the situation, Phil and Linda devised a plan. Both of them would set out in different directions for short periods of time before reporting back to the sarcophagus. Phil defended this plan by thinking there had to be a clue somewhere, some kind of sign that would show them the way home. By splitting up, they could cover more territory in less time. Sooner or later, Phil realized, they would be trapped here once the Vrishnis decided to pull out of the Council and take off for greener pastures. It would be a lot safer for all of them to escape nice and quiet-like before Malik came charging in with the cavalry, he thought. The whole idea was crazy. None of them should have been there. Perhaps subconsciously Phil's psyche was performing some kind of test to see how far he could go before insanity set in. Once it did he was sure everything would start making sense.

The sheer magnitude of Jovii's complexity kept Phil in constant awe. Only a thin line separated reality from

fantasy. Most times he couldn't tell the difference.
Besides the variety of spacecraft, the main gallery consisted of mountains of light that looked incredibly beautiful, functioning for purposes he could only imagine.
Wraithlike forms, concentrated into energized balls of light, flashed by in highways of translucent tubes that reached to all corners of the giant chamber. Everywhere he looked, cylindrical columns of whirling atoms manifested themselves as blinding towers of luminous energy. And overshadowing it all were the cells.

Stepping inside one of them made Phil's skin crawl. There was a subdued, funereal atmosphere about them that brought on sordid memories. It was like when he was a kid, his parents used to force him to go with them to pay his respects to some distant relative he never met or knew, and never wanted to meet or know even when they were alive. That's what he felt like now—an intruder. Human flotsam, representing earth's five indigenous races, were lined up in perpendicular rows like stalks of corn in a corn field. Confined in cocoons of blue fluorescent light, their waxen features appeared to be held in a state of suspended animation. Every cell Phil entered held up to twenty of these unfortunates, their frozen faces portraying an air of unsuspecting peacefulness. Some were fully clad, some nude, others wore only the scantiest of clothing, as if they had just been summoned to a 'come as you are' party. Future ova and sperm contributors, Phil thought sadly. It was like walking among a bunch of mesmerized zombies.

From their style of dress, Phil saw that many of them were seamen and airmen. They seemed to come from different time periods, he noted, and their uniforms spelled a wide range of nationalities. One luckless fellow stood out from all the rest in his cell, his twisted lips set in a sardonic grin. He was wearing a policeman's uniform and sporting an unusually thick mustache and bushy eyebrows.

It was Sergeant Putnam! And there was no way he could get him out either, Phil lamented silently to himself. Every time he approached one of the lighted capsules was like walking toward an open furnace. The heat became unbearable and he had to quickly back off. The whole scene repulsed him, making him terminate his tour through the cells, never to return.

At every turn, Phil found himself irrevocably drawn toward the spacecraft on the ground floor. This was where it was happening, he decided. This was where a truly remarkable force was being consummated between the machines and the solar fires raging outside. Some of the smaller ships were being force-fed life-giving energy into the very fabric of their skin. Running his fingertips lightly over their surfaces, Phil could feel microscopic spores nursing like sucklings. These craft were living, breathing organisms! Scientists had speculated that some UFOs could be biological life forms, but to actually confirm their wild hypotheses was mind-boggling.

One of these life forms had a peculiar lozenge-shaped configuration, approximating the same dimensions as an old-fashioned Philadelphia streetcar. It had brilliantly lit reddish-orange light emanating from apertures along its sides. By exercising a little imagination, which wasn't too hard to do in this indecipherable world of oddities, Phil and Linda imagined the craft as a geomorphic trolley. Because it provided an earthly model to boost their morale, they made it their rendezvous point as well as their inspirational symbol.

Phil was returning from one of his exploratory trips when he spotted Linda standing next to the trolley, a perplexed look on her face. In the lessened gravity, he landed beside her in double-quick time. Before he had a chance to ask her what was wrong, she greeted him with an impatient nod.

"I thought you'd never get here," she snapped. Her concentration was totally centered on the lighted assembly in front of her.

"What's going on?"

"Look for yourself!"

From the trolley's innards emerged a strange-looking creature that literally floated down to them on a silver cloud. He scanned Phil and Linda with unblinking, mechanical eyes. His pupils would repeatedly widen and narrow like a camera lens being constantly adjusted. He was about five feet tall and extremely thin, his body wrapped in a form-fitting suit with a hood over his pointed head. His nose was long, almost spiked. His mouth was a precise slit as if incised by a surgeon's scalpel. He opened his hand, palm up, toward Phil, revealing what looked like a large agate. Phil hesitated. "It looks like he wants you to take it," Linda urged.

As soon as Phil's fingers closed over the strange object, a series of thoughts and word patterns bombarded his brain. He closed his eyes and concentrated, trying to sort out whatever message it was communicating. It was as if a computer started to type out words to him.

"It-is-time-for-your-return-to-earth. Do-not-delay. You-must-not-wait-for-your-male-companion. His-inhibitive-thoughts-will-not-allow-him-to-continue-the-journey-with-you."

Phil looked at Linda with a sinking feeling. The words had settled like lead shots in his stomach. He was sure it was a message from Malik. It sounded like he was abandoning Steve and Lucienne to the wolves.

"Phil! Look!"

Phil followed Linda's pointing finger. A light mauve mist that had magically appeared inside the trolley suddenly revealed Steve cradling Lucienne in his arms. Steve's specter-like body seemed to be walking toward them and yet, he didn't seem to be moving at all. His face looked gaunt and lifeless.

"STEVE!"

"He can't hear you, Phil," Linda explained. "That's a hologram we're looking at."

Phil and Linda could see them as clearly as if their images were being flashed on a movie screen. But she was right, Phil confessed. It was nothing but an illusion.

"What have you done with them?" he yelled. He reached out to grab the creature who had handed him the marble, but it was like grasping thin air. The alien had turned into a disappearing marionette, its dilating pupils diminishing to the size of pinheads before vanishing completely.

"Let's get back to the cell," Linda encouraged. "Maybe they're trying to trick us into thinking they're gone."

By the time they arrived back to the cell, the sarcophagus was empty and Steve was nowhere to be found. Phil and Linda looked at each other guiltily. Now what? Phil wondered. It was too late for recriminations. "Phil! Look at your arm!"

"What are you talking about?"

"Your arm!" Linda reached over and twisted Phil's left forearm so that the fleshy part of it was exposed.

"See for yourself!"

Phil looked down in amazement. His scar was turning a bloody red! He could see the linked triangles as plain as day emerging through the soft material of his uniform. "Does it hurt?" Linda asked.

"No…no it doesn't," Phil mumbled, as if in deep thought. Then, as if bursting out of a thick fog, the significance of it suddenly dawned on him. Intuitively he sprinted for the doorway, grabbing Linda's hand in the process. "Come on! I think I've found our ticket out of here."

CHAPTER 31

Phil and Linda raced back to the trolley. Something was compelling Phil to probe beyond the glittering mask of Jovii, to search even deeper into its mysterious labyrinth of arcane life forms. This unexplained realm of the space station divulged a whole new breeding place of mutations Phil had never dreamed were possible. It was like walking through a waking nightmare—blobs that looked like jellyfish, crabs with metamorphic shells and shapeless amoebae-like invertebrate which were thought to be omnivorous by earth scientists. Crazy as it sounded, these transmogrifications were as much a part of the cosmic enigma as the aliens themselves. They were always in play when reports of bizarre looking creatures were linked with UFO sightings. Phil construed this part of Jovii to be where it all began, a breeding place for experimental DNA samples to nurture and mature. Perhaps someday the Vrishnis would find the right biochemical reaction to empower their own DNA strands to replicate new ones, Phil opined. He remembered what DNA was all about from his high school days in biology class. In a way, he felt sorry for the alien's predicament, but even sorrier for the humanity that was in those cells waiting to be used as specimens.

Suddenly Phil felt a burning sensation coming from his arm. It was almost as if someone were holding a flame against his skin. He stopped, pulling Linda aside. His scar! It was beginning to sizzle like a branding iron.

At the same time, something weird was happening. One of the spacecraft parked near them had suddenly come to life. With disbelieving eyes, Phil's first thought was that he had finally gone over the edge. He was hallucinating like a mad hatter. Thankfully, that wasn't the case...at least not yet. Somehow he had triggered a reaction in one of the machines; a nuts-and-bolts machine, one that was fifty-foot-in-diameter with a bubble top, wrap-around windows, a pewter base and a string of lights spinning around its middle... a vimana!

As the duo stood and watched in fascination, a narrow ramp magically appeared from a rectangular doorway, extending all the way down to their feet. The glowing interior exuded a nebulous atmosphere of fluorescence that looked suggestively warm and inviting.

"It looks like someone is extending us a welcome," Phil said nonchalantly. Inside he was jumping for joy. Now he knew why Ninlil taught him all he wanted to know about a vimana. Certainly it was under the Controller's orders. From the beginning the old master must have taken a liking to the rugged firefighter. Intuitively he knew Phil, and the other humans, would be held hostage once Jovii withdrew from the Council's control. Voila! Stage right...a vimana. The Controller gave them all a means to escape and Phil wasn't about to pass up the opportunity. For the time being, he would leave Malik worry about Steve and Lucienne.

Phil grabbed Linda's hand. It was cold and sweaty. She began to pull away, her eyes fearful. Phil suddenly

realized his wife was reliving her experience in the cave.
He should have anticipated her reaction. Linda had been
beamed directly aboard the mothership. She had never
seen the inside of a vimana before.

"There's nothing to worry about, kid. I've been
through this before. Com'n, trust me." Phil could tell she
wasn't overcome with enthusiasm, but, after giving her
husband a 'you'd better be right,' kind of look, she shuffled
up the ramp beside him. No sooner had they stepped across
the threshold, than the outer hull sealed itself soundlessly
behind them. The garish brightness they had left behind,
was instantly replaced with the soft glow of diffused
lighting inside the vimana. The dead silence made it seem
as though a coffin lid had just closed over their heads.

Phil led Linda up the gradually inclining corridor.
It was so rote in his memory from innumerable practice
sessions with Ninlil, he knew just how many steps to take.
He stopped, facing a blank wall. He knew that, at this spot,
on the other side of that wall, was the control room.

"Listen carefully," Phil said sternly. He was afraid
he was going to screw it up. "Just hold my hand and step
through when I do. And for god's sake, don't let go." It
was imperative she followed his instructions implicitly, he
thought. If their hands slipped apart, his wife would
instantly be part of a new wall decoration...inside the wall!
It was his first solo with somebody else other than Ninlil.

"Step through wh...!"

Phil didn't give her time to think about it. He
gripped her hand tightly, took a deep breath, remembering
Ninlil's mantra of staying focused, and pulled Linda
through the wall with him. A slight tingling sensation

washed over him. Phil had focused his mind into manipulating an energy force inside his brain the alien hybrid had called the Power of the Ki. In the blink of an eye, he and Linda were standing inside the control room.

A cry of amazement escaped Linda's lips. Phil was just as surprised although he didn't dare show it. Whatever happened from now on, he had to show complete confidence in what he did or decided to do in order to get one-hundred per-cent cooperation from Linda. He knew she wasn't ready to go to hell and back with him in blind obedience just yet without some degree of trust he could instill in her. Her defenses and thinking processes were slow. He had to be careful. With the slightest provocation he believed his wife could easily slip back into her defensive mode.

A quick sweep of the small room told Phil it was empty. He would have bet anyone that he and Linda were the only ones aboard. It seemed that was the way it was supposed to be. Linda kept giving him a guarded look.

When Phil began advancing toward the console, his legs suddenly felt as though they were filled with lead. It only took an instant to realize the reason why. Somehow the ship was acting under its own power, supplying its own gravitational field. He and Linda were back to some sense of normalcy again.

The strange hieroglyphics and the perplexing retinue of blinking lights on the console told him about as much information as if he were standing inside the cockpit of a Boeing 747. He desperately tried to recall what Ninlil had taught him. Basically a vimana was built as a shuttle craft. Once in space, the vimana automatically stayed within the confines of the energy fields that traversed the intergalactic voids. Being propelled in one of them was like being sucked inside the eye of a tornado. He remembered that punching a preprogrammed monitoring device would start the whole process working.

Phil feverishly began playing his hands over the console's smooth surface, methodically working his way around the panel. Odd-looking symbols began to appear on the overhead monitors as well as small built-in units inside the console. He was looking for one sign in particular, the only one that made any sense to him at all. Drops of nervous perspiration began to bead his forehead. After a few tense moments of watching his mad scrambling, Linda came over and placed a worried hand on his arm. She probably thinks I'm going daft, Phil thought. He gave her a nervous smile and resolutely continued his search.

Suddenly there it was, etched in brilliant glowing lines, three interlocking pyramids fastened together like arthritic fingers. The symbol was highlighted inside one of the console's monitors. It was the exact duplicate he had espied earlier with the Controller, the same symbol that years ago he and his mother were branded with. It was the earth sign from the start, made up, he suspected, by the same aliens involved in building the Great Pyramid and the two smaller ones of Giza, in Egypt. It was just a matter of pushing a button to start a new sequel of maneuvers into the computer. To Phil, it was the same as pushing the start button in a slot machine to start the graphics going.

The room automatically dimmed. All the overhead monitors suddenly blinked on. At the same time, a flash of light filled the screens. Then blackness. A picture emerged. One of the monitors was showing the image of a large, twisting energy tube. It was emitting a pulsating, greenish phosphorescence that resembled a gigantic glow worm snaking through a black sea freckled with diamonds. The sequence of events were startling. On another monitor, a white blip flickered allusively. At no time did either of them feel any movement or sound from the spacecraft.

"It's gotta be us," Phil muttered.

"What is it?" Linda demanded.

"An energy beam, my dear. A space-time warp through space. That's how the aliens travel. We're in one now, I believe. That's also how they can enter and leave different planet's atmospheres without burning up like shooting stars. That's how we're going to get back, through one of these wormholes. The ship's already on auto-pilot. It looks like we've got a free ride home."

"How do you know that, Phil? And…and walking through walls. What's happening to you?"

Phil had overlooked the fact that his wife hadn't attained the level of awareness he had gained from his communion with the aliens. All she could rationalize aboard Jovii was the all pervading sense that Steve and Lucienne, including Captain Smollet, were never coming back or were already dead. However, Phil still kept the faith in Malik. Somehow the firefighter knew that his friends were safe and still alive. I guess now was as good time as any to let Linda in on his little secret, Phil thought.

"Let's sit down and I'll tell you all about it, kid," he reassured her. "It's a long story."

CHAPTER 32

Earth Day Plus Twelve

Phil and Linda were in the ship's propulsion chamber when a terrific jolt knocked them to the floor. They stood up, only to be hurled to the floor again by another blast. Linda screamed and Phil cursed. This was no time for civilities, he argued with himself.

"We've got to get back to the control room!" Phil shouted as he dashed toward the corridor, remembering to grab hold of Linda's hand before reaching the wall.

After a few more hammering blows and one particular corkscrewing toss that left them in a tangled heap, Phil and Linda eventually managed to reach the control room. Luckily the walls had some flexibility, Phil fancied, or else they would have sustained some broken bones along the way. What he initially guessed was happening proved correct; the reason why the vimana was reacting like a bucking bronco. The monitors confirmed it. The energy tube was going crazy. They had arrived.

"Oh god. Look!" Linda was staring out through the view screen, her body crazed with shock. She began to shudder as she stood steadfast, gazing with disbelieving eyes. This picture was all too familiar to Phil. Chaos was everywhere on a rolling rock obsessed with self-destruction.

Phil's line of sight reluctantly followed the writhing vortex they were in as it disappeared into a heaving, boiling cauldron of fire and smoke. Rising from the ashes were winds spewing massive showers of sparks and liquid flame high into the stratosphere. Subterranean fissures were thrusting newborn land to the surface where there was once fathomless ocean. Nothing was recognizable. Floating chunks of solidified lava made the whole scene look like a jigsaw puzzle yet to be assembled. From Phil's perspective, the original path of the tube they were traveling in had centered somewhere over one of earth's oceans. Where they actually were was anybody's guess.

"Phil, what's happening? Is...is that the earth?"

"Yes. The earth changes have started."

Linda knew, without having to ask, what that meant. A muffled cry poured from her lips as she smothered them with her fist. Her maternal instincts wouldn't hold back. "The kids?"

"Yes. Like I said, Malik assured me our family and friends would be spared. So would Lucienne's."

Phil jockeyed himself into position beside a control lever, one of three which had popped up the moment the earth sign was activated. The handgrip looked like a joystick of a video game, he thought. He remembered that four buttons were recessed in the lever itself. One button operated the main power unit, the others proportionately governed the electrical charges of each sphere in the propulsion chamber. By increasing or decreasing their voltage, the attitude and speed of the craft could be controlled.

But then, Ninlil's warning flashed through his mind. As long as they stayed inside the energy tube, they were safe. Within earth's atmosphere, the vimana used the earth's geomagnetic field for power. It was also the energy tubes' lifeblood. Phil dreaded what would happen without its protection. The fact that the geomagnetic field was being slowly inverted, reversing its polarity, gave them little chance of keeping their protective envelope intact for much longer. Already it was being severely tested. Once the tube disintegrated, earth's thermal barrier would take over, and they would be caught in its grip. The gates of hell were waiting for them on the other side. His eyes locked onto Linda's in a resigned expression of helplessness. There was nothing they could do but wait it out and pray. He crawled over to her and held her in his arms. If Malik was going to make a grand entrance, now would be as good a time as any, Phil prayed under his breath.

Time itself took on a new dimension. To Phil, it was meaningless to know how long it took before your next roller-coaster drop might be your last...five seconds, a minute, five minutes. It was nerve-wracking. If the vimana wasn't plummeting out of control, it was pitching and yawing in stomach wrenching twists and turns. It was almost anticlimactic when the energy tube lost its signal and disappeared off the screen. Only a running scale remained that showed a series of unintelligible markings that were constantly changing. It would be reasonable to assume, Phil thought, that it was measuring atmospheric gases. It suggested only one thing. Vicious volcanic winds (scientists called plumes) had reached up and stripped the vimana of its protective cover before dumping it unceremoniously into an ocean of rarified air. Phil figured the automatic pilot was down. His only remaining hope was that the vimana could sustain enough punishment getting through earth's fiery reentry without burning up. Once that was achieved, the Marianas Trench in the Pacific, at a depth of over thirty-six thousand feet, would do nicely to ride out whatever was happening on the surface.

Easier said than done. By the time Phil got back behind a control lever, the conditions outside had deteriorated drastically. The vimana started shaking as if something was trying to tear it apart. As the buffeting intensified, it was underscored by an ominous screeching noise that reminded Phil of a blown transaxle in a car, except indescribably louder. He concluded from that sound that the machine couldn't stand much more punishment. Several lights had flickered off on the console and the liquid inside the attitude indicators had darkened and gone still.

Phil clutched the control lever in desperation and tried maneuvering the wildly bucking machine. But his tremulous fingers, relaying electronic signals to the spheres, proved no match for the growing air turbulence raging outside. A tremendous groan suddenly erupted from deep inside the spacecraft. It was as though its innards were crying out in pain.

Without any warning, the vimana became a replica of a rocket taking off. The control lever was savagely ripped out of Phil's hands and he suddenly became airborne. He heard an anguished chorus of screams in the background, then realized it was his and Linda's matching contraltos as their bodies collided in mid-air before somersaulting to a stop somewhere between where the wall and the view screen joined together. The spacecraft had done a version of a death spiral and was now savagely spinning in an uncontrollable crash dive. The resultant centrifugal force kept Phil and Linda pinned down like a couple of mannequins buried in cement.

Linda began to sob. Gathering his remaining strength, Phil reached over her quivering body and held his wife tightly. Below them, through the view screen, they were getting a bird's eye view of the maelstrom coming up to engulf them. The heat was building rapidly. They were now entering the earth's troposphere, the last of its fiery shields. Phil could see the outer hull of the vimana begin glowing a cherry red. He estimated their speed as that of a falling meteor. The noise of the hull breaking up filled their ears with agonizing, ear-shattering snaps and pops that sounded like a can being crushed in a giant's fist. "SHUT YOUR EYES!" he yelled at the top of his voice. It made no difference. Linda couldn't hear him anyway. She had feinted.

The incinerating heat overtook them quickly. From Phil's perspective, the survivors on earth probably saw the UFO as nothing more than a blazing ball of light.

CHAPTER 33

Earth Day Plus Thirteen

Phil woke up looking at a powder blue sky with
white cottony clouds floating by. The sun was a blazing
golden-yellow. The air was fresh with the scent of Lily-of-
the-Valley. It reminded him of his mom's favorite flower.
Spread-eagled alone on the side of a sloping hill, he
casually glanced down and saw his attire had reverted back
to a standard jumpsuit. He recalled it was the same skin
tight material he had worn the first time he met Malik.
Struggling to his feet, he could faintly hear birds chirping
in the background. A stand of maple and birch, partially
shading a patch of wild flowers, stood at the bottom of the
hill. The site looked awfully familiar. Wherever he was, he
felt safe and secure. In the distance he could see a modern
city with lofty walls of stone and concrete. To his left, not
more than a block away, stood a tall suspension bridge
spanning a wide, rushing river. The water flowing around
the pillars was swift and silent, alive with glistening eddies.
He would have bet anybody it was springtime, when the ice
is melting and the currents are surging strong between
lakes. The Great Lakes! It was the first thing that came to
mind. If true, the bridge had to be the Ambassador Bridge.
It spanned the Detroit River between Windsor, Ontario and
Detroit, Michigan. The river then took a dogleg to the
right, its fast current following the land's contour not far

from where he stood before emptying into Lake Erie further down the coast. But something was different about the skyline, he thought. The buildings seemed to have an architecture all their own; old-fashioned dregs from the past. He focused his attention on one building in particular. He studied it for several minutes. Yes, now he recalled. It was the old Colton building in downtown Detroit. It was one of the original skyscrapers. It always had that Elizabethan flair that made it stand out from the construction boom of the eighties. But he had thought the building was torn down years ago to make room for a new convention center. Phil shrugged his shoulders in resignation. There was little doubt left. It was the city of Detroit in the days of his youth.

Phil started down the hill toward the trees. Just below him, over the tree line, was a wharf with attached steps leading down to the water. Through the branches he caught sight of a wooden ferry boat heading across the gap toward it. There was no sign of Linda. Phil wasn't particularly concerned at the moment. For the present, it seemed their lives were predetermined, and, according to Malik, it didn't include dying. He was starting to get nervous. As he kept walking toward the river, for the first time in his life, he felt he was living in a bubble. The bubble kept expanding to include more and more surprises. Sooner or later, that bubble was going to burst. And when it did, he was afraid of what he was going to discover.

A distant toot on a steam whistle made him stop and look up. Down by the riverbank, the ferryboat was just tying up to the dock. A few minutes later a crowd of people emerged. The sounds of laughter and talking filled the air. Phil wasn't surprised at the men and women's attire, or their hair-do's. Definitely the style during his high school days, he recalled. Something made him pause. A lone figure had broken away from the rest and began climbing the hill toward him. It was a man wearing a checkered flannel shirt with double pockets. A man who was favoring his right leg. There was only one person he knew who had a limp and would wear a long-sleeved shirt in summery weather. Phil's heart skipped a beat. The fedora hat, cocked at a rakish angle, was the giveaway.

"DAD!"

Phil choked out the word. It was him, flesh and blood! He appeared the same as he always remembered him. Phil broke into a run toward him, stumbling and falling in his excitement. He hastily picked himself up, continuing his mad scramble down the hill, keeping his eyes fixed on his dad's extended arms waiting to greet him.

"Oh Dad...Dad, is it really you?" Phil hugged him tightly for fear it was only an illusion. He could feel his strong arms squeezing him back affectionately.

"Yes...yes, it's me all right, Son." His voice sounded strong, reassuring, just what Phil needed to hear at the moment. Then he held Phil at arm's length and scrutinized him closely. "You haven't changed much. You look as trim as the last time I saw you."

Phil gave him a puzzled look.

"You probably don't remember, do you?" His dad had a big smile on his face. His shiny gold tooth, the one that had replaced one of his molars while he was in the army, gleamed under the shadow of his fedora. That was his trademark, along with the faded pair of gabardines he liked to loaf around in. Phil remembered crawling up on the lap of those worn trousers on many occasions when he was a little boy.

"Dad, what is this place? What are you doing here?" He wasn't thinking too clearly at this point or he would have known the buildings, the bridge, the ferryboat were only make- believe, that his dad wasn't really standing there in front of him, that it was all an illusion.

"It's my home for a while, Son. My turn to move on will eventually come. But don't fool yourself. I'm as real to you now as if I were back in your time." He gave Phil an extra squeeze as he draped his burly arm around his son's shoulders. Then he led him down the slope to the nearest tree and indicated for Phil to join him under the shade. The scent of Lily-Of-The-Valley seemed strongest here. The whispering breeze, soughing gently through the branches, made a faint rustling sound that lulled him. The feelings Phil was deriving from this place felt so good, he wished he could stay here with his dad longer than he knew he could.

The wharf was a short distance away. The ferryboat's truncated bow, securely butted against the wooden planks, made a creaking noise that carried its mournful tune to them. Oddly enough, nobody else was around to hear it.

"Dad, I don't know where to begin." Phil's voice cracked. "Cayce's predictions are all coming true. My friends and I have been chosen to stay behind after the earth changes. I've seen what it looks like…it's horrible…millions of people. Linda and I were taken by aliens. I met a deity named Malik. He said the New Age was coming. I stole a vimana and…"

"Slow down son…slow down. I know where you're coming from. It's a learning process. It's a bumpy trip, that's for sure. But just think of the growing experience you will gain from this. You've been given the chance to take shortcuts very few souls even dream of." His words held a wistful edge to them. "But it's not like you to be so bummed out." His dad arched his eyebrows in that familiar fashion of his whenever he was displeased. "Hell, you've been in tougher scrapes than this before. Remember the duplex fire?"

Of course, how could he forget it? It happened shortly after he had finished basic training. He was part of a search-and-rescue team, looking for victims reportedly trapped on the second floor of an old tenement. Somehow he had become separated from his crew and found himself alone in the middle of a room so thick with smoke he could have cut it with a knife. The fire had eaten into the attic space and was fully involved by the time it reached him. Usually when a fire vents itself, the firefighters can see well enough to find an exit. Not this time. Where Phil was situated, he was in a dead-end hallway. A thick pocket of smoke was trapped, with no way of escaping, except through a blackened window at the end of the hall. Unfortunately Phil didn't know that, or he could have held his breath long enough to reach it. So. he did what he was trained to do, follow the wall back to a doorway or window that offered him a way out.

To every law enforcement officer that protects the streets or a firefighter battling fires, there is always

Murphy's Law to contend with. It never fails. If something can possibly go wrong, it will. In Phil's case, it did. The regulator on his air tank froze up. It was in the middle of winter and the outside temperature was minus three degrees Fahrenheit. It turned out the duplex was abandoned and without heat, the temperature inside was not that much warmer. It seemed his exhalations, ridden with moisture, formed a pinch of ice just large enough to block the valve shut that opened and closed the airway to his air tank. Phil remembered going down for the count, choking and gasping all the way till he hit the floor. Down there wasn't much better either.

"Uh-huh. I remember what happened quite well, Dad." Flashes kept coming back. An ancient skylight in the roof collapsed over his head. That allowed a perfect vent for the trapped smoke to escape. It was just short of a miracle that not one shard of glass had rained its deadly guillotines on Phil. Somehow he was able to deliver himself out of a fog of semi-consciousness long enough to get out safely. "But how did you...?"

"Just because you can't see me on your wave length doesn't mean to say I can't see you on mine. You're destined for better things than dying in some rat hole, Son," he explained. "You had your whole life ahead of you yet. I remember you were dating that cute nurse then. Later, you brought in to the world two fine kids that wouldn't have happened otherwise. There were times when you had to learn through hardships. But now, that's all behind you. You have more important things to think about."

His Dad's words brought a hollow feeling to Phil's disturbing thoughts. Also a touch of sadness. Phil realized his meeting with his Dad was nothing more than an interlude, a brief respite in order to renew his resolve. The blueprint had already been drawn. Earth would not remain the same upon his return. A period of adjustment and rebuilding lay ahead. All well and good, he reasoned. But, something else was stirring in Phil's brain that he couldn't quite put his finger on. Something his dad had said. His turn would come eventually. It seemed his dad was in neither heaven nor hell, but in a holding place for souls waiting to be reincarnated. Apparently reincarnation was a big motivator and was the fastest way to work off your karma. Free will was still the determining factor. To Phil it smacked of a subtle reference to fate—from the time you are born, you resume the long road back to the Source. There always exists the probability of something occurring in your future that will block your path, regardless of free will. The definitive word is probability. Simply put, it is based on the assumption that something will occur eventually, no matter what or how long it may take. It is written that probability will influence all occurrences in the long term. The unknown factor. It could be the answer he was looking for, something Cayce touched upon in several of his readings. It was an edict that kept repeating itself over and over again in his subconscious, something that Ninlil had once said to him—do not always believe what you see, but see what you believe. The first part was self-explanatory. If you believed in something strong enough, it would happen. That's what he gathered from the second part. In Phil's case, how could he believe in something that would never happen. He lost hope of a compassionate God long ago. Phil was still waiting for God to show mercy for the most defenseless of all His flock, but he wasn't holding his breath on that one either.

Just then a soft swishing noise interrupted Phil's reverie. He nonchalantly turned his head toward the sound. The ferryboat was just pulling away from the dock. "Remember that ferryboat?" Dad interjected. "It used to take us to Boblo Island."

"I sure do," Phil replied. Back in the sixties, Boblo Island was the closest thing to Disneyland. His family used to have so much fun together then when he was young, he recalled. But after Jeremy was born, things changed. "What happened, Dad? I remember when you and Mom used to be so happy."

"Yes, I know. I thought when your brother came along it would help your mother and I stay together, but, I'm afraid, all it did was drive us further apart. That's why I left. I knew as long as I stayed around, you and Jeremy would never get any peace and quiet."

"But why, Dad?" Phil persisted. "It was like everything fell apart. I missed you terribly when you left." The long-ago memory was like a raw sore that had festered so long in his mind he had to have it expunged once and for all.

His father looked at his son beseechingly. His soft gray eyes were shaded with remorse.

"It wasn't your mother's fault, Son. It was my own stubbornness. I just couldn't understand at the time why God allowed it to happen."

Phil wasn't sure he was hearing correctly. Allow what to happen? He didn't have to ask. It seemed his father was going to explain regardless, if for no other reason but to relieve some mysterious burden he had been carrying around all these years. "Remember when I told you about the time your mother and I brought you to Duchesnay Falls?"

Phil nodded.

"You wandered off while we were making love. By the time we realized you were gone, we had no idea you might have fallen into the creek. It's when we started looking for you..." Dad shook his head to shake the cobwebs of time away. Phil noticed he was having a difficult time finding the right words.

"That's when we ran into them...beings from another world. Their saucer was hidden high up in the bush where nobody from the highway could see them."

Phil was completely stunned. If a bomb had exploded next to him, he wouldn't have been more surprised.

"Your mother and I tried to escape, but they shot a beam of light at us that stopped us in our tracks. They took your mother inside the ship while they left me there, paralyzed, for what seemed like hours."

It was hard to believe what his Dad was saying was true. Yet, hearing him describe what must have been an horrific experience, especially for his mother, Phil was left with a deeper understanding of something he had puzzled over ever since his dreams of the little people began.

"Soon afterward, your mother started having these terrible nightmares," the old man continued. "Our regular doctor referred her to a Doctor Jessup. Besides being a psychoanalyst, he was also a hypnotist. He was able to regress her memory back to the time of the abduction. It seemed she was implanted with something. It was only later we found out she was pregnant with Jeremy."

Any outsider listening to his dad's discourse wouldn't have questioned it, Phil thought. Everything pointed toward he and Mom conceiving Jeremy during their lovemaking session at Duchesnay Falls. But that was not the case. "There's something else that happened to me in the war besides having my knee blown apart, Son, something only your mother knew about. I think that's why the aliens didn't take me too. The land mine that tore up my knee also prevented me from ever having children again."

Another bombshell just went off. Things like this just didn't happen in real life, Phil exclaimed to himself.

"At the time I couldn't cope with it," his dad went on. He tilted his head back against the tree and closed his eyes. "That's why I left, Son. It was better that way."

Phil and his dad sat in abject silence for a few moments. All that could be heard was the screech of a seagull high overhead. His dad's confession explained a lot of things. Jeremy's amazing knowledge of the universe, for instance, and his deep-felt misgivings for Planet Earth. Phil lifted his eyes toward a universe that covered a multitude of different species reaching out to be heard. Cayce predicted that the earth changes could be staved off by a higher consciousness of being who were most desirous to return through reincarnation. Many Atlanteans were in that pool of thought. The Old Testament had many allegories and metaphors about angels who were reincarnated as messengers of God. Many theologians have always thought it was the truer version of the Bible. A plethora of secular changes were made in The New Testament by Constantine the Great and the Council of Nicaea in 325 AD, and in Constantinople in 381 AD. that made it suspect of being a conspiracy. What was so important that the life and teachings of Jesus Christ, as mostly written by the apostles in the New Testament, had to be compromised by Church intervention? Reincarnation. Any references to it in Christian doctrine was considered heresy and condemned from that day forward. Scholars have debated for centuries whether there was a hidden agenda that may have influenced Constantine to hide what may have been told about Jesus from his original teachings. Historians claim something was confidentially revealed behind closed doors at the Council of Nicaea that was never recorded. According to Cayce's thousands of readings of past lives, eliminating reincarnation from Judeo culture was tantamount to denying Jews the right to communicate directly with God. History shows many new sects branched out and started their own religions during that same period. Their fight for parity continued through the Crusades.

Phil blinked his eyes to clear the sound of distant voices. He and his dad stood up. Phil's gaze was fixed on a pinpoint of light just hovering above the horizon. What looked like a star washed out by the sun's brightness took on new significance as it steered toward the hill where he and his dad were standing. It quickly began taking on distinctive form and substance. It piqued Phil's curiosity. "Look, Dad!" He pointed toward the strange light. "What is that?"

Dad squinted his eyes and held up his hand to block the sun. A few seconds passed before a gleam of recognition broadened his face.

"I've been expecting them," was all he said.

They watched as a shiny object plummeted down from the lower stratosphere. Phil judged it falling faster than a jet. A growing, pulsating energy source as bright as a miniature sun suddenly manifested itself into a elliptically shaped spacecraft. It stopped on a dime, remained stationary high over the bridge for a brief second, then began a slow, curving descent in their direction. Its dimensions were as big as a modern sport stadium.

Phil and his dad began walking partway up the hillside to obtain a better view. The mysterious craft was giving off an intense luminosity. As it drew nearer, its details became more pronounced as the luminosity diminished proportionately to their speed. Neither one of them could hear a sound. Through the subdued glare Phil could make out multiple rows of windows encircling the ship. Its bulk eclipsed the sun like a giant's hand smothering a firefly. It quickly dropped from view to the other side of the hill. He glanced at his dad questioningly.

"I believe you got guests, Son. Come, let's go greet them." To Phil's perspective, the spacecraft had looked strikingly familiar.

CHAPTER 34

Earth Day Plus Thirteen

Cresting the hill, Phil and his dad surveyed the grandiose spectacle before them. The spacecraft had landed in a large empty space reserved for, as a sign was advertising, a new roller coaster that would be breaking ground soon. Next to it was a crop of evergreens that looked like little toy trees in a train set. Phil continued to survey the scene closely for any sign of movement on the giant ship. He saw that it wasn't as big as Jovii, but respectable nonetheless. Reverting to his kid days, he couldn't help compare it to a Buck Rogers space cruiser. It looked sleek and fast. It rested on four cylindrical struts that supported a combination of multi-colored lights rotating around a bulging perimeter. A large rounded dome with rectangular windows crowned the huge superstructure. He could see movement behind the openings.

"Dad, what's going on?" All of a sudden he got the feeling the balloon he was walking in for so long was getting ready to burst. His dad gave Phil a sly wink and said, "If you don't hurry up, you're going to miss the show." Phil began high-stepping it down the hill. A small group of people were just detaching themselves from beneath the shadow of the spacecraft.

Oh my god! Phil's pounding heart began to beat faster with every stride. They're not who I think they are, are they? he panted.

But they were! Even from a fifty yard distance, Phil could pick out Linda's slim features as she walked next to two more familiar figures. He broke away from his dad at the same time Linda began running toward him. They hungrily gave each other a bear hug and a quick kiss.

She gasped, "Oh, Phil. You won't believe what's happened. Lucienne's back! She's back!"

Peering over her shoulder, Phil tried to focus with bleary eyes on the rest of the group.

There was Malik, appearing the same as he saw him last, standing off to the side dressed in immaculate white. In fact, everyone's attire duplicated his own Everyone human, that is. Nearby were what looked like the two hairy bipeds he and Linda had confronted at the cove. Their gangly arms drooped to their sides, their fiery eyes closed, they stood like large stuffed toy gorillas. They didn't look so scary now, he thought. But it was the couple who were walking hurriedly to greet him, arm in arm, that almost made his knees buckle. If it wasn't for his wife's support, Phil's legs would have completely collapsed. It was Steve and Lucienne, giggling and grinning from ear to ear. Yet, that was only part of the shock awaiting his benumbed senses.

"You look as handsome as I've always pictured you, Phil," Lucienne said in her soft voice. She had dispensed with the sunglasses, her eyes shone with vibrant recognition. She was seeing Phil for the first time.

Phil was speechless as Lucienne gave him an affectionate hug, then stepped back, looking him up and down before adding somewhat kiddingly to Steve, "So that's what Paul Anka looks like, huh? Classy." Somehow Phil mumbled something unintelligible, his mind still too shell-shocked to think of a witty reply. Then Steve came up and gave his friend a hug and a warm handshake. "It's good to be back among the living, eh?" His voice had that old Errol Flynn timbre to it again.

"You Canucks sure know how to scare a guy," Phil retorted half-jokingly. "I gave you all up for dead."

"And we would be, pal, if it wasn't for that guy over there," Steve declared, nodding his head toward Malik as the celestial was slowly approaching them. Malik waved as he saw Phil looking in his direction. Phil started to wave back but stopped short when he spotted a man dragging a few paces back. It was someone he was used to seeing for years when growing up, and occasionally since. He had a big grin on his face as he came up to Phil.

"Jeremy!" was all Phil's vocal chords could muster. His brother's light complexion, pear-shaped eyes and slender features seemed to stand out sharper now that the story was told, but it didn't take away the love and commitment they shared. Phil reached out in welcome.

"Hi, Brother," came the reply as both brothers wrapped their arms around each other tightly. "I thought I'd tag along, just in case. I figured you could use some of my star wisdom," saying it with tongue in cheek.

"I'm glad you could make it," Phil choked. An idea suddenly struck him. Now would be a good opportunity to introduce his dad to everybody.

"Dad," Phil hollered over his shoulder. "Come meet..."

As he swung around his words caught in his throat. He wasn't there. Phil could have sworn his dad was right behind him a moment ago. Somewhat flustered, he looked in all directions. It was when he happened to glance up that he saw a solitary figure, wearing an old fedora, standing on the brow of the hill waving to him.

"DAD...DAD...NO! COME BACK!" Phil started toward him but Malik's presence stood in his way. Malik gently put his hand on Phil's arm. The firefighter could feel a deep warmth radiating from his touch.

"Your father cannot return with us, Phillip. His mission is done. Now you must return to your world where you belong and he must return to his."

A tremor ran the gauntlet of Phil's backbone. It sent a shiver right through his body. He knew Malik was right, but still...couldn't he make an exception so he could be with his dad just one more minute? He looked at Malik, pleading with his eyes. He beseeched him. Surely Malik could read his mind. Please grant me this one last request.

Linda came over and slipped her arm around her husband's waist. "Come, darling. It's time to go home."

Phil held on to her for support as they slowly made their way back to the spacecraft. He looked back to get one last glimpse of his father raising his arm, his fingers touching his forehead in a farewell salute.

CHAPTER 35

Earth Day Plus Fourteen

All of them were ushered into a large, rotunda-like room. It was not at all what Phil had come to expect aboard a spaceship. Instead of being surrounded by a superior technology that pushed the envelope by ordinary standards, this alien craft could not be described in any way alien. It had a wide balcony circumventing its upper half, while its lower half was decorated with a luxurious resort atmosphere of beautiful paintings and murals on the walls, including statues portraying busts of people with unusual Nordic features. Sandwiched in-between all this was a colorful assortment of sofas, chairs and plush carpet. Doorways led off to unknown destinations and TV monitors seemed to be everywhere. Phil was pleased to discover it had all the trappings of accommodating ordinary-sized humans instead of three-and-a-half-foot humanoids with hypnotizing eyes and automatons that carried automatic stun guns.

Inside lighting came from suspended globes that glowed a milky white. Most intriguingly, several men and women stood on the balcony. They were human in form, perfect specimens, just like Malik, with silvery suits and long golden hair. Some were leaning on the banister looking down at the visitors, while others were engaged in quiet conversations among themselves. It all looked so informal. Phil saw that they were joined by some forty other people. Malik said their little party was only one of many that would reach out to every corner of the globe. There would be more to follow after them. They were the first contingent of "chosen ones," he had said, as were others who had preceded them in other earth cycles. They were to begin the healing process.

Malik stood in front of the group and began to speak in a gentle voice. Phil could hear him quite clearly even though he was standing a few feet away. It was as if a built-in receiver was amplifying the words inside his head. "Each of you will learn how to foster understanding...how to tune into different vibrations...how to sensitize yourselves to others so that you can become better receptors, "said Malik. "You will accomplish this by channeling your energies through a third eye, a psychic eye, that will give you the power to attune yourself to a person's aura. The auras' colors will tell you about that person, about their positive and negative tendencies. This will enable you to help those who want help. By so doing they can break loose from their earthly bonds and attain spiritual freedom. Do not be discouraged by initial failures. Let the love of the Creator be your guide."

The entire group was led into a large darkened room. There, in the center, suspended in mid-air and slowly rotating as if on a spit, was the largest diamond crystal Phil had ever laid his eyes on. It was the size of a small house. Rays of iridescence flowed outward from its shimmering surface, like heat waves radiating off hot pavement. Phil immediately could feel its hypnotic qualities infiltrate his consciousness. Changing light patterns bandied back and forth inside its multifaceted prism like a giant sparkler. The colorful streamers of light captivated his attention, fascinating him as would a schoolchild at a fireworks display. He listened raptly to its subtle whisper. 'The peace and comfort you derive from this light will be manifest in you. Touch it and share in its power.' Phil could feel its energy field beginning to draw him out, strengthening his resolve.

Tentatively, Phil reached out. Lucienne, standing next to him, gave him a confident smile. He suddenly realized her reborn eyes, aglow with anticipation, would give her a new awareness of life. He could feel some of those same emotions stirring in him as a steady flow of kinetic energy coursed through his veins. He could feel its insurgent powers swirling about inside his body as though he had just received an overdose of adrenaline.

Sounds, vibrations, all blending together to form nerve receptors in his brain. Phil was amazed that his perception was greatly heightened by the crystal. He could actually receive thoughts without his brain having to pick up on them through mental telepathy. It was like taking a short cut through someone's auditory system. His temporal lobes enabled him to activate a subliminal process that was humanly impossible to duplicate. He could actually communicate in whatever language he chose and only be understood by the person he was talking to. It was an extraordinary gift from God to help him accomplish his tasks.

Suddenly Phil could feel his wife's touch next to him. She was also gazing into the crystal, captured by it.

Then, as if by some unspoken command, the rays separated before them. A portal embroidered with a bluish-white light appeared. It was an opening through which they could see luxuriant foliage and a vault of blue sky. The foliage was part of a verdant forest interspersed across the horizon with an assemblage of lakes, rivers, plains and mountains. Both saw it as a tapestry condensed into an overall view of what earth looked like at the beginning of their journey.

Phil pulled Linda toward him. It was as if an unseen force was holding Phil back from going through the opening. He was frightened.. It was the first time in his adult life he was really afraid of where he stood with God. For most of his career as a firefighter/paramedic, he kept God at bay in his own personal life. He had become disenchanted with a merciless and uncaring Being who continued to persecute youngsters that could not fend for themselves. He defiantly stood up against a Power that he challenged more times than not. Phil lost count of the amount of times he literally begged for God to stop the carnage. He had given up and was now at the point of capitulation. He looked over at his wife. She knew her husband's dilemma. God would not forget his mockery. Then, she looked again. She couldn't believe what she was seeing on her husband's face. He was hearing something she wasn't. Then came the game changer. It was a voice she was also hearing this time; a most holy, angelic voice that sent both their hearts flying through space. *Allow the path of My love for humankind stand true. Let your free will roam the passages of My House until your condemnations are no longer.* It was at that instant Phil's bitterness against God vanished completely. A heavy weight had just been lifted from his soul. At last he felt truly unencumbered with doubts. God's mercy had always been there when he asked for it. It was just that it was never needed to begin with. God's love was always there first. There was never any suffering in God's house. The souls of the innocents Phil had thought perished were in God's hands long before rescuers arrived on the scene.

The portal was still there, still waiting, beckoning them both to enter.

Phil gave Linda a sidelong look. By the look on her face, she saw wonderment in her husband's eyes. She was ready to follow his lead. He squeezed her hand and pulled her nearer. She answered with an intrepid squeeze of her own. Phil gave her one of his best Bogie impersonations as they stepped through the portal together: "This could be the beginning of a beautiful friendship." Even she had to crack a smile at that one.

CHAPTER 36

November 24—9:07 P.M.—Bruce Peninsula

Phil could feel cool, circulating air nuzzling his face and neck. It wasn't exactly comfortable, he thought, because it was downright cold. He was freezing. He began to stir. He felt as if he had just dozed off for a minute. He could hear the sound of the car engine purring in the background. He bolted straight up, wide awake.

Like a gushing cataract, Phil's brain was suddenly inundated with an outpouring of nightmarish scenes. Linda's hollering and screaming…the mad dash to the car…hairy creatures with glaring red eyes staring down at them.

Phil whirled around in his seat. It was pitch black outside. There was a gibbous moon shining through his side window, but still more than enough light, he thought, not to warrant such darkness. It took him a minute to get reoriented. No wonder. The windshield and windows were covered with snow. It was snowing outside! He turned on the wipers. He gazed into the darkness in the direction of the clearing, silently praying he wouldn't see anything moving. A solid mass of trees and underbrush, covered with an inch of snow, blocked his view.

A touch on his shoulder made him jump three inches off the seat.

"Sorry. I didn't mean to scare you," came a feminine voice next to him. His wife's voice had a sleepy texture to it, intermingled with a scratchy yawn.

"What hap...!" Linda's sentence snapped off into a stifled shriek as she suddenly remembered where she was. She instinctively crouched down in her seat and began curling into a defensive ball.

"It's okay, it's okay," Phil soothed quickly. The last thing he wanted to hear was her screaming in his ear again. "I think they're gone. Quit worrying. I would venture to guess we're alone now." The memories of what happened came rushing back. It all happened in a matter of seconds. But, according to the dashboard clock, there were two hours missing.

Linda paused, then began to relax a little. Her eyes became furtive darts as they surveyed the scene in front of her. "I'm cold, Phil."

Phil then realized the air conditioner was blowing out cold air. He shut it down and turned the thermostat in the opposite direction. It was a far cry from earlier when he was trying his best to keep him and Linda from melting to death.

Suddenly a toneless voice cut in on the radio, preset to catch all emergency news broadcasts. "Good Evening. This is Oliver Schumacher reporting. The date is November 24th—the time, 9:15 P.M. Eastern Standard Time. Here are the latest news developments from the BBC...Scientists from around the world are still puzzled by the sudden stoppage of the tilting earth. Emmett Carlysle, the world renowned astronomer from the Laboratory for Planetary Studies at Cornell University, declared it a miracle. He was quoted as saying the event was unprecedented in the history of the planet. The earth's rotational imbalance returned to its former axial tilt of 23.4 degrees at 20:07 Greenwich Mean Time. At this hour, St. Peters Square at the Vatican in Rome is filling with thousands of people waiting for Pope Thomas to make an announcement of the many visions of the Blessed Virgin Mary being reported around the world. Also, Chinese troops massing at the Pakistani border are voluntarily retreating back to a demilitarized zone until the United Nations sets up permanent sanctions between countries. The Organization for Environmental Studies has reported new laws dedicated to world-wide anti-pollution will be forthcoming in the next council session. It will be strictly enforced, through the U.N. Protection League. Stand-by for further bulletins on this BBC station...

Phil and Linda stared at each other with the same question on their lips. What happened to them in the past two hours? Phil lighted up the face of his watch. The cadmium dials confirmed the missing time. He remembered driving straight through to Tobermory after leaving the cove, stopping briefly only to see that they weren't being followed. Strange. Now they were back at the cove, or did they ever leave it to begin with?

"Stay here. I'm going to go check the clearing."

He opened the car door and was thankful to be confronted by cold air, the norm for this time of year in this latitude. He only wished he would have brought a warmer jacket. Grabbing one out of the trunk, he was halfway across the road when he was intercepted by Linda tugging at his sleeve. "Don't leave me here all alone," she chided.

They cautiously edged their way into the deeper shadows of the trees. The woods were alive with the night sounds of nocturnal creatures. Somehow it gave them a comforting feeling to know things were back to normal. When they reached the clearing, they found it empty. Linda was the first to begrudgingly admit that they hadn't been dreaming, at least not in the normal sense. Both of them recalled being taken into the spaceship by aliens who looked like Adonis's with their long golden hair and handsome Nordic features. One of them described what they were going through as a learning process—interacting with simulated 3/D enhanced images—the fifth dimension. Virtual Reality was not a kid's game in the world of UFOs and extraterrestrials. It was in that medium that Phil and Linda were chosen to act out a scenario of life and death with the good and evil forces of free will. It was in that medium that they saw the results of mankind's disrespect for Universal Law. It was in that medium that they saw the earth changes that would occur if the lifeblood of their planet continued to be spilled. Their subconscious would retain the memories of those events.

Phil and Linda knew the score. They were privileged to have witnessed the divination of a miracle first-hand. Do not always believe what you see, but see what you believe. Phil finally saw what he wanted desperately to believe. God's mercy. In His good graces, a reprieve was given to humankind. How long it lasted depended on humankind's adherence to Universal Law. It was God's Ten Commandments to the universe.

For several minutes Phil and Linda stood still, quietly absorbed in a stream of consciousness. It was like being inside an open cathedral, Phil thought. Strangely enough, neither one of them were in any hurry to leave. They knew something had happened to them that had changed their lives forever.

Phil started getting anxious. "We may as well take off, kid. Captain Smollet said he'd wait up for us."

As they turned around to continue their journey, Phil spied a multitude of V-shaped formations of tiny bright lights streaking across the heavens. Perhaps, he figured, they had another call to make; another rogue planet that had to be saved. Only time would tell if he would ever have to see them again.

THE END